Dead End on the Camino

Elyn Aviva

Pilgrims' Process, Inc., Boulder, CO

DEAD END ON THE CAMINO

ISBN: 0-9710609-1-6

Library of Congress Control Number: 2001090346

Printed in the United States of America

0 9 8 7 6 5 4 3 2 1

TO GARY
My companion in life and on the Camino

Acknowledgements

I want to acknowledge the pervasive impact the Camino de Santiago has had on my life. For more than twenty years I have been drawn back, like an iron filing to a magnet, to learn more about the Camino and to experience the pilgrimage again and again. The ancient traditions, layers of meaning, and rich historical associations of the Camino—and of the Milky Way—formed the inspiration for this novel.

I have also been inspired by the many pilgrims to Santiago de Compostela (and beyond) who walk in the footsteps of their ancestors. They understand the complexities of embarking on a quest and the determination required to reach a goal.

To the best of my knowledge, the historical information, descriptions of locations on the Camino, and anthropological observations in this novel are accurate, although the modern-day characters, events, and the Brotherhood of the Knights of Santiago are, of course, fictitious.

The Caminos de Santiago

The four pilgrimage roads in France join together to form one Camino across Spain

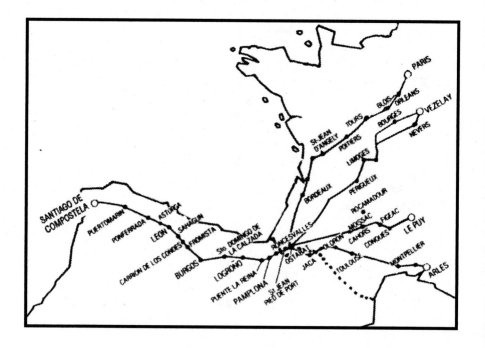

Prelude

A tall man in a hooded white robe held a flickering candle up to the rows of bookshelves in the dark room. Shadows shrouded his face. He reached up and pulled down one book, examined it, and then replaced it. He took down another, examined it, and re-placed that one too. After inspecting several other volumes, he se-lected one and carried it over to a nearby writing desk. He smiled with grim satisfaction. This book would fit his purposes well. It was undistinguished in appearance, and a heavily embossed leather panel had been glued on top of the plain leather front.

Putting the candlestick down, he reached beneath his robe and pulled out a small leather bag and a thin, sharp dagger. The jewel-encrusted crosspiece was decorated with a simple scallop shell. Inserting the dagger's point, he slit the top of the panel loose from the leather beneath.

Although he was alone in the room, he worked surrepti-tiously, hiding his actions from view. Suddenly he looked up from his task, his brow furrowed with concern. Had he heard a stifled cough? The muffled clank of sword against armor? He hurried over to the heavy wooden door and checked the lock, his sandaled feet slapping against the stone floor. Relieved that he heard nothing more, he returned to work.

He slipped his hand inside his tunic and drew out a thin, gold medallion, dangling from a green velvet ribbon. He cut the ribbon and held the medallion up to the candle's flame, admiring the way the intricate designs glittered in the flickering light. The metal was warm from his body's heat, slightly damp from his sweat.

With a weary sigh, he slipped the gleaming medallion into the pocket he had formed between the leather panel and the cover of the book. Then he took a small bottle out of the suede bag, dabbed the contents on the open slit, and pressed it shut. Picking up the book, he examined it in the candle's light. Satisfied that his work would pass undetected, he put the book down on the table and reached for a piece of vellum, a pen, and ink.

He began to write:

"14 June, Year of Our Lord 1493"
"Most Honored Master:
I have done as you ordered . . . . "

The sound of his labored breathing and his pen scratching across the vellum filled the silent room. Abruptly, he stopped writing and listened intently. Then he continued the task he was so anxious to complete.

Suddenly there was a loud pounding on the door.

He looked around frantically for a place to hide the letter.

The heavy wooden door started to splinter with the force of numerous hatchet blows. He could see the glow of torches and hear the eager shouts of soldiers. The door burst open, and soon he lay dead on the floor, his white robe stained with red.

One

If I hadn't sneezed, none of this would have happened. But who could have known that my allergy to mold, mildew, and boring archival research would lead to murder, mayhem, and—but I'm getting ahead of myself.

It all started when my nose began to twitch. Muttering "Damn this dust!" I dug a wrinkled piece of Kleenex out of my canvas shoulder bag. Once I had the Kleenex in hand, the sneeze subsided, lying in wait somewhere behind the bridge of my nose. Tricky little devil. With a sigh, I leaned back in my squeaky library chair and stared at the tattered, leather-covered books on the table.

That morning Brother Mateo, one of the archivists at the National Library of Madrid, had brought me ten newly discovered books, found together in a decaying box in a damp cellar in a village in north-central Spain. He had carried them gently, like newborn puppies, and carefully laid them on the wooden desk before me. I had smiled insincerely and thanked him profusely. I didn't share his enthusiasm for the musty, worm-eaten tomes. All I wanted to do was to end my library research quickly—but honorably—and find something more productive to do for the rest of the summer.

Distastefully, I selected one of the books at random. It was about the size and thickness of the paperback mystery I was reading, but I knew from experience it would be a lot less interesting. The deeply embossed leather front panel was covered with furry, moss-green mold, as was the rest of the book. Centuries ago, the covers had been fastened with thin leather straps attached to riveted brass fittings. Now only three tarnished brass pieces and a fragment of one frayed strap remained. The book had obviously seen better days, but whether its current state resulted from use or abuse, I couldn't tell.

I began turning the cream-colored vellum pages, trying to read the faded handwriting. My knowledge of modern Spanish is quite good, but the ornate fifteenth-century writing was full of abbreviations, elaborate swirls, and unknown expressions. Besides, the ink had faded to a light purple, making the words even harder to decipher in the dim light that found its way through the distant, dirty windows of the room.

My nose twitched uncontrollably. I complained to myself, "Whatever made me think I'd enjoy archival research? I'm a cultural anthropologist, not a historian—and I hate mold."

As I reached around to get another Kleenex from my bag, my elbow hit the book, sending it flying off the table. It landed on the stone floor with a crash that seemed to reverberate throughout the cavernous room. I glanced around quickly. Fortunately, I was alone.

When I picked up the book, I saw that the spine had split from the impact. What looked like a piece of paper was wedged between the leather spine and the binding. I tried to pull it out, but it was stuck fast. Taking a nail file from my bag, I attempted to pry the paper loose. After carefully twisting it back and forth, I managed to extract a yellowed, concave piece of vellum. It crackled and split as I unfolded it and pressed it flat. With great difficulty, I translated the nearly illegible message:

14 June, Year of Our Lord 1493
Most Honored Master,
I have done as you ordered and hidden our most important treasure from those who would take it from us under the guise of sovereignty. We and only we are the true Knights of Santiago, and we cannot let this greatest treasure of all fall into the hands of those who have destroyed us.
I will reveal the details when I talk with you, but know now, in case anything befalls me, that the path begins where our comrades in faith and battle, the Knights of Charlemagne, lie resting. Only the true pilgrim who follows the Milky Way will reach the treasure, and only if St. James the Apostle guides him. I have made a key to the treasure—"

The letter ended abruptly.

My knowledge of Spanish history was sketchy, but I knew that the Order of the Knights of Santiago was a military brotherhood that fought against the Moors during the Reconquest of Spain in the Middle Ages. It was named for Santiago—St. James the Greater, the first of the martyred apostles and the patron saint of Spain. Along with fighting Moors, the Knights of Santiago protected pilgrims traveling the Camino de Santiago, the 500-mile-long pilgrimage road that led from the French Pyrenees across Spain to Santiago de Compostela, supposed burial place of the saint. I'd done my Ph.D. research in Sahagún, a village located on the Camino, so I knew something about the pilgrimage.

I also knew that in 1492 Columbus discovered America, Ferdinand and Isabella conquered Granada, the last Moorish stronghold in Spain, and the Jews were expelled for the final time. But I had no idea what happened in 1493, the date on the letter.

I turned the fragile paper over in my hands. Who had hidden the letter—and why? What was the treasure and where was it? Maybe Brother Mateo would have some ideas. After all, medieval history was his specialty.

With a start, I realized bells were ringing: it was 2 P.M. Closing time. Leaving the books on the table as required—there was no way to take that mysterious tome with me—I went to find Brother Mateo. On the way, I passed a Xerox machine. After setting it to "darkest," I managed to make a barely legible copy of the letter, which I put in my bag. Then I continued down the hall to a small wooden desk hidden behind the doorway to a storage area.

A plump, gray-haired figure in a white, hooded robe was dozing in a chair, his head resting on his folded arms on top of a cluttered desk. He snored lightly. Standing over him, I could see the bright pink circle of sunburned scalp above his tonsure. I cleared my throat softly so as not to startle him.

He jerked his head up and looked around wildly for a moment, eyes unfocused, then sighed with relief. "Oh, it's you, Noa. For a moment I thought—"

"Don't worry, Brother Mateo. Your secret is safe with me."

"Do you think anyone saw me?"

"No, of course not. Your desk is hidden behind the doorway."

His eyes looked bleary and bloodshot and his skin had a grayish tinge. A few days before I had found him slumped in his chair, unable to stand. He had made me promise not to mention his dizziness to anyone; he was afraid he would lose his job if they knew.

Concerned, I asked, "Are you feeling all right?"

"I had a doctor's appointment this morning. He tells me I have a minor problem with my heart. Nothing to worry about," he said, dismissively. "How are you?"

"I'm fine, except I'm allergic to the mold in all these old books. Doesn't it bother you?"

"After all these years, I must be immune. Besides, I have a higher calling that protects me."

"You mean the brotherhood?" I said, half-jokingly.

"The brotherhood?"

"You told me you belonged to a brotherhood, that's all. Remember?"

"Of course. So I did." He changed the subject. "I haven't been well, you know, and my son has brought me disturbing news."

"Your son, Brother Mateo? I thought you were a friar."

"I belong to a special brotherhood. We are permitted to marry."

"It sounded unusual, but if I knew little about Spanish history, I knew even less about Spanish religious orders. "So what was the bad news?"

"An international smuggling ring is stealing some of our most treasured patrimony. These people will do anything for money."

"That's terrible!"

"Yes, terrible. But I am just an old, tired librarian. What can I do?" He looked at his watch in surprise. "Is it really that late?" He started to get up.

"I want to show you something before you go."

I held the letter out to him, but he pointed to his watch. "I'm sorry, but it will have to wait—I've got a meeting to go to—and I'm late already." Noticing my disappointment, he added affectionately, "Surely it will keep until tomorrow?"

"I suppose so," I said, wryly. "After all, it's already waited 500 years."

He was straightening up his desk, not really listening. "Good, good." Then, with a start, he turned and looked at me. "500 years?"

He reached for the yellowed vellum and unfolded it. His hands started to tremble and his color suddenly grew much dingier.

"Have you read this?" he asked.

"Yes, but it didn't make much sense. A treasure hidden on the Milky Way? What could that mean? It's probably a hoax, though why anyone would bother . . ."

With shaking hands, he put the letter in the center drawer in his desk. Then he locked it with a large wrought-iron key that dangled from his corded belt. With an effort, he stood up, holding onto the desk to steady himself.

I reached out to help him.

He brushed off my hand and lurched off, his sandals slapping unevenly against the polished stone floors.

"Brother Mateo—" I called after him, but he just increased his speed.

I walked slowly back towards the main lobby, puzzling over his abrupt departure. What had upset him so? The letter? I shook my head. I probably shouldn't take it personally. After all, he had said he didn't feel well, and he was late to an important meeting.

Fred Gubser, a historian I had met that summer, was standing by the main entry to the library. When he saw me, his pale, freckled face turned red. I don't normally have that effect on people, but Fred had a crush on me. The library guards were funneling people out the door. I looked for Brother Mateo, but he was nowhere in sight.

Fred and I stepped out of the cool shelter of the library into a scorching July day filled with the stench of melting asphalt and diesel exhaust. Blinded by the sunlight, I groped in my shoulder bag for sunglasses.

Eyes shielded behind dark lenses, I said, "They say that Madrid has three months of heaven and nine months of hell—just which do you suppose this is?"

Fred laughed appreciatively.

Unwilling to confront the heat, we stood poised at the top of the flight of marble stairs. In the distance, I saw Mateo trotting down the sidewalk, white robe flapping against his legs. I was surprised at how quickly he was moving, given his bad heart.

In a thin, reedy voice that somehow matched his appearance, Fred asked, "Are you going home now?"

My room would be hot enough to grill a cheese sandwich. The only window opened onto a small patio, but I kept the metal window blinds closed when I was gone to keep people from climbing into my room from the patio. When I was in the room I could open the blinds, but then noisy conversation entered along with the stifling air. It was a bit better at night, but not much. Sometimes I wondered if that's why the room was so inexpensive: it could only be used half the time.

Fred repeated his question. "Are you going home?"

"No, I think I'll find a nice, shady sidewalk café."

"I was going to ask you to have lunch with me. After all, we Americans should stick together, don't you think?"

"Not really."

"Oh." His face smushed like a dried apple.

I patted his arm. "Don't take it personally."

"Well, how about tonight, then? We could get something to eat and then see some flamenco dancing. How about it?"

It was difficult to imagine spending an evening with Fred. He was just too bland. But, after all, there were worse things than bland. A lot worse. I should know. I glanced at him. He was waiting expectantly for my reply. Bland, yes, but also patient—and appreciative—and eager.

"I suppose so," I said hesitantly.

"Great. I'll pick you up around 9 P.M."

"Let's meet at the Plaza Santa Ana, across from my hostel."

"I can hardly wait!"

"Right. See you then." Eager to escape, I ran down the marble staircase to the sidewalk, leaving Fred, still hesitating, at the top of the stairs.

I strode down the Paseo de Recoletos, scurrying from one patch of shade to the next, and wondered if it had been wise—or fair—to succumb to Fred's ardent invitation. After all, adulation can be boring. On the other hand, so was the prospect of another evening alone. Besides, maybe I could find out something about the Knights of Santiago. And the letter. The letter.

After walking past blocks of stores and cafés shuttered against the heat, I arrived at the 300-year-old Plaza Mayor. I strolled by vendors selling bullfight posters with your name and the date added for a small fee, flamenco dolls and plastic gold-tone castanets, multi-colored Indian silk scarves edged with fringe, brass peace-symbol earrings and hair ornaments.

Passing through a stone arch I entered the huge, sunlit square. Two sides were lined with café tables, most of which were empty, but I saw someone I knew: Sue Ellen Jackson, an American art historian doing research in Madrid. We were both staying at the same inexpensive hostel.

Sue Ellen was sitting at a table in the corner, shaded by a bright green- and white-striped umbrella advertising Heineken. She saw me and waved languidly. I waved back, then walked over to her, staying inside the shaded arcades until the last possible moment.

She looked remarkably cool in a pale pink gauze sundress, her deeply tanned legs crossed at the knees, a high-heeled sandal dangling lazily off of one of her feet. Her shoulder-length blond hair fluttered gently as a faint breeze sighed through the plaza.

Once I had asked Sue Ellen how she managed to look so cool and comfortable when the temperature was well over 95° and the humidity was close to 100%. "Heredity," she had explained in her molasses-coated voice. Her family had lived in Charleston for generations.

Sipping from a half-empty glass filled with dark red liquid, a slice of lemon, and tiny ice cubes, she looked up at me and smiled idly. "Hi, Noa. My, don't you look bedraggled."

I knew I looked bedraggled, but I wished Sue Ellen hadn't mentioned it. My jeans felt damp, my T-shirt was clinging to my back, and a telltale splotch of sweat was spreading under each arm. I didn't have to look to know it was there; I could feel it. The only good thing about humidity was that my hair developed corkscrew ringlets, which I rather liked. I was bedraggled from the heat, the humidity, and the excitement of finding the letter. Funny how excitement could be exhausting.

I pulled up a metal chair, scraping the legs against the uneven cobblestone pavement. The chair was hot to the touch so I sat down gingerly, expecting my pants to sizzle when they hit the surface. They didn't.

Glancing at her nearly empty glass, I asked, "What are you drinking? Bitter Kas? "

"Campari. Looks the same since you can't see the alcohol."

"In this heat?"

"Now, Noa, lighten up. Don't take everything so seriously."

That's just what Peter had said before I left New York for Spain. At the time I had been furious, and, given the context, I had good reason. But maybe they both had a point. All work and no play. A type one on the Enneagram. Why couldn't I learn to work hard and still find time to enjoy myself? Peter managed to. Sue Ellen managed to, and she was doing an important art history project at the Prado Museum. At least that's what she said she was doing, though I never saw her working on anything more serious than the next social engagement. But that wasn't fair, I chided myself. After all, since I was usually working, how could I know what Sue Ellen did with her time?

"How's the research at the library?" Sue Ellen asked. "Find anything interesting?" She drummed her long, pink-tipped nails against the top of the white enamel table.

Preoccupied with memories of my last fight with Peter, I replied offhandedly, "I found a letter about hidden treasure."

Blue eyes glittering, Sue Ellen leaned forward, her tiny pink tongue peeking out between her frosted pink lips. "Hidden treasure?"

Sue Ellen took another drink from her glass and signaled gracefully to the black-jacketed waiter who was hovering nearby. Pointing at her drink, she indicating she wanted another one. I ordered iced coffee.

Leaning towards me conspiratorially, she asked, "Now, what were you saying about treasure?"

I wished I hadn't said anything. Determined to tell her as little as possible, I said, "In the Middle Ages, Sahagún was the site of the most powerful Benedictine monastery in Spain. My fieldwork was on life in Sahagún today—but I thought I might get a new angle if I could read original historical documents in the National Library. Peter thought so too. In fact, he encouraged me to come here this summer."

"Peter's your boyfriend, isn't he?"

"Well, not exactly." I searched for the right words. "Sometimes he is, sometimes he isn't."

"Oh. One of those," said Sue Ellen, smiling slyly.

I wondered how Sue Ellen could possibly know what "one of those" was. I wasn't even sure myself, and I sincerely doubted that Sue Ellen had ever had the kind of relationship I currently found myself in. I didn't even know what kind of relationship it was, and I was right in the middle of it—or had been, before I left for Spain. Now it was hard to know *where* I was.

Sue Ellen prompted me again. "The treasure."

The waiter returned, balancing a black lacquered tray on his arm. With a flourish, he placed a small white bowl of thyme-coated green olives on the table and replaced Sue Ellen's empty glass with a full one, the outside beaded with condensation. He placed a narrow cylinder of glass filled with ice and a large mug of steaming espresso in front of me. I poured the coffee over the ice, which crackled and rapidly melted. Then I added some cream and stirred it with a long-handled spoon, taking my time, watching the swirling pale ribbons turn the dark-chocolate-colored liquid into mocha-colored, my mind swirling around like the cream. The letter, Peter. . .

"So you're doing archival research you don't like and Peter got you into it—"

"Come on, Sue Ellen, quit twisting my words. What's the matter with you today, anyway?"

She chewed on her lower lip. "Sorry, Noa." She took a large gulp of Campari. "I'm upset about some money problems back home, that's all."

"I hope it's nothing serious."

"Nothing that winning the lottery wouldn't cure." she said, taking another long swallow.

"If I can help, let me know." Not that I could, of course, but it seemed like the right thing to say. Too often, I found, I said what seemed like the right thing to say. Except around Peter.

"What were you saying about Peter?"

"I wanted to go back to Spain, and Peter suggested a way to get funding—"

"And leave him for the summer?" Sue Ellen sucked on an olive, puckering her lips at the tartness.

This time, I refused to rise to the bait.

"And the mysterious letter?"

Wishing I had been more cautious to begin with, I replied, carefully, "I found a letter about the Knights of Santiago, hidden in an old book. Know anything about them?"

Sue Ellen stared at her glass, which was already half empty, and rubbed one of her pink-tipped fingers around the damp rim. "Not really, but I think the seventeenth-century painter Velázquez was one. That famous painting of his, The Meninas, shows him in a black cloak with the blood-red cross of Santiago on his chest."

I was puzzled. "I thought the Knights were a religious brotherhood."

"Maybe the membership requirements changed by the seventeenth century."

Two young men in Hard Rock T-shirts and extremely tight blue jeans—so tight they made me worry about what they were doing to their chances to produce future generations—were walking quickly in our direction. "Friends of yours?"

Sue Ellen glanced casually over her shoulder. "Why, it's Jorge and Antonio. They said they were going to take me out for lunch, but they're late." She glanced at her watch.

I shifted uncomfortably on the hot chair. "Look, Sue Ellen, do me a favor. Don't mention the letter to anyone."

"Why not?"

I paused, trying to find a reason she would believe.

"I don't want to look gullible, that's all."

"I'll think about it. Promise you'll keep me posted?"

"Of course."

After taking a long drink, Sue Ellen asked, "By the way, I'd love to see the letter. Maybe I can help you figure out what it means."

"Sorry, I don't have it with me." After all, I thought, always a stickler for honesty, I don't have the letter, Brother Mateo does. I only have a copy.

The two young men arrived with effusive apologies. They invited me to join them for lunch, but I declined. "Three's fun, but four's a crowd," I explained, much to their puzzlement.

Sue Ellen raised one eyebrow. "Waiting for someone? What would Peter think?"

"Too bad he'll never know," I replied sadly.

Laughing, Sue Ellen put her cool hand lightly on my shoulder. "We'll talk more later."

They strolled off, arm in arm, Sue Ellen in the middle, her high heels clicking arhythmically on the uneven stone pavement of the plaza.

I finished my drink and then finished Sue Ellen's, grimacing at the warm, cloying dregs. The waiter came over with the tab. Sue Ellen, as usual, had forgotten to pay for her share. She said she was having money problems, but she wasn't the only one. Irritated, I paid the bill and resolved to ask her to pay me back next time I saw her.

I ambled through deserted streets to Retiro Park and sat down on a cool stone bench shaded by trees by the side of a small lake. Drowsy from the heat, I thought about how to learn more about the Knights of Santiago. The libraries were closed for the day, but the bookstores would be open again after 5 P.M. I could ask Fred this evening. But I'd have to be discreet. I laughed aloud. Why worry about being discreet? Surely I didn't believe the treasure was real, did I? I was gullible—Peter always said so—but not *that* gullible.

But the letter looked so real. And the way it was hidden seemed so authentic.

My mind in a whirl, I leaned back on the bench, watching the lethargic tourists stroll by and listening to the babble of languages, while I kept thinking about the letter. Not the long-awaited letter from Peter—after all, the mail took 10 - 14 days each way, and I'd only been in Spain for a month— but rather, *the* letter, as I was beginning to refer to it to myself.

Rummaging in my bag, I found the Xeroxed copy and stared at the faint, nearly illegible words. Brother Mateo had seemed upset when he saw the letter, but that didn't mean it was authentic. It probably just meant his heart was acting up. After all, why would the letter mean anything to him? He was just a tired, old friar-librarian, to paraphrase his own words.

Torn between skepticism and enthusiasm, I wondered what I would do if the treasure were real and if I actually found it. The things I wanted were things money couldn't buy: love, professional success, an interesting life. On second thought, I realized money could certainly buy an interesting life. Travel. Freedom to do research where and when I wanted. No more struggling for grants. No more living in hot, dingy rooming houses. No more counting pesetas.

I shook my head firmly, trying to dispel such dreams. I was a firm believer in hard work, not in unearned good fortune. I never even played the lottery. With a sigh, I slipped the letter back into my bag. Then, stretching out on the hard stone bench and using my bag as a pillow, I sleepily closed my eyes.

Two

I jerked awake to the sound of shrieking children. Groggily, I sat up, retrieved fallen hairpins from the grass, and twisted my hair back into its coil. Then I straightened my clothes and went to find a bookstore. After asking a few people, I ended up on a narrow, twisting street, the Calle de los Libros, near the Puerta del Sol.

Picking the Librería Paco at random, I pushed open the heavy, creaking door and walked in. The air was thick with cigarette smoke, heat, and dust. Through the haze, I saw walls lined to the ceiling with shelves piled high with books. An overflowing storage room behind the main counter increased the sense of barely controlled chaos.

The chain-smoking clerk informed me there was nothing on the Knights of Santiago. He ought to know, he asserted, since he kept a list in his head of everything in stock and where to find it. To emphasize his point, he tapped his head hard with his hand, scattering cigarette ashes on the floor. I left quickly.

The next bookstore looked like a twin of the first one, except that the air was less polluted. A smiling young clerk pulled a teetering ladder over to one wall and, climbing up and down the rickety steps, returned with a large volume. After blowing off the dust, I saw it was a beautifully illustrated book about the shields and weapons of the Brotherhood of Santiago in Burgos. Unfortunately, as far as I could tell, this group was totally unrelated to the Order of the Knights of Santiago.

I tried several other bookstores without success before deciding to quit for the day. A faint, hot breeze stirred the mop-head leafy tops of the plane trees as I walked back to my room. My room was as hot as an oven, and a faint whiff of olive oil and garlic-scented air crept in through the open slits. Maybe a bath would cool me off. I undressed, put on the raspberry silk bathrobe I had bought on a splurge—justifying the extravagance by telling myself it was lightweight, great for traveling, and, besides, it was on sale—grabbed my toiletry kit and a towel, and hurried down the dimly lit hall to the bathroom.

Stretching out in the big, claw-footed tub filled with cool water, I soaped myself with Magno, the scented black glycerin soap that never failed to remind me of when I first met Peter, the year before.

I had taken a break from fieldwork in Sahagún to visit a couple of friends on sabbatical in London, friends who taught at a university near mine in New York. P.D.P. Murphy, a British-born colleague of theirs at SUNY, had dropped by. P.D.P., known as Peter by his friends, was spending the summer in England doing research on an obscure medieval woman writer.

He had thick, curly brown hair, just beginning to be salted with gray, piercing blue-gray eyes, an aquiline nose, and an absolutely outrageous grin. He was in his mid thirties, a little—but not much—older than I. And he was just a few inches taller—I'm 5' 7"—which was just right, since I hate being loomed over by tall men. His voice was deep and vibrant, and he had a wonderful English accent. Not, of course, that that made any difference.

Thinking about Peter was as excruciating, and as unavoidable, as wiggling a loose tooth. With a sigh, I surfaced from the bath water, lifted the showerhead from the wall bracket, and gave myself a brisk massage, being careful not to spray water on the floor. As was usual in Spain, there was no shower curtain. Then I dried myself with the small, stiff towel provided by the landlady, so different from the luxurious Turkish towels at the Hotel San Marcos in León where Peter and I had stayed the summer before.

I stared at the wavery reflection that stared back at me from the small, poorly lit mirror over the sink. Long, auburn hair, pale skin, hazel, almond-shaped eyes that tilted up at the corners, high cheekbones, a nondescript nose, a sensuous mouth—or so I had been told—and a firm chin.

"I know, I know," I said aloud, fogging the mirror with my breath. Below the chin I was not so firm, due to a weakness for fried chicken and Lindt chocolate.

Someone jiggled the doorknob and then started pounding on the door.

"Just a minute!" I called out as I wrapped the towel around my head, put on my bathrobe, and grabbed my toiletry kit. Hair still dripping, I went back to my room to get ready for the evening with Fred.

Deciding what to wear was a challenge. I didn't want to look alluring but I wanted to look good. Vanity, vanity. I finally put on a teal gauze tunic and skirt, belting it with the antique Navajo concha belt my parents had given me. Then I dumped the contents of my shoulder bag on the bed and put a few essentials into a small straw purse. The Xeroxed letter fell out and I read it again in the fading light. Hidden treasure. Most precious treasure. A key. Was the letter just a hoax, an idle game played by some long-dead joker? With a sigh, I put the letter in the drawer of the nightstand. Even if it were real, what difference would it make. How could I ever find the treasure?

Stretching out on the bed, I tried to read the Elizabeth Peters murder mystery I had bought at the Rastro, Madrid's Sunday morning flea market. But the room was stifling, so I went out to the communal lounge and sank into a faded, overstuffed chair in the corner. The slowly revolving blades of the ceiling fan barely stirred the sticky air. After a while, another lodger came in and turned on the television. "Dallas," dubbed in Spanish, blared forth.

Unwilling to listen to "Dallas," especially in Spanish, I left the hostel, walked over to the Plaza Santa Ana, and sat down at one end of a wrought iron bench, next to a young couple who were embracing passionately and noisily. I supposed they lived at home and this was their only place for recreation. It was a warm summer night, and children played hopscotch, old men nodded off on the benches, vendors sold ice cream cones and lottery tickets, and the line in front of the nearby pay telephone cabinet grew longer and shorter and longer again.

At 9 P.M. Fred arrived, slightly out of breath. "I hope I haven't kept you waiting," he gasped.

"Not a bit."

"Gee, Noa, you're really beautiful."

"Why, Fred—" I replied.

"That outfit you're wearing makes your hair look like burnished copper. And your eyes are so beautiful—what color are they, green?"

"Actually, they're hazel. They change color depending on what I'm wearing. But really, Fred, what's with the flattery?"

A flush spread over his pale, freckled face. "I just had to tell you, that's all. I hope you don't mind."

"Why should I mind?"

"Well, I know there's someone else in your life."

"That doesn't mean I can't enjoy myself." After all, I thought ruefully, Peter probably is. I stood up briskly. "Where to?"

"Have you eaten yet?" I shook my head. "Let's hit a few *tapas* bars. Then we can go listen to some flamenco."

"Sounds good."

We walked towards the Plaza Mayor, passing a number of small cafés that offered a variety of appetizers, called *tapas*. Lured in by the succulent seafood display in the window, we entered the Bar Zamora. The long counter was lined with people smoking, drinking sherry, and eating, all at the same time. We had to peer over their shoulders to see the plates of appetizers on top of the bar. Deep-fried squid rings, garlic-drenched shrimp, cayenne-dusted potatoes, stuffed mussels, assorted olives and onions on tiny bayonets, a casserole of something unknown floating in an inky broth—to name just a few. After catching the attention of the bartender, we pointed at several *tapas* and retreated to the relative quiet of a corner table.

"You realize," I pointed out, "that the *tapas* cost more if you sit at a table instead of standing at the bar."

"I know, but I want to talk to you in comfort."

"What do you want to talk about?"

"Well, you interest me." He smiled shyly. "You're not like most women I've met."

"I bet you say that to all the women."

He hesitated a moment, then asked, "How can I get you to take me seriously?"

"You can't," I said, gently. "But don't take it personally."

Just then our *caracoles con perejil y ajo* arrived, and we started prying the tiny, garlic-scented snails out of their parsley-sprinkled shells. Next the *tortilla española* arrived, accompanied by a plate of sliced French bread. Actually, it was Spanish bread, but it looked just like French baguettes. We put the thick squares of egg-and-potato omelet on top of the bread, making an open-faced sandwich, and washed them down with sherry.

While savoring the sweet, nutty flavor of the sherry, I thought about the best way to approach Fred about the letter. I decided to be direct. Sort of. "How about helping me solve a problem?"

"I'd be delighted."

"You're an expert on Spanish history, right?"

"Well, I won a prize for my dissertation."

"What do you know about medieval Spain?"

"Not much. My specialty is nineteenth century. But go ahead and ask."

"What do you know about the Knights of Santiago?"

"They were a powerful military-religious order, as I recall. They still exist, you know."

"They do?"

"Yes, but they no longer go around on horseback killing infidels." He laughed nervously at his joke. I smiled encouragingly. "Franco made some of his followers Knights of Santiago. It's like an English knighthood or something." He took a deep swallow of sherry. "Tell me, why are you so curious?"

"I found a letter that mentioned them."

"Oh?"

I added cautiously. "And something about a treasure."

"Where'd you find the letter?"

"In a book."

"In a book? You mean, reproduced in a book?"

"No. Hidden in it. Know of any long-lost Spanish treasures?"

He shook his head.

"Can't say that I do."

"Not that I believe the letter, of course. But in the Southwest, where I grew up, people often talked of lost treasure—the Lost Cities of Cibola, for example. Not that anyone really believed in them, of course." Except me, of course.

Fred thought a moment. "In Spain there have been a number of elaborate frauds. The idea seems to be, that just because you can't find proof for your pet historical theory doesn't mean you aren't right. If you can't find proof, you make it up."

"Really?"

"Really." He continued, "A great deal of the early historical record was destroyed during the Reconquest. So some of the more enterprising Spaniards have manufactured elaborate fake burials, fake documents—not to mention fake artwork—to prove what they believed about the past."

"Oh." I said, thoughtfully.

"Your letter might not be a fake, but you have to be cautious." He paused. "Many of the great frauds—the false documents claiming taxation rights, for example—had to be 'accidentally' discovered. Your letter, however, was hidden, so it would appear that it was meant not to be found."

"Unless that's just part of the fraud."

He looked at me intently. "Just how and where was the letter hidden?"

"In a book." I tried to sound off-handed, though my voice was shaky. "Well, it's probably not important. I was just curious."

"I'll ask around. Maybe someone else will know more about the Knights of Santiago and hidden treasure than I do."

"Thanks. But be discreet, will you?"

"Of course, but why?"

"I don't want to look gullible." Even to my ears that sounded a bit limp as an excuse. Truth was, I didn't want other people to know till I had figured out what I wanted to do about it. If it were genuine. If.

Between mouthfuls of potato omelet, Fred asked again, "Where'd you say you found the letter?"

Stalling for time, I signaled to the waiter. When he came over, I ordered fried squid rings.

"Where'd you find the letter?" he pressed.

Grudgingly, I replied, "In the spine of a book."

"What kind of book?"

"Just a book." I added, irritated, "Look, I'm sorry I said anything. Let's change the subject, Okay?"

"Sure."

We ate in silence, using what was left of the bread to mop up the garlic and parsley sauce surrounding the empty snail shells.

After a few minutes, Fred cleared his throat and said, "You say you grew up in the Southwest? Where, exactly?"

"All over, though mostly on the Hopi Reservation in Arizona. My dad was—still is—a part-time Indian trader and part-time artist; my mother is a high-school English teacher and part-time writer. We moved around a lot, depending on which reservation school had a vacancy."

The waiter brought the squid rings, and I squeezed a slice of lemon over my half. "We could have stayed in one place, but my folks liked to move around. Every few years we'd pack what we could fit into the car—actually, it was a jeep—and move."

"What about what wouldn't fit?"

"It was left behind or given away. My folks thought that was a good way to keep from getting attached to things. They said people and ideas mattered, not possessions."

Fred leaned back in his chair.

"Sounds like a fascinating childhood."

"It had its moments. I suppose that's why I became an anthropologist—the perpetual outsider, always living in a foreign culture."

"Was it that bad?"

Startled, I said, "I didn't mean to make it sound bad. It was exciting, and different—and challenging. I can imagine much worse."

"Such as?"

"Growing up in a big city. Living all of one's life in one place."

"Sounds like the way I grew up, in Philadelphia. Compared to your upbringing, it was pretty boring."

"Well, you're not boring," I said ingenuously.

"Thanks, Noa."

I chewed on the remaining squid ring, wondering why I felt compelled to make people feel better. Fred *was* boring. I didn't need to say that, but I didn't need to deny it either. I was always polite, smoothing things over, making people feel good, even at my own expense. Case in point: I really didn't want to tell Fred the details of the letter, but I found it hard not to answer his questions. I finished the glass of sherry.

After Fred paid the bill, we headed for the *cuevas*, cave-like rooms built into the steep steps on the west side of the Plaza Mayor. The sound of flamenco music wafted out of the open doors of several of the clubs, and slim, black-suited men in pointy-toed boots leaned against the outside wall, urging tourists to enter their establishments.

We entered a smoke-filled room and managed to find two seats together at a tiny table at the back of the room. A heavy-set, black-dressed guitar player sat in a wooden chair in the corner of a small, raised stage; beside him, tapping a cane, stood an old, dark-haired man, also dressed in black. His eyes closed, he chanted the *cante hondo*, the deep mournful flamenco music of southern Spain.

After the third song, three plump dancers in flounced polka-dotted dresses swept onto the stage and started to tap their high-heeled shoes and click their castanets in time to the music. Soon they began to beat out intricate staccato rhythms with their heels and to inscribe complex patterns in the air with their gracefully twisting hands. Sometimes the singer accompanied them with his cane, sometimes the guitar player joined in.

A Spanish friend once told me that flamenco songs were always tales of love and betrayal, passion and death. Looking at the intense, rapt faces of the performers I believed it, even though I couldn't understand the lyrics.

We sat wedged together against the wall, breathing cigarette smoke and alcohol fumes, nibbling at a bowl of salted almonds, unable to hear each other over the music. Which was just as well, since I wanted to avoid any more questions about the letter. Somehow our waiter found his way through the maze of tables to refill our sherry glasses and the bowl of salted almonds.

Soon I was mesmerized by the complex strumming of the guitar, the clapping of the dancers' hands, and the repetitive tapping of the singer's cane. Elbows on the table, I stared at the gaily costumed dancers swirling and twirling and rapping their heels in hypnotic rhythms on the wooden dance platform. The husky voice of the singer filled the room like fragrant smoke, swirling into corners, floating over the background murmur of the crowd. What was he singing about—lost love? Lost treasure?

With a start, I realized the lights were bright and the waiter was hovering nearby, waiting to be paid. We pushed our way through the crowd and into the fresh evening air. I took a deep breath and held it a moment.

Flushed from the music and the sherry, I turned to Fred and exclaimed enthusiastically, "That was wonderful!"

He smiled warmly. "It was my pleasure."

He started to put his arm around my shoulder, but I moved deftly away. His hand dropped to his side. I said, "You're awfully nice, Fred, but you shouldn't waste your time. There's really no future in it."

"Don't underestimate me, Noa." Abruptly, he grabbed me and kissed me hard. I tried to draw away, but he held my arms tight and kissed me again, mashing his lips into mine.

I jerked away angrily. "Take me back to the hostel. Now."

When we reached the hostel, Fred turned to me, his voice shaking. "I'm sorry Noa. It must have been all that emotional music—and the sherry. I hope you're not angry."

"It's late and I want to go to bed."

"Okay. Goodnight, Noa."

"Goodnight, Fred."

He looked as if he wanted to say something more. I didn't give him the chance. I turned quickly, opened the front door, and ran up the three flights of stairs to the hostel.

A group of boarders had taken over the lounge and were drinking beer and arguing loudly, drowning out the sound of hoof beats in the old Western movie on the television. They waved to me and invited me to join them, but I wasn't in the mood.

Damn! I let the situation get out of hand. So much for having just a little fun. So much for trying to "pump" Fred for information. Who did I think I was, Mata Hari?

My room was still too hot and I couldn't sleep, so I decided to go back downstairs. I peered out the door, making sure that Fred was gone. Even though it was nearly midnight, the streets were full of loud, gesturing groups of people moving from bar to bar, of lone individuals hurrying to unknown rendezvous. A young couple strolled down the sidewalk, holding hands, followed by a tall man in a white robe, his face hidden by his hood. He walked slowly, thoughtfully, his fingers clicking the beads on his rosary. His eyes seemed to flicker as he walked by.

I passed a brightly lit telephone cabinet, then stopped in surprise and looked again. The phone booth was empty, a rare occurrence in Madrid. On a whim, I stepped inside and tried calling Peter.

"P.D.P. Murphy here. Who are you?"

"Hi, Peter."

"Noa! What a surprise to hear from you."

"Pleased?"

"Why wouldn't I be?"

"I never know."

"A little uncertainty adds spice to life—"

"Or indigestion."

"Only if you've got a weak stomach. Now, Noa, we agreed to take each day as it comes. Besides, this way, we never take each other for granted."

"You mean, we never take anything for granted."

"Life should be exciting—"

"I know, I know. By the way, talking about excitement—something happened at the library today."

"I wait with baited breath."

"I found a letter hidden in the spine of a fifteenth-century book."

"Ah, the letter in the old book-spine routine. What does it say?"

"It's written by someone in the Order of the Knights of Santiago and talks about buried treasure on the Milky Way. Make any sense?"

"Not really. Though the Knights of Santiago rings a bell."

"Last summer we stayed at the Hotel San Marcos in León. That was their headquarters."

Silence.

"Remember?"

"Of course."

Silence.

"Peter—"

"Of course I remember the hotel, and the halcyon days of yore, your golden hair forming a halo on the pillow—"

"My hair's auburn, remember? That must have been someone else."

"Ah, my dear, there has never been anyone else—except my ex-wife, my golden retriever—"

"That must be the golden hair you're thinking of. To think, I've been supplanted by a dog."

"Seriously, Noa, of course I remember the hotel and the Camino de Santiago, but you said something about the Milky Way. Wasn't there a film by that name?"

"Yes, by Buñuel, called *La Vía Láctea*—'The Milky Way'—about a pilgrimage to Santiago. The Camino is sometimes called the Milky Way because there were as many pilgrims as stars in the Milky Way. Sometimes the phrase refers to a pre-Christian pilgrimage road that existed before the Camino de Santiago but went past Santiago to a place called Finisterre."

"Your command of esoteric knowledge is truly impressive."

"You forget, Peter, I did my fieldwork in Sahagún, a town on the Camino, so I couldn't help learning something about it."

"Self-deprecating as always. Now, tell me more about the letter."

"Actually, I was hoping you could tell me."

"Delighted. My scholarly instincts are aroused."

"I hope that's all that's aroused."

"My dear, with you so far away, how could it be otherwise? Now tell me, what can I do to help?"

"Can you discreetly find out about the Knights of Santiago? And about tales of hidden treasure?"

"Discretion is my middle name. But whom should I talk to? It's not my field, you know."

"Try Rupert Nicholson in the History Department at SUNY. I've talked with him once or twice, though I don't think he'll remember me."

"Rupert Nicholson? I don't think I've met him. Then what should I do—mail you the dope?"

"You're so cute when you try to talk American. Don't mail it to me—that would take too long. I'll call you in a couple of days."

"Okay."

"How're things?"

"Fine."

"Up to anything interesting?"

"Not really."

"What a relief."

"This idle chit-chat is costing you money—"

"Ah. I must have called at a bad time."

"Not exactly, but I am going out, and I'm late."

"Okay. Good-bye."

"Call me in a day or two. I'll see what I can find out for you."

"Thanks for the help."

"Think nothing of it."

"Peter—"

He had hung up. I sat down on a nearby bench, feeling depressed. Slowly, I walked back to the hostel.

It was after midnight, so the street-level door to the building was shut. I inserted a key into the lock and pulled on the large flat knob in the middle of the door. The lock gave a satisfying click and I pushed it open. I pressed the light switch and hurried up the three flights of stairs to the hostel, listening to the timer ticking off the seconds. Breathless, I reached the door of the hostel just as the light went out.

My room was still hot, but no longer unbearable. With a weary sigh, I got undressed and stretched out on the bed, feeling a faint, cool breeze waft over my body. Closing my eyes, I realized how tired I was. Tired of thinking about the mysterious letter, of wondering about Peter's dinner plans, of worrying about Mateo, of quizzing and being quizzed by Fred. Soon I fell asleep.

Suddenly I was awaked by someone tapping on my door. I groped in the dark for my robe and stumbled sleepily over to the door.

"Who is it?"

"It's me, Sue Ellen."

I opened the door part-way. A slightly disheveled Sue Ellen stood in the brightly lit hallway, smiling.

"I'm so sorry. Were you sleeping?"

"What else would I be doing?" I grumbled.

"You never can tell. I'm sorry I woke you, but I just got in. Let's have lunch together tomorrow."

"Lunch?"

"Lunch. At Café La Trucha. My treat."

"Your treat?" I asked suspiciously. "What's the occasion?"

"Does there have to be an occasion?" Sue Ellen's eyes darted past me to the darkened room. "I just want to talk to you about something, that's all. Surely you don't mind, do you?"

Groggily, I replied, "Of course not. What time?"

"How about 2:15?"

"Okay. See you then."

"Sleep well."

"You too."

I locked the door and staggered back to bed, too sleepy to spend more than a moment wondering why Sue Ellen was being so friendly.

Three

Soaked with sweat, I struggled awake. A dream fragment surfaced behind my eyes, then submerged. Another surfaced and I held it for a moment: I was fleeing from a black-cloaked figure riding a jet-black stallion. The hoof beats thundered closer and closer. His robe billowed out behind him like bat wings, his eyes glowed like red-hot coals—I tripped, falling beneath the stallion's flaying hoofs. He reached down and hacked at me with a blood-stained sword grasped in his skeletal hand. The dream fragment blurred and faded.

Another fragment surfaced: With my bare hands, I was try-ing to dig up a treasure chest buried deep in the sand. Waves broke like thunder on the jagged rocks nearby. My hands were bleeding, staining the golden sand pink, and the sticky, pink-streaked sand kept flowing back into the hole. At last, straining with the effort, I managed to pull up the heavy wooden chest. I pried loose the lock, lifted up the jewel-encrusted lid, and found—I couldn't remem-ber. Wearily, I rubbed my eyes.

Trying to dispel an overwhelming sense of dread, I got out of bed, walked over to the sink, and splashed cold water on my face. After a few minutes of yoga stretches and deep breathing, I was less trapped in the shadowy borderland between wake and sleep.

I put on a fresh pair of blue jeans, a white T-shirt decorated with petroglyph designs, and my Berkinstock sandals. Then I fastened my concha belt around my waist, put on large silver hoop earrings and a heavy silver chain hung with assorted good-luck charms. No harm in a few preventive measures, I thought, half jokingly.

Awake, dressed, I took the Xeroxed letter out of the nightstand drawer. In the harsh morning light, it seemed even less likely that it was real. And even if it were real, the treasure was probably long gone. I shivered, remembering my nightmare. Already the treasure was disturbing my sleep, and all I'd done was find the letter. I hadn't even begun to look for the treasure, if there were any. It was obvious I wasn't cut out for this kind of adventure.

I left the letter on the nightstand, locked the room, and fled outside. Squinting against the bright daylight, I crossed the street to a small bar that served good espresso and cheap *media lunas*, a dry, sugar-coated approximation to the French croissant. Having breakfast there was a habit and, after last night, I needed all the habits I had to help me feel centered.

I stood at the long, polished wood counter and smiled at the bartender. With an answering smile, he went over to the electric grinder, pushed a button, ground some coffee beans, pressed them into a small metal basket, and slipped it into the espresso machine, all in one fluid, practiced motion. While I listened to the hissing of the espresso machine building up pressure, I looked around the room.

Three workmen in faded blue overalls stood at the other end of the bar, gesturing emphatically and arguing in loud voices; a young couple sat close together at a nearby table, whispering intently; a priest in a white robe, his face hidden by his cowl, sat silently in a corner, warming his hands on a large cup of *café con leche*.

After pouring cognac into the coffee cups of the workmen, the bartender brought me a steaming mug of espresso and placed the sweet roll on a plate beside it. The espresso had a thin topping of light-beige foam, called *crema*, a sure indication that it was fresh. While I sipped my coffee and nibbled my slightly stale roll, he told me the temperature in the café the day before had broken all records, and the forecast was for even hotter. He seemed proud of the fact, as if he personally had something to do with it. Maybe he was just proud that he had survived. Another customer called him away, and I was sorry that our conversation ended. His voice had built a fragile barrier between me and my nightmares. I finished my coffee and left a generous tip.

When I reached the library, Brother Mateo was pacing nervously near the guard desk inside the front entrance. As I came in the door, he started moving shakily in my direction. I heard someone call my name and looked around. A man standing next to one of the exhibit cases began striding toward me.

Thick black hair curled gracefully over his forehead. His olive skin was darkly tanned; his eyes were dark, his nose slender, with flaring nostrils; his lips curved in a sensuous smile. He was wearing an off-white linen shirt and taupe linen slacks, expensive-looking leather loafers but no socks. A very faint scent of musk and leather wafted through the air around him.

"Noa? Noa Webster?" He sounded both surprised and pleased.

I nodded, puzzled.

"Don't you remember me?" He asked.

I looked at him with what I hoped was a friendly but noncommittal expression. "Should I?"

His smile faded abruptly. "I could never forget you—you and your gorgeous auburn hair. You made quite an impression on me."

Try as I might, I couldn't remember who he was or where I had met him.

"Surely you remember me," he said, making it sound like a command. He waiting a few moments, then said, with more than a hint of disappointment in his voice, "I'm Jack, Jack Merlot. I'm in Art History at SUNY."

I was still puzzled. "Where did we meet?"

"At that departmental bash. Don't you remember?"

"Of course! How could I forget." Although obviously I had done just that. I wondered which bash it had been, and who had taken me there. It must have been Peter. Otherwise, Jack would have made a much more lasting impression.

We shook hands, and Jack held onto mine until I pulled it loose. "I'm surprised you remembered my name."

"How could I forget you or your name. You were named after Gauguin's autobiography, Noa Noa—isn't that what you told me?"

"That's right," I said, flattered that he remembered so much of what must have been a brief encounter. "What brings you to Madrid?"

"I'm spending the summer in Europe, and I wanted to see more of Spain, including this library. Did you know it has a world-famous collection of over two million volumes and more than 100,000 prints?"

"Really?" I hadn't bothered to check.

"They have some beautiful rare manuscripts from the tenth century. I was just admiring some on display." He gestured towards the glass case where he had been standing.

Still smiling—I was beginning to feel like an idiot, but he was smiling, too—I said, "What a coincidence to run into you here."

"I suppose it is a bit much, but stranger things do happen. Years ago in Thailand I ran into an old friend with someone who was not his wife. Were they surprised!" Jack chuckled at the memory. I found myself laughing with him, as if we were fellow conspirators.

A guard started to approach us, wagging his finger.

"We'd better keep our voices down," I whispered.

He whispered back, "What are you doing here? I didn't think you were a historian."

"I'm not. I'm a cultural anthropologist. But I'm looking through old manuscripts about Sahagún, a small town in north-central Spain."

"Find anything interesting?"

"Possibly."

The guard strode toward us.

Jack touched me lightly on the arm. "Let's go somewhere where we can really talk."

Regretfully, I said, "I'd love to, but I have to work." Seeing the startled look on his face, I realized I had, in essence, said I preferred examining musty manuscripts to renewing our acquaintance. Even I had to admit that was taking my work too seriously.

With a quirky smile, he asked, "Do you mind if I come with you? Old manuscripts fascinate me."

I looked at him in surprise. A true scholar, hidden behind that gorgeous front. "Are you sure you want to? You'll probably find it boring."

"How could I, with such charming company?"

"If you really want to . . ." I was beginning to feel like a blushing schoolgirl being asked out by the captain of the football team—not that I ever had been, or had ever wanted to be.

"I wouldn't miss this opportunity for anything. Believe me."

Looking around, I noticed Brother Mateo was no longer in sight. I wondered what he had wanted to see me about—if, in fact, he had been waiting for me. Well, he knew where to find me.

In the corridor leading to the study room we ran into Fred, who took one look at us and bolted like a frightened rabbit. The room was, as usual, deserted. There, piled on the table, were the books I had been examining the day before, but they seemed slightly rearranged. Frowning, I stared at the subtly altered heap.

"Something the matter, Noa?"

"I'm not sure, but I think these books have been rearranged."

"Is anything missing?"

Looking quickly through the disordered stack, I replied, "I don't think so."

"Maybe the janitor was here."

"Could be. But that would be the first time all summer."

I sat down and selected the mold-encrusted book in which I had found the letter. Jack pulled up a chair.

"What are you looking for?"

"I'm trying to get a new angle on Sahagún, the village where I did my fieldwork. It was the site of the most important Cluny monastery in Spain, back in the eleventh and twelfth centuries, and the history of the town is really quite interesting—townsfolk battling the feudal monastery, that kind of thing."

"Wasn't that unusual?"

"Very. Sahagún was an unusual place. Merchants and craftsmen from all over Europe lived in Sahagún. They were a very independent bunch. They took care of the various needs of monks, visiting kings and nobles, and the pilgrims traveling the Camino de Santiago."

"Fascinating." He said, as if he meant it. He reached for the book and I handed it to him. "It looks like it's been kicked around a lot."

I winced. "It is old, after all."

"The spine's almost falling off."

"So it is." I reached for the book.

Jack held onto it and examined it more closely. "You started to say you'd found something interesting. What was it?"

Torn between discretion and excitement, I hesitated a moment—but only a moment. "I found an old letter hidden in that book. At least I think it's old."

"A letter? That's just about as unlikely as running into you in the National Library. And almost—but not quite—as intriguing." He turned the book over. "You think the letter's old but you're not sure?"

"The date on the letter is June 14, 1493, but it could be a fake. A friend of mine was telling me there have been a number of faked documents in Spain."

"Your friend is right."

"So the letter is probably a fraud."

Jack glanced up from the book. "I've had a lot of experience examining old manuscripts. In fact, that's one of my specialties. I can tell you if the letter's real."

It seemed to good to be true. I'd wanted someone who could tell me if the letter was real, and here he was. Maybe the biblical line was right: ask and ye shall receive.

While I watched, Jack painstakingly inspected the binding of the book, then ran his hands over the inside and outside of the covers. His fingers explored each crack and spot. Idly, I wondered what it would feel like to have those long, sensuous fingers exploring the back of my neck, my shoulders . . . . With a start, I realized his fingers had stopped moving and he was saying something.

"There's something strange about the cover. See how the front panel has been loosened at the top?"

He held the book up to the light. "It sticks out too much." He started prying at it with his well-manicured fingernails.

"Jack! You're destroying the book—"

"Don't worry, Noa, it's just a battered old book. Nobody will care. Besides, nobody will know." Jack reached into his pants pocket, took out a monogrammed, silver folding knife, and clicked the blade open. Before I could stop him, he slit the panel of the book.

There was a glint of gold. He shook the book upside down, and a gold medallion the size of a silver dollar rolled across the table. I reached for it and held it in my hand.

"My God," I whispered. "This must be the key."

"What key?" Jack whispered back.

"The letter said there was a key."

"What else did the letter say?" His voice throbbed with excitement.

"Something about a treasure and the Milky Way. And the Knights of Santiago."

"Where's the letter?"

I stared at the gold medallion. "I gave it to one of the librarians."

Shaking his head in disbelief, he said, "You gave it to one of the librarians?"

I nodded.

He touched my hand, which was clutching the medallion. His fingers were warm and vibrant on my skin. "I'd really like to see the letter."

"Brother Mateo has the letter. I'll ask him to show it to you."

"Great. Let's do it."

Stunned—and vaguely uneasy at the casual way Jack had destroyed the book—I slipped the gold medallion into the watch pocket in my jeans. Then I led Jack to Brother Mateo's office. He wasn't there. Jack said he'd wait for him to return and then he'd rejoin me. I left him pacing the room and returned to stare at the mutilated book.

Half an hour went by, and I was getting very nervous. Just as I decided to go look for Jack, he returned and slumped down in the chair next to me.

His voice was thick with frustration. "Mateo wouldn't tell me anything."

"That doesn't sound like Brother Mateo," I said, puzzled. "He's always been quite cordial.

"He acted like he'd never heard of the letter."

"I don't understand. I gave it to him yesterday."

"Are you sure?"

"Come on, Jack!" I replied, angrily.

"Sorry, Noa. I don't know what got into me," he said apologetically. "The excitement of the hunt, I guess."

"Tell me what happened," I demanded.

"First I tried to talk to Mateo in English, but he pretended he didn't understand."

"Maybe he didn't."

"Then I tried Spanish. My Spanish isn't very good, but it's good enough. He still pretended he didn't know what I was talking about."

Thoughtfully, I said, "Brother Mateo hasn't been feeling well, but I can't believe he doesn't remember the letter. Besides, I saw him lock it in his desk drawer. I'd better go talk to him."

On the way to Brother Mateo's office, we ran into Fred again.

Fred glanced uneasily at Jack. "Noa, I've *really* got to talk to you—"

"Not now, Fred. Later." Next year, for example, I thought to myself.

I glanced back. Fred stood rooted to one spot, staring intently after us, hands clenching and unclenching at his side. I shivered slightly.

When we reached Mateo's office, the old man wasn't sitting at his usual spot. His desk appeared to be even more disorganized than usual, but before I could look it over, I found Mateo crumpled on the floor behind the door.

I held my ear to his chest but could hear no heart beat. Frantically, I started to loosen his clothes. A gold, sword-shaped cross of Santiago hung from a chain around his neck.

Just then a hooded, white-robed figure dashed from behind a cabinet and darted through the door. Jack ran after him, and I heard the sound of his shoes striking on the marble floor as he chased the man. A few minutes later Jack returned, panting hard.

"I couldn't catch him. One minute he was running down the corridor; next minute—poof!—he was gone." He looked at Mateo, lying still on the floor. "He's dead, isn't he?"

I nodded silently, still kneeling beside the motionless form.

"He was all right when I left him," he said defensively.

"I'm sure he was."

I noticed a scrap of crumpled paper lying next to his limp form. Bending down, I picked it up. It was barely decipherable but I made out a few words: "the Brotherhood . . . beware . . ."

Jack came over, took it from my shaking hands, and tried to read it. He shook his head and gave it back to me. "What's it say?"

"Something about 'the Brotherhood . . . beware . . .'—at least I think that's what it says." Without thinking, I slipped it into my pocket.

Jack glanced nervously around the room, then strode over to the desk. "The desk's been torn apart. I bet that white-robed monk did it. I wonder if he got what he was looking for." He started searching through the now-unlocked desk drawers.

I looked up from where I was kneeling, surprised. "What are you doing?"

"Looking for the letter, of course."

I looked up at Jack, tears in my eyes. "The doctor told him he had a bad heart. Maybe someone surprised him or upset him. Are you *sure* he was okay when you left?"

He glanced up from his search of the desk. "Of course I'm sure. He denied knowing about the letter, but he looked fine."

"But he's dead!"

"Maybe the man in white killed him," he said.

"What?" I gasped.

Seeing how upset I was, he tried to reassure me. "Just joking. He must have died of a heart attack. There's nothing mysterious about that. But something mysterious is going on, and it has to do with that letter. Which is definitely not here." He looked at Mateo, lying unmoving on the floor. "Let's get out of here."

I suddenly realized we hadn't told anyone what had happened. "Of course! We've got to get help right away—"

"It's too late for help, Noa. He's dead. But we should tell the authorities. I'll come with you." He reconsidered. "On second thought, you go. I'll keep watch." He hesitated again. "No, I'll come with you. You're so upset, it'll be easier for you if I do the explaining."

When we located the nearest security guard, Jack explained we had found Mateo lying dead on the floor. The security guard accompanied us back to Mateo's office. He took one look at Mateo and shook his head sadly.

It was a shame, he told us, but not unexpected. He pointed at his chest. Bad heart. He would call the ambulance immediately, even though it was pointless.

Having done all we could for Mateo, we went back to the study room and sat down at the table. Jack picked up the battered book. I stared into space.

Abruptly, Jack asked, "What are you going to do with the medallion, Noa?"

I came out of my daze. "The medallion?" I reached into my pocket and took it out.

On one side was a spiral design formed by the Roman numerals from I to XIII. Between each numeral was a symbol. On the reverse side was a labyrinth inscribed on top of a scallop shell. A hole had been drilled near one edge of the medallion, and a shred of green ribbon still clung to it.

Jack reached towards the glittering metal. "It might be better if I take care of the medallion."

"I can't imagine why." Ignoring his outstretched hand, I unfastened the heavy silver chain around my neck, slipped the medallion on it, and put it back on. The medallion was partly hidden by the dangling good luck charms.

"Do you really think someone killed him?" I asked hesitantly.

"Of course not. You've been reading too many murder mysteries. Mateo died of a heart attack. But his desk was searched and the letter is gone. And we know that a man in a white robe was there and fled."

I shuddered and looked uneasily around the room. Leaving the mangled book on the table, we strode out of the library and past the ambulance that had pulled up in front. Fred was standing at the edge of the group of onlookers. He waved urgently at me, but I ignored him. I wanted to get as far away as possible from the scene of Mateo's death.

Jack and I walked silently down the tree-lined Paseo. Suddenly, I started to tremble uncontrollably, and Jack gently pulled me close.

"What is it, Noa?" He asked, brushing a strand of hair from my forehead.

Sobbing, I mumbled, "I keep thinking of Mateo. He was my friend. He was alive and now he's dead. Just like that." Tears trickled down my cheeks. "He has—had—a son, and I never even met him. I never will. Not that that matters, really. I guess I'm not making much sense." I found some Kleenex and blew my nose loudly.

He held me close. "Dear Noa."

I sniffled. "I feel responsible, somehow. After all, I gave him the letter." I looked at Jack. "Do you think that's what started this whole thing?"

Tenderly, he wiped a tear from my cheek. "It's natural to feel guilty, Noa, but don't. Mateo had a heart attack, that's all. It's not your fault." His voice turned husky as he asked, "But what about us? What do we do now?"

His words were like a splash of ice water, startling me out of my tears. I drew away, puzzled. "What?"

"After all, we've got the medallion."

I'd forgotten for a moment. Instinctively, my hand went up to my throat.

He continued intensely, "Or rather, you've got the medallion. I found it, but you've got it. Someone else has the letter but no medallion. One's no good without the other." He touched my arm, as if to draw me closer. "If only we had the letter, we could have the adventure of a lifetime. But without the letter we can't do anything. What a lost opportunity!"

I said softly, "I made a copy."

"You made a copy?" He repeated.

"It's not a good copy, but it's a copy."

He smiled slowly. "You're my kind of woman."

"But, Jack, you can't tell from the copy if the letter is real."

"It's real, all right. The medallion's real, and so is the letter. Trust me."

If there's one thing I hate, it's being told "trust me." In my experience, that's usually a set-up for a major breach of confidence. But then, what do I know? Maybe I've just had bad luck too often. Or been attracted to the wrong kind of man. I started to demand a more concrete explanation, but just then I heard chimes: it was 2 o'clock.

"I forgot! I'm supposed to meet a friend at La Trucha."

"I don't want to leave you, Noa," he said slowly. "You've been through so much—"

"Well . . ."

"Besides, we have a lot to talk about."

It felt good to have him with me. I still felt shaky from Mateo's death. And besides, I thought, fingering the medallion, we did have a lot to talk about.

Shoulders touching, we walked quickly up the street to the café and, pushing open the frosted art-deco glass doors, we sat down at a marble-topped, wrought-iron table. A trio played chamber music in the corner. Unlike most Spanish bars, this one was not smoky; apparently the patrons preferred cleaner air. Or perhaps the air circulation system was better.

We were a bit early—Sue Ellen wasn't there yet. While we waited, Jack ordered a selection of *tapas*, fried squid rings, marinated octopus, and spicy potato salad. I had no appetite, but Jack was ravenous. And thirsty. He ordered a bottle of white Marqués de Murrieta and kept refilling our glasses.

Flushed with excitement and wine, he leaned towards me. "It's a wonderful world, isn't it? Just yesterday, I was alone and bored. Today, I'm planning to take off on a treasure hunt with a gorgeous woman."

I protested, "Now, wait a minute, Jack. I haven't agreed to go anywhere."

"It's a once-in-a-lifetime opportunity!"

"That's what they all say. There's probably no treasure—and even if there was, it's probably long gone."

"Someone took the letter. There has to be a hidden treasure." Jack said tensely.

He drained his glass and looked intently at me, then started to take one of my hands in his. I drew it away and held my wineglass tightly with both hands.

Gently, he asked, "What's the matter? Afraid?"

I looked away. "Maybe."

Taking a deep breath, he began, "Look, Noa, Mateo died under mysterious circumstances. Maybe the man in the white robe killed him." I gasped. "More likely, he found Mateo collapsed on the floor and took the opportunity to ransack his desk. He grabbed the letter and made off with it."

He reached out to touch my hands. I started to jerk away, then relaxed, feeling the energy tingling through his fingers to mine.

"You've been badly shaken by Mateo's death." He stroked my hand, reassuringly. "You care deeply about your friends. And you're no fool. You know this treasure hunt could be dangerous. But, Noa, I can take care of you. You don't have anything to worry about."

Warily, I glanced at him.

Looking deeply into my eyes, he said, "If you're afraid to go, give me the medallion and the letter so I can go. But Noa, I don't want to go without you. I want to find the treasure, but I want to do it with you." He added, under his breath, "How can Peter be such a fool!"

I jerked my hands away from his light caress. "Peter? You know Peter?"

"Yes, I know Peter. And I know that Peter is a fool to let you go. Maybe he just doesn't care—"

"What are you talking about?"

Jack continued talking, almost to himself. "You made a big impression on me at that party, but I didn't stand a chance, not with Peter around." Suddenly, his face lit with a flash of understanding. "Is that it? Are you worried what Peter will say if he finds out we're together?"

Actually, I hadn't thought that far ahead. I was still in shock.

"Peter didn't seem very lonely the last time I saw him."

"What?" I exclaimed, the wineglass slipping from my fingers.

Jack mopped up the spilled wine with a monogrammed hand-kerchief, which he wadded up and dropped in the ashtray.

He refilled my glass. "Did I say something that upset you?"

I took a deep breath and a long drink. "Let's drop the subject, okay?"

Suddenly the door opened and sunlight streamed into the room. Sue Ellen entered, framed in light. She paused for a moment and looked around. The backlighting from the sun made her peach-colored silk dress semitransparent. She was not wearing a slip. Her shoulder-length blond hair swung loose around her face, surrounding it with a golden halo. Involuntarily, I held my breath. She spotted us. Swaying on her high heels, she strolled over to the table.

She nodded at me, then turned a dazzling smile on Jack. "Well, hello!"

"Do you two know each other?" I asked, surprised.

Sue Ellen replied in her best Southern drawl, "I don't believe we've had the pleasure."

Much to my amazement, Jack ignored her and stared at his wineglass.

She slid into the empty chair between us. "Noa, aren't you going to introduce us?"

"Sue Ellen, this is Jack. Jack, this is Sue Ellen."

"Hello, Jack," she purred. "What brings you to Madrid?"

He stared at his wineglass and replied, "Good luck, I guess."

Nonplused, Sue Ellen twisted a strand of corn-silk hair around a pink-tipped finger. Then she fished in her purse for a cigarette, found one, and looked expectantly towards Jack. He didn't move.

"Jack, dear, don't you have a light?"

He seemed to come out of a daze. "Sorry, Sarah, I don't smoke."

"The name's Sue Ellen," she replied, irritated.

He continued to stare at his wineglass.

Uncomfortable, I started drawing a design in a puddle of wine.

Sue Ellen leaned towards me and hissed, "Really, Noa! What's going on?"

I wasn't sure I knew why Jack was ignoring her, but I tried to explain anyway. "We were in the middle of an important conversation."

Sue Ellen stood up. "Come on, Noa, let's go to the powder room. Excuse us, Jack."

We walked to the back of the restaurant and opened the door with the flamenco-dressed female silhouette on the front. Sue Ellen took out a matchbook, lit her own cigarette, inhaled deeply, and leaned back against the red and black brocade-covered wall.

"Just what is going on?"

Evasively, I asked, "What do you mean?"

"You know what I mean."

"My librarian friend, Brother Mateo, just died."

"Oh, I'm so sorry, honey," she said, sincerely. "Was Jack there too?"

"Yes. We found Mateo just after he died."

"Well, I wondered what the matter was. It was obvious something strange was going on—Jack couldn't even remember my name!" Obviously, that was unheard of for Sue Ellen.

She inhaled deeply and tapped the ashes into the sink. "Want to talk about it?"

"Maybe later."

"By the way, where did you meet that gorgeous man?"

"Jack?"

"Who else."

"We ran into each other at the library."

"Known him long?"

"We met at a party back home. Why?"

"I just wondered."

"Why?" I replied, puzzled.

"He just isn't your type, that's all."

"Oh? And just what is my type?"

"Now don't get huffy, Noa. You've had enough trouble holding on to Peter—and I'm sure he's not half the man Jack is." Sue Ellen went on breathlessly, "Jack's got a kind of magnetism—he practically radiates danger—it's hard to explain, honey, but I've been around a lot of men and I can smell it."

Like the hound after the fox, I thought. Or the pig after the truffle.

"I know I told you to loosen up and have some fun, Noa, but I really didn't think you'd do it so soon." Sue Ellen gave a deep, throaty laugh. "Take it from me, you're just not ready for a man like Jack."

I laughed at the absurdity of the conversation. "Come on, Sue Ellen, you're just jealous."

"Me, jealous of you? That'll be the day."

"Don't underestimate me, Sue Ellen."

Sue Ellen dropped her cigarette in the sink. It sizzled and went out, leaving an unpleasant smell of wet, burnt tobacco. She turned abruptly and swayed out of the room. I followed behind.

Jack was sitting at the table, staring off into space, drumming on the tabletop with his graceful fingers. Sue Ellen placed her hand gently on his shoulder.

Smiling sweetly, she said, "Noa told me something dreadful happened at the library. I'm sure you've been a great comfort to her, Jack." She rubbed her lower lip with her pink-tipped finger. "Maybe we can get together later and talk about it, hmm? Noa and I are staying at the same hostel."

She turned and sauntered out of the café, stopping to chat at several tables on the way out.

Coming out of a deep reverie, Jack looked intently at me. I was trying hard to control myself. Breathe in for five, out for five, I told myself, using yoga practice to help expel the anger I felt. Anger at Sue Ellen for saying I couldn't handle Peter? For saying I couldn't handle Jack?

After watching me breathe for a few minutes, Jack raised his glass for a toast. "Well, Noa, are you ready for the adventure of a lifetime?"

My hand went to the gold medallion hanging from the chain around my neck. It was obvious, now that I thought about it, that Mateo had been badly shaken by the letter. And now he was dead, indirectly—or perhaps directly—because of the letter I had given him. Although it wasn't really my fault, I felt guilty. There was nothing I could do about his death, but I could do something about the letter. I could find the treasure.

I stroked the medallion slowly. It felt warm to the touch. I thought about Peter, who apparently was having a wonderful time without me. I thought about Jack, who wanted to have a wonderful time with me. And what did I want? I wanted to forget about death and disappointment. I wanted an adventure. Slowly, I nodded my head.

With a deep sigh of relief, Jack reached out to touch my hand again. This time, I didn't draw away. "I have a feeling this will be the most exciting adventure—and the best company—I've ever had."

He called the waiter over and ordered a bottle of their finest champagne. The waiter returned with an ice-filled silver bucket, a tripod, two fluted glasses and a towel-wrapped black bottle. He showed the gold label to Jack.

Jack looked at it with disdain. "Is this the best you have?"

The waiter nodded, surprised.

Condescendingly, Jack said, "Then it'll have to do."

The waiter cut the foil and then carefully worked the cork loose. It popped explosively, and white foam shot out of the bottle and ran down the sides onto the table. He poured the foaming liquid into our upraised glasses, shoved the bottle in the bucket, and left.

"A toast to the future!"

"To the future!"

We clinked our glasses together, spilling more champagne onto the already damp tabletop.

Jack took a deep swallow and leaned back in his chair. "So. The adventure begins. Actually, it began the moment I ran into you at the library." His expression became thoughtful. "But just where do we begin?"

I licked the tingly, lemon-scented foam off my lips. "The letter says the road begins where the Knights of Charlemagne lie buried. It also says that Santiago will lead the way on the Milky Way."

"Santiago—that's St. James. Or St. Jacques, in French. And my name's Jack." He laughed infectiously. "So far so good, though I won't be leading the way—I'll be following your lead. But what's the Milky Way? And where do we begin?"

Thoughtfully, I replied, "The Camino de Santiago was also called the Milky Way. And the Knights of Charlemagne—some of them, at least—are supposed to be buried at Roncesvalles, near the beginning of the Camino de Santiago."

"Then that's where we'll start." He drank more champagne. "You said there was a key."

"That must be the medallion."

"Any idea how to use it?"

"We'll have to figure it out when we get there."

"Sounds good. Let's go!"

"But how do we get to Roncesvalles?" I asked, just beginning to deal with the reality of this adventure. "Maybe there's a train or a bus—"

"No problem. I rented a car for the summer." Impatiently, he glanced at his gold Rolex. "Where are you staying?"

"At the Hostel Amargo, just up the street from here."

"I'll meet you in half an hour in front of the hostel. Will that give you enough time to pack?"

I nodded.

"The sooner we get going the better."

I drained my glass of champagne and stood up.

He stood up, took out his wallet and tossed some large pe-
seta bills on the table. We walked together in silence up the street
to the hostel. Jack opened the door and stepped inside with me.
There he embraced me tightly. He smelled of expensive cologne
and adventure. Releasing me, he said, "See you in a half an hour.
And be sure you bring the letter!"

Four

I hurried up the stairs to my room. Somewhat winded, I stood in the corridor, searching for my room key. Then I noticed I didn't need it. The door was slightly ajar.

Cautiously, I pushed it open and peered inside. Sue Ellen was reclining on my unmade bed, looking at the Xeroxed letter.

"How the heck did you get in?" I said angrily, as I marched over and grabbed the letter.

She smiled at me, unperturbed. "I told the landlord you had borrowed a dress and I just had to have it back. He was very understanding."

"Out!" I said, pointing at the door.

Sue Ellen examined her fingernails. "Why?"

I sputtered, "Why?"

"Now, Noa, you're not being very friendly. We have plenty to talk about. Like your friend Jack. And that letter."

I took one look at her grinning face and wanted to slap it. Instead, I stomped over to the wooden wardrobe in the corner, found my battered blue backpack/suitcase, and started packing.

"What are you doing?" she asked.

"Packing."

"Where are you going?"

"None of your business."

"This has something to do with the letter, doesn't it? Remember, Noa, you promised to keep me posted and I promised not to tell anyone."

She had a point. But why was I the only one who felt compelled to play by the rules? I muttered, "I gave the letter to Brother Mateo."

"He's the guy you found dead, isn't he?"

"Yes." Why did I keep blurting out the truth whenever she asked? I felt like Pavlov's dog.

"There's a connection between the letter and his death, isn't there?"

I was beginning to realize that Sue Ellen wasn't as dumb as she acted. She had always reminded me of the popular girls I had envied in high school, coasting through life with dates every weekend and flawless skin. They were dumb, but nobody cared. I, on the other hand, had been plump and pimply and shy. And smart. And nobody cared. At least you could outgrow being fat. You couldn't outgrow being dumb.

"What?" I said, realizing she was waiting for me to say something.

"The letter has something to do with his death, doesn't it?"

Ignoring her, I went over to the washstand and started packing my toiletry bag.

"Did you tell the police about the letter?"

"Why should I?" I replied defensively. "The two things probably had nothing to do with each other."

"Come on, Noa, level with me. After all, I'm your friend."

"With friends like you—. If you must know, I gave the letter to Mateo and he's dead. From a heart attack. That's the extent of the connection. Satisfied?"

"So why are you rushing off in such a hurry?"

"Jack and I are taking a trip on the Camino de Santiago, that's all. We want to get away for a while. After all, Mateo's death has been rather upsetting."

Sue Ellen snorted. "I don't believe you. Besides, what would Peter think?"

"Oh, damn Peter! Who cares what he thinks."

"My, my, Noa. You really are acting out of character." She chewed on one of her long, pink fingernails. "I think you should take me along. For your own sake."

I stared at her in amazement.

"You should take me along to protect you from Jack. Besides, I know you're going on a treasure hunt and I don't want to be left out."

"Absolutely not." I started going through the wardrobe, pulling out clothes, including a nightgown and a robe. Although I liked to sleep nude, modesty might be advisable. I grabbed a pair of dressy sandals.

"Please, Noa, it would mean so much to me," she pleaded.

Determined not to capitulate, I refused to look at her.

Sue Ellen's voice changed from sugary-sweet to threatening. "Let me put it this way. If you don't take me with you I'll tell the police."

"There's nothing to tell."

"Of course there is. You found a letter about a hidden treasure and you gave it to Mateo, and then you found Mateo dead. From a heart attack. Or so you claim. And now you're leaving town suddenly. Sounds pretty suspicious to me, and it will to the police."

"You have a way of twisting things—"

"Noa, you should know by now that I get what I want. And I want to come with you. You and Jack." She looked off into space.

I looked at my watch. It was time to meet Jack. I shrugged my shoulders and said, "You win. I don't have time to argue."

Sue Ellen jumped up from the bed and ran to the door. "I'll be packed in a jiffy."

"You'd better be," I said angrily. "Meet me downstairs."

I closed the suitcase, looked quickly around the room, and grabbed my camera bag from the top of the wardrobe. On the way out, I saw the landlady dozing in a lounge chair, so I told her I'd be gone for a few days—and not to rent my room. Then I ran down the stairs to the street.

A gleaming silver Mercedes was parked at the curb, its motor purring. Jack opened the passenger door from inside, and I tossed my bag onto the back seat and slid in. Then I turned to him.

"Sue Ellen wants to come too."

He slammed his fist against the steering wheel. "How'd she find out?"

"She already knew about the letter, and she was waiting for me when I got back to my room. She says she'll tell the police."

Jack gripped the wheel so tightly his knuckles turned white. "It's just a stupid threat. She doesn't know a thing. I don't want her along." He glanced at me. "Do you?"

"Of course not."

Abruptly, Jack slammed the Mercedes into reverse, then forward. Tires squealing, we drove off. I looked in the right-hand rearview mirror and saw Sue Ellen rush out the door. She stood on the sidewalk, hands on her hips, watching us speed away.

We drove out of town on the autoroute that headed northeast to the Pyrenees. At Medinaceli we turned off the superhighway onto Route 111, the most direct way to go from Madrid to Roncesvalles.

I leaned back, enjoying the look and feel of the Mercedes. Oiled teakwood dashboard, state-of-the-art computerized controls, golden-tan glove-leather seats, teak and leather trim on the doors, velvety, gold-colored carpet. Idly, I wondered whether the leather seats smelled that good naturally or whether the scent was artificial. In one of the numerous mail order catalogues I received back home, I'd seen an advertisement for a spray to make your car smell new. Maybe there was a spray to make your car smell expensive.

Jack's long, slender hands rested lightly on the steering wheel, but I noticed his air of indolence disguised intense concentration and rapid reflexes. He drove with expertise on the narrow, winding roads, swinging skillfully around slow-moving trucks, effortlessly evading the traffic that darted out unexpectedly from side roads.

The miles flowed by as we sped through rolling hills, past terraces of vineyards, fields of golden grain, olive groves, sunflower fields, and acres of what looked like tiny molehills. The mounds hid white asparagus, covered with earth to keep the stalks from turning green.

Every so often I stroked the gold medallion around my neck. Where would the treasure hunt take me, I wondered, and what would I find along the way? I felt a strange sense of foreboding, and fragments of last night's vivid dreams flashed through my mind, then faded away.

After several hours, Jack interrupted my musing. "I don't know about you, but I'm getting hungry. And tired. Any idea where we should stop for the night?"

I opened the glove compartment and pulled out the road map. "Pamplona isn't far from here, and it's only 50 kilometers—about 30 miles—to Roncesvalles."

"Sounds good. Pamplona ... that's Hemingway country, isn't it?"

I nodded, remembering a literature-class discussion of *For Whom the Bell Tolls*. Or was it *The Sun also Rises*. As I recalled, the characters had gone trout fishing and run with the bulls. At least the men had. What had the women done? Waited patiently?

Jack thought a minute, eyes narrowed. "I suppose there's no rush to reach Roncesvalles. Even if whoever stole the letter has the same idea we do—to start looking for the treasure at Roncesvalles— he won't be able to find anything without the medallion."

Jack's reminder that someone else was looking for the treasure made me shift uncomfortably on the soft leather seat.

"Know any good hotels?" he asked.

"I've never been to Pamplona."

"In that case, let's just head into town and see what we find."

Hesitantly, I said, "Jack, I don't have much money. We'll have to be careful where we stay."

Jack looked at me in disbelief. "We're on a once-in-a-lifetime adventure and you're worrying about the cost of a hotel room?"

"It may seem absurd to you," I replied stiffly, "but I'm an assistant professor of anthropology at a small college, remember? And my summer research grant isn't very big. If I spend it all now, I won't have anything to live on for the rest of the summer."

He laughed and patted my knee, letting his hand linger a moment on my skin. "Don't worry, Noa. I said I would take care of you and I will, starting now. I've got plenty of money."

"Is that why you rented a Mercedes?"

"I like fine, responsive cars, almost as much as I like fine, responsive women. Besides, it's one of the few cars you can rent in Spain with air conditioning."

I remembered the five-star Hotel San Marcos in León. "Even the best Spanish hotels usually don't have air conditioning in the rooms."

"Spain is so backwards."

Defensively, I replied, "Of course, that does help conserve energy."

"Why worry about the future? We should enjoy the present— in luxurious comfort, if at all possible."

Soon we reached Olite, a small country town south of Pamplona. As we sped by, Jack saw a sign for a three-star *parador*, the Principe de Viana. Abruptly, he spun the car around and headed down a narrow cobblestone road, then through a huge stone archway. In front of us was a castle with multicolored pennants fluttering gaily from its turrets.

He looked surprised. "Is this the hotel?"

"Must be. Some of the government-run *parador*s are converted monasteries and castles."

I stayed in the car while Jack went inside to ask for a room. He returned, whistling a dance tune.

"No problem. They had one room left."

"One room?"

"Only one. And I had to bribe the clerk for it." He grinned. "You're not worried about spending the night alone with me, are you?"

Annoyed, I replied, "If I 'spend the night' with you, Jack, I want it to be out of choice, not out of convenience."

"Don't worry, Noa, you can trust me. You have my word as a gentleman."

I looked at him skeptically.

"Besides, the room has two beds," he said, laughing.

Feeling a bit foolish, I laughed along with him.

We parked the car and walked through the arched stone entryway to the hotel. It was like stepping into a medieval castle, with modern conveniences. The main salon had an enormous stone fireplace. A gleaming suit of armor stood next to it. The gray stone walls were covered with huge oil paintings, framed in gilt, and the cavernous room was furnished with velvet sofas and leather lounge chairs. In one corner, several guests watched television.

Walking past the main desk, I noticed a framed poster of Pamplona's seven-day-long Festival of San Fermín, the Sanfermines held in July. I turned to Jack. "No wonder the *parador* is so crowded. We've gotten here just in time for the running of the bulls."

"I've always wanted to do that."

"You and Hemingway," I said, wondering why anyone would want to try to outrun a charging herd of smelly, sharp-horned beasts.

The bellboy took our bags and led us up two flights of stairs to our room. While Jack tipped him, I walked through the leaded-glass double doors that opened onto the private balcony. Spread out before me were a thickly wooded pine grove and the low mountains of Navarra. I leaned on the ornate wrought-iron railing, breathing in the evergreen-scented air and listening to the sounds of birds settling in for the night. Somewhere in the distance, at the edge of the Pyrenees, was Roncesvalles. With a sigh, I stepped back inside, leaving the doors open.

Jack was waiting. "Which bed do you prefer?"

I chose the one closest to the bathroom. Then, feeling suddenly awkward about sharing a room with a stranger, no matter how charming and attractive—or maybe because he *was* so charming and attractive—I paced nervously around while Jack unpacking his leather Hartmann bag. On top of a massive wooden bureau in the corner, I found a folder full of embossed stationery and a brochure describing the *parador*.

I sat down in a large leather-covered, rosette-studded armchair. "Interested in learning about the history of our hotel?"

He glanced up at me and smiled. "Sure, why not."

"According to this, our hotel was originally a thirteenth- or fourteenth-century castle-fortress, converted by Charles III of Navarra into his summer palace. Rumor had it that Charles once hired three matadors to fight bulls in the main courtyard. The oldest part of the castle was converted into a *parador* in 1966." I could tell that Jack wasn't really listening, and neither was I, so I put down the brochure and stared out the open balcony doors.

He went into the bathroom to shower and change clothes. When he came out, he was dressed in a fresh linen shirt, pale gray linen trousers, and a chamois-colored suede jacket. He looked good and smelled even better. I took a deep breath, let it out slowly—I seemed to be doing a lot of deep breathing these days—and headed for the bathroom.

The bathroom was not quite as nice as the one at the Hotel San Marcos. No black Magno soap, for one thing; this *parador* provided a different line, something green and herbal. And no Peter. But there were compensations. Or might be.

After a quick shower, I dried myself off with a voluminous white bath sheet and sprayed myself liberally with Obsession. Then I put on a halterneck turquoise silk dress. The dangling silver charms and gold medallion looked a bit garish against the silk, but I didn't want to take any of them off. A touch of mascara, a touch of blusher, a little lipstick, guaranteed not to smear.

I looked at my reflection in the full-length mirror. Not bad, I decided, then blushed. Was I really trying to attract Jack? Looking my reflection straight in the eye, I admitted that Jack was extremely attractive—Sue Ellen was absolutely right. But no matter what Sue Ellen thought, I was woman enough for him. Not that I planned to do anything about it, of course. After all, I didn't quite trust him, yet. Still, he was a delightful change from the surly, inept men I had known and from Peter's sardonic, intellectual vacillation. Speaking of which, just what was Peter up to, anyhow? Jack said he hadn't looked too lonely when he saw him, so maybe he *had* wanted me out of the way for the summer.

I twisted my hair back into a bun and left the bathroom. Jack took one look and let out a low whistle. "Not only do you look great in jeans, but you look marvelous all dressed up. Even better than I remembered."

I blushed again. "Let's go."

The hotel dining room was elegant—and nearly empty, since it was only 10 P.M., early for dinner by Spanish standards. Floor-length red and gold tapestry curtains covered the windows and most of the walls, matching the upholstery on the chairs. An elaborate crystal chandelier tinkled delicately in the gentle breeze from the ceiling fans. The hostess led us to a damask-covered, candle-lit table for two.

The waiter came over and handed each of us a large menu hand-printed on antique-looking parchment. While we looked at the menu, he recited the specialties of the day. I saw the prices and frowned. Jack placed his hand gently on mine.

"Dinner's on me, Noa, now and for the rest of the trip. So is the hotel room."

I started to protest, but he shook his head emphatically. "I insist. Actually, you'll be doing me a favor."

"I will?"

He smiled. "Yes, you will. I like to travel in style—fine cars, fine wines—that kind of thing. It's an expensive habit, but one I just can't seem to break. You would probably choose to stay in a cheaper hotel and eat at a cheaper restaurant, given your financial constraints."

"Of course."

"But you and I are traveling together. We can hardly stay or eat in different places, and I won't lower my standards. I know you don't have much money, so it wouldn't be fair to make you— in effect—pay for my habits. " He grinned disarmingly.

"But—"

"Besides, it's much more enjoyable for me if I have someone to share this with.

"But—"

"Don't misunderstand. I'm not trying to 'buy my way' into your confidence—or your bed."

How had he known what I was thinking?

He continued. "Not that I'd object if that's where I end up, of course. But that's a different issue. Let's just consider my paying our expenses as an exchange."

I looked at him suspiciously. "For what?"

"Translation services."

I laughed at the unexpected reply.

"Your Spanish is much better than mine, and so is your knowledge of Spain. So let's call it a fair exchange, all right?"

"All right," I replied, still laughing.

Jack turned to the waiter, who was waiting, apparently oblivious to our conversation, and ordered the specialties of the house, whatever they might be, and the best local wine. After some discussion, the waiter returned with a bottle of red wine from Bodegas Ollara. Jack inspected the label, inhaled the bouquet, then took a sip and rolled it around in his mouth. He leaned back, contented.

"One unexpected pleasure of this trip—aside from your company, Noa—is that I'm doing something I've wanted to do for some time."

"What's that?"

"Sample the finest Rioja wines. We're right in the middle of the best wine-growing region in Spain."

My Epicurean experience had been limited by my meager budget, so I had to take his word for it.

Dinner began with *entremeses:* several kinds of cured ham, mayonnaise-and-olive stuffed eggs, smoked trout on toast, several aged cheeses, and succulent white asparagus. I could definitely get used to this kind of life, I decided.

The main course was rabbit with snails, redolent with garlic and onions and wine. For dessert, we split a slice of rum-soaked *tarta helada*, a dense, creamy ice-cream torte. Surreptitiously, I loosened my concha belt a notch.

The waiter brought espresso and then returned with a small wooden box, which he opened with a flourish. The scent of fine tobacco filled the air. Jack took a cigar and the waiter lit it for him. Normally, I detest cigar smoke, but this smelled marvelous, a mixture of cured leather, spices, and fresh-plowed earth after rain.

Watching the glowing coal of the cigar brighten and fade, I observed, "Given all that's happened today—meeting you, finding the medallion, Mateo's death, taking off for Roncesvalles—I feel surprisingly good. I have to admit, I haven't had this much fun in a long time."

A trickle of white smoke escaped his lips. "Adventure becomes you, my dear." He tapped the gray tip of ash into an ashtray. "Why don't we go to the lounge and have a drink?"

Soon we were seated next to each other on a deeply cushioned red velvet sofa.

I smiled happily at Jack. "This is the way to live. But are you sure you can afford this?"

"Don't worry about me. I do a lot of outside consulting. Besides, what better way to spend money than on good food, fine wine, and delightful company."

The barmaid came over and Jack ordered two Lepantos. We swirled the amber-colored cognac in the large brandy snifters, watching it cling to the sides of the glass. It looked like honey. The aroma reminded me of a flower garden in full bloom. I leaned back—and reclined unexpectedly into Jack's waiting arms. He kissed me deeply.

Startled, I broke away.

He looked surprised. "I didn't think you'd mind."

"It's just that everything has happened so fast."

"Maybe for you," he said huffily, "but I've been waiting for this moment for a long time."

Disconcerted, I stared into my glass of cognac. Jack shifted on the couch, then looked at his watch. "We'd better go to bed."

I looked at him warily.

"To our separate beds. Trust me."

As we walked across the lobby past the large color television, I noticed the late news program was on. It showed a narrow street lined with people; more people leaned out of flower-laden balconies of the houses on each side of the street. Down the middle marched a procession of dancing giant figures dressed like Moors, followed by a group of men in white clothes with red sashes and bandannas, playing drums and flutes. Darting in and out of the crowd were squat, monstrous creatures with enormous papier mâché heads.

"What are those?" Jack asked.

Glad to talk about something neutral, I explained, "It's a parade of the *gigantes*—giants—and *cabezudos*—'bigheads.' They use similar figures in the feast day parades in Sahagún, too. The giants are supposed to be reenacting the conquest of the Moors, while the bigheads play practical jokes and shoot off fireworks. They must be part of today's Sanfermines celebration."

"Oh," he said, disinterested.

Eager to stall, I said, "Maybe they'll show the *encierro*."

As we watched, the camera cut to an overhead shot of glistening, black-skinned animals with pointed white horns running in a tightly clumped pack, their massive heads tossing from side to side as they stampeded up the narrow street. Racing in front of them and at the side were men of all ages, most of them dressed in white and red. I could almost smell the sweat, the danger, the fear. A man darted into a vacant doorway and plastered himself flat against the door. One of the bulls lunged at him and missed. The animals thundered past on their way to the *plaza de toros*. In just a few moments, it was over. My hands were damp. I started to wipe them off on the skirt of my dress, then remembered it was silk.

The newscaster announced that two runners had been seriously injured in the *encierro* that morning: one was trampled, the other gored. He added that there was some discussion in the city council of limiting the number of foreigners who could run with the bulls, since it was usually the foreigners who got hurt. On the other hand, nobody wanted to discourage the influx of tourists to the city. I translated for Jack.

"That was it? All of it? But it happened so fast!"

"They do it each day for a week." I shook my head. "I don't understand what the attraction is. Do you?"

Jack looked at me, one corner of his mouth turned up in a crooked half-smile. "It's Man against Nature, against Fate with a capitol F. It's like race car driving. Or treasure hunting. Or making love to an exciting woman. It makes life worth living."

We started to walk away, but I stopped abruptly when I heard the newscaster announce that the police were investigating the mysterious death of a librarian at the National Library.

"Did you hear that?" I asked, forgetting his Spanish wasn't good enough.

"What?"

"The police are investigating Mateo's death."

"So what?" He said dismissively.

"They suspect foul play. Shouldn't we do something?"

"Surely you don't want to offer to help!"

"Why not? We know more about what happened than anyone."

"Not more than the killer," Jack pointed out.

"It's not clear Mateo was murdered. They're investigating it, that's all."

"Believe me, that means they think he was murdered."

"Even more reason to go to the police. Mateo was my friend," I said stubbornly. "Besides, it's our duty to go to the police."

Eyes narrowed, Jack replied, "Who the hell cares about duty! What do you think this is, some grade-school picnic?" He took a deep breath. "Look, Noa, if we talk to the police we'll be held up for days, maybe even have to go back to Madrid, and we haven't done anything wrong. Besides, we'd be in danger."

I waited for him to continue.

"If we go to the police, whoever killed Mateo will find out and *our* lives will be in danger. Besides, given what I know of Spanish police, we'll be in jail under suspicion and the real murderer will be free and hunting for the treasure. Mateo's treasure."

"You've got a point. Several, in fact." I conceded.

"That-a girl! I knew you had the right spirit."

"I guess there really isn't anything we could tell, except about the man in white." I thought for a moment. "I know. I'll call anonymously."

"No, Noa—"

"Yes, Jack. They won't know who called, and it might even help us if they could catch the man in white."

"Maybe you've got a point."

I went to a pay phone and got information for Madrid. Then I called the number for the police station there. In my best Spanish, I explained that a white-robed man had been seen fleeing Mateo's office. Then I hung up.

"Feel better?" Jack asked.

"Somewhat."

I still felt badly, but, logically, I knew that Jack was right. We knew we were innocent but the police didn't. And the thought of Mateo's murderer—if it was murder—finding the treasure made me sick. It was bad enough that Mateo was dead, but it would be even worse if his murderer benefited from the death. Besides, maybe it wasn't really murder. I still clung to that bit of hope. Or was it denial?

Distressed, I stumbled up the stairs to our room. Jack followed behind and gently turned me towards him. I looked away.

"Remember, Noa, this is the adventure of a lifetime! There're risks, but so what?"

"Peter's always talking about adventure—"

"What can Peter know about adventure," he sneered. "Besides, why bring up Peter? It's just you and me, Noa. Together in a romantic castle in Spain." He put his arm around me.

Peter.

I twisted away and started towards the staircase.

"Where are you going?"

"I just remembered I promised Peter I'd call tonight."

He reached for me and held me tight.

I struggled unsuccessfully. "Jack, let go!"

Reluctantly, he released me. Furious, I glared at him and rubbed my arms.

"Noa, I'm sorry. Forgive me. I'm just jealous. You mentioned Peter, and I just lost control."

Somewhat mollified, but not much, I said, "I told Peter I'd call him. I asked him to find out about the Knights of Santiago."

"I don't want too many people in on this." He thought a moment. "Look, Noa, don't say anything about me."

"Why not?"

"I'd rather you didn't, that's all."

"Why not?"

He looked away from me. "It might make Peter nervous."

"Oh, really, Jack!"

He continued quickly, "It would damn well make me nervous if my girlfriend was running around Spain with another man."

I started down the stairs, Jack following close behind. I stopped and said, coldly. "Surely you don't plan to listen in on the conversation."

"Of course not. I just want to make sure nothing happens to you."

"What on earth could happen to me between our room and the main desk?"

"Don't forget what happened to Mateo."

I shivered and hurried down the stairs. At the reception desk I asked to make an international phone call. The clerk took the telephone number and put the call through on the desk phone. Jack hovered nearby, and I motioned to him to go away. He went into the bar but sat where he could see me. I turned my back on him.

At last, the call went through.

"Un momento," the desk clerk said and handed me the receiver.

"Hi, Peter, it's me."

"Ah, the dulcet tones of my fair lady calling me from the Spanish Steps—"

"Aren't those in Rome, sweetie?"

"Well, so my geography's a bit weak. How goes it?"

"It goes apace. Actually, I am happily ensconced in a medieval castle."

"With a benighted knight in shining armor?"

"He's no knight, but I suppose so."

Startled, Peter asked, "Where are you and who are you with?"

"I'm in the *parador* at Olite, near Pamplona."

"That's the 'where'; who's the 'who'?"

"Jack."

"Jack?"

"Jack Merlot."

"Who's that?"

"Don't you know him?" I asked, surprised.

"I don't think so."

"He says he knows you. He's in art history at SUNY."

There was a pause. "I don't remember him. But then, I meet so many people—"

"And you only remember the attractive female ones, right?"

"Ah, that you can read my mind, despite the distance, only demonstrates the depth of our attachment. But seriously, Noa, where did you run into him?"

"In the National Library."

"And what are you doing with him in Olite?"

"Peter, do you really want to know?"

Silence.

"Far be it from me to inquire about your private life." He sounded miffed. "After all, you are a 'free agent,' as they say."

"As are you, as you keep reminding me. But really, Peter, it isn't like that. We found the gold medallion, and now we're on a treasure hunt."

"Wait—back up. Start over."

With mounting excitement, I explained, "We found the medallion—the key the letter talks about—and then Brother Mateo died—or maybe he was killed, though I really don't think so—and then Jack and I took off for Roncesvalles. That's where the treasure hunt begins. At least I think it does."

"Of course. Now I'm with you." There was a pause. "You mean there really *is* a key?"

"Yes! Jack found it in the same book where I found the letter. Come to think of it, that's kind of odd, isn't it? Why would someone hide the letter and the key in the same place? Anyway, it's a gold medallion engraved with thirteen numerals, with strange symbols between each one. On the back is a labyrinth in a scallop shell. But that's not what I called about."

"No?"

"No. Remember, you said you'd find out about the Knights of Santiago and lost Spanish treasure. Any luck?"

"I called Nicholson right after you called me. He knows something about the Knights of Santiago, but not much, since his specialty's modern Spain. Anyway, he gave me a couple of references, which I looked up." He paused. "While you've been gallivanting around Spain, my dear, I have been buried in the dusty stacks of the library, doing your bidding."

I laughed. "Come on, Peter, was it that bad?"

"Actually, it's been rather fun. I fancy myself a combination of Peter Wimsey and Hercule Poirot."

"Not Sam Spade?"

"Definitely not. He ain't got no class. Ahem. In a nutshell, the Knights of Santiago were married knights sworn to protect pilgrims on the Camino de Santiago and to defend Spain against the Moors."

"A little more detail would be helpful," I said, wryly.

"Just a minute. Let me look at my notes." Papers rustled. "The Order of St. James of the Sword was officially founded in 1175, although a related group had been protecting pilgrims to Compostela from the mid 1100s, and another group—I'll skip that. Anyway, in 1175 Pope Alexander III approved the Rules of the Order. The Order were broken into five groups or divisions, called *encomiendas*, one each for León, Castile, Portugal, Aragón, and Gascony." I heard him shuffling some more papers. "The Order based its rule on St. Augustine's."

"What's that mean?"

"It means the rules by which they led their lives. St. Augustine's as opposed to St. Benedict's, I suppose. Church history is not my specialty."

"Nor mine."

"Canons—a kind of clergy—looked after the spiritual welfare of the knights, who took vows of poverty, chastity and obedience, while canonesses tended pilgrims in separate guesthouses and hospitals. Each *encomienda* had a governing board of thirteen selected brothers, representing Christ and his apostles, as did the Great Council, called the '*Trece*,' the 'Thirteen.' They were the celibate commanders who elected the grand Master.

"The Order was quite unusual because married knights could be full members. At certain times of the year the knights had retreats, and during Lent and Advent they slept apart from their wives, but otherwise they lived normal married lives."

"I guess that 'normal' is pretty relative."

"Right you are. The Knights wore a white habit, a kind of white cloak, with a red cross on the shoulder."

I remembered the white robe Mateo had worn. "They wore white?"

"With a red cross of Santiago on the shoulder."

Mateo's robe had been plain.

"The bottom arm of the cross of Santiago is pointed and resembles a sword blade. The cross is called the *espada*, or sword, and was nicknamed '*el lagarto*,' the lizard. Later, the Knights also wore a black tunic with a red *espada* on the chest."

"That's what Velázquez is wearing in that famous painting, I forget the name—"

"Las Meninas? I do believe you're right. The motto of the Order was '*Rubet ensis sanguine Arabum*'—'May the sword be red with Arab blood'—and they used the battle cry, '*Santiago y cierra España*'—'St. James and close ranks Spain.'"

Impatiently, I broke in. "This is all very interesting, Peter, but what about treasure? What did your sources say?"

"Not much, I'm afraid. Although originally appointed by the Trece, the top Masters were eventually appointed, or at least confirmed, by King Ferdinand and Queen Isabella. This happened fairly late in the game. In April of 1477 Ferdinand and Isabella gave the last 'real' Master of St. James, Alonso de Cárdenas, the standards and the insignia of the Order. He led the Order in the war against the Moslems, which continued for another ten years and culminated in the conquest of Granada on January 2, 1492, when the Moors were kicked out of Spain.

"After that, the Catholic Kings no longer needed the Order of Santiago, but they didn't want to destroy it. They wanted to control it. It was immensely powerful and wealthy. It has been estimated, and I quote, that 'soon after 1500 the Order of Santiago possessed 94 commanderies with an annual revenue of 60,000 ducats.'"

"How much was that?"

"A lot of money, I gather. The last 'real' Master, Alonso de Cárdenas, died on July 1, 1493—got that date, Noa?—just a few weeks after your mysterious letter was written. King Ferdinand appointed a Cardinal to govern the Order in his name. I'll spare you the details of who did what to whom, but when Ferdinand died in 1516, Prince Charles, the future Emperor, became administrator. In 1523, Charles V officially took over administration of the masterships of Santiago, with the approval of the Pope.

"By mid century all of the military Orders—there were others—were little more than a way to provide royal favorites with titles, places and pensions, even if canon law still regarded the Orders as religious. As late as 1536, The Knights of Santiago rebuilt their second *encomienda*, San Marcos in León, but more as a palace barracks than fortress."

"That's the hotel where we stayed last summer. But you haven't said anything about treasure."

"That's because I don't know anything. All I have is a hunch. The last 'real' master died in 1493, just after your letter was written. Maybe he saw what was happening to the Order and had the treasure hidden, and then he died before he could tell anybody. Or else the person who hid the treasure died before *he* could tell anybody."

"At any rate, something happened, and nobody found the letter, or the medallion."

"Until you came along."

I glanced around and saw Jack watching me intently.

"Noa, are you still there?"

"Just thinking. Let me see if I've got this straight. The members of the Order usually wore white, were married, were fighting men—they were knights, after all—and had lots of money. And the Crown took them over for all practical purposes in 1493, but they were still active in 1536 or so, when they rebuilt San Marcos."

"That's about it."

I pulled the Xerox copy of the letter out of my purse and read from it. "But what's 'the most important treasure' that the man who wrote the letter hid from 'those who would take it away under the guise of sovereignty'?"

"Got me. Gold? Jewels?"

"Something worth killing for, that's for sure."

After a moment, Peter said breezily, "Not that I'm worried or anything as mundane as that, but did you say Mateo was murdered?"

"I really don't know. The police are investigating. We found him dead—"

"Who's we?"

"Jack and me."

"Let me get this straight. You and Jack found Mateo dead."

"He had a bad heart. It was probably a heart attack."

"Probably a heart attack."

"But it could have been murder. A monk in a white robe ran out of the room and down the hall. Jack took after him but couldn't catch him. And Mateo's desk had been ransacked and the letter was gone."

"Sounds suspicious to me. Did you tell the police?"

"No, we didn't." I hesitated. "Maybe Mateo had been looking for something and tore his own desk apart. Or maybe he gave
someone the letter. At the time, there didn't seem to be any reason
to tell the police. The security guard was sure Mateo had had a
heart attack. Besides, I guess I was in shock."

"I see."

Defensive, I said, "When I heard Mateo might have been
murdered I called the police anonymously and told them about
the man in white."

"And then you and Jack took off to Roncesvalles. Makes perfect sense."

"It did at the time, Peter. Besides," I chuckled, "I was just
following your advice."

"My advice?"

"You're always telling me I should lighten up and have more
fun. I've done it all for you." I heard choking sounds at the other
end of the phone. "Did you say something?"

"Not a word. But seriously, Noa, it does sound dangerous.
Are you sure you can handle this?"

"Of course," I replied, sharply. "Why not?"

Peter spoke soothingly. "Of course. Why not? Bon voyage
and all that. Just promise to keep in touch, okay? And at the slight-
est sign of danger, run like a rabbit in the opposite direction."

"Actually, Peter, I'm really enjoying myself. We had a wonderful dinner and the most delicious cognac—"

"Is this a treasure hunt or a pleasure hunt?"

"Jealous, are you? But why? Jack says you seem to be enjoying yourself quite a bit these days."

"He does, does he?"

"He says he saw you somewhere with someone."

"That's not very precise, you realize. He could have seen me
with my aged mother, or my tax accountant, or—" He paused.
"Ah, I know. He must have seen me with Natasha, that volup-
tuous brunette I met in Acapulco, though how he could have seen
us there—"

"Ta, ta."

"Talk to you later. I will wait by the phone for the next in-
stallment."

"Peter—"

"Hmm?"

"Thanks a lot."

As soon as I hung up, Jack hurried over and asked nervously, "Did you mention me?"

I smiled, remembering the conversation. "Only in passing."

He looked relieved. "What did you learn about the Knights of Santiago?"

"Not much, except that they wore white, though later some of them wore black, and they were quite wealthy, and the Crown viewed them as a threat."

"And the treasure?"

"Nothing."

"Are you sure?" he pressed.

"Don't you trust me?" I bristled.

"Of course I do, but maybe Peter said something more important than you think."

Placated, I explained, "There isn't much to tell. Apparently the Knights of Santiago lost their autonomy in July 1493 when the last 'real' Master died. Then Ferdinand and Isabella took over the Order. But the Order stayed around for a long time afterwards as a sort of prestigious private club."

"So what's the treasure?"

"Got me."

Thoughtfully, Jack said, "The last Master must have been the one who hid it or had it hidden. The timing's right. You say the Order was quite wealthy at the time?"

I nodded.

"Well, I hope the treasure hunt's worth it." He turned towards me and smiled a slow, sensuous smile. "Actually, I know it's worth it. It's given me the chance to be with you."

Torn between amusement and annoyance, I replied, "You don't quit, do you?"

"Should I?"

We went back upstairs and to bed. I carefully kept my distance.

Five

I woke up at the sound of a door slamming, followed by water splattering in a tub. Pale, lemon-colored light streamed through the balcony windows, gently illuminating the rumpled bed next to mine. Where was I? And with whom? Suddenly it all came back. I was on a treasure hunt with a handsome, mercurial stranger named Jack.

With a shiver, I jumped out of bed, threw on my robe, and stepped out onto the balcony, breathing in the fresh, pine-scented air. While listening to the early morning chirping of unidentified birds, I began carefully untangling my hair with my fingers; giving up on the delicate approach, I started yanking the snarls loose, taking strands of hair with them.

A faint, potent combination of herbal soap and musk-and-leather cologne wafted through the air. I started to turn around just as he put his arms around me and nuzzled my neck.

"Good morning, Beautiful," he whispered into my ear.

"Jack—"

He tightened his grip as I started to move away.

In a husky voice, he said, "Noa, I'm only human. I left you alone last night, but you can't expect me to ignore you this morning. You looked gorgeous with your hair spread out on the pillow like a halo of flame. It was all I could do not to wake you with a kiss."

I pried his arms loose and stepped away.

Irritated, he asked, "What's the matter? Thinking of Peter?"

I chose not to reply.

"Peter is such a fool. How he could leave you—"

"You've got it all wrong."

"You mean you left him?"

"Nobody left anybody!"

"So you and Peter aren't a couple?"

I brushed my hair back and took a deep breath. "It's complicated."

He tried to nuzzle my neck again, but I moved away. "You know, Jack, I can't decide if you're more interested in me or the treasure."

He grinned crookedly. "Why should I have to choose?"

I slid past him, grabbed my cosmetic bag and the jeans and T-shirt I had worn the day before, hurried into the bathroom, and slammed the door after me. The room smelled of herbal soap and masculine cologne. After wiping the steam from the mirror over the sink, I took a long look at myself. Jack said that my hair looked "like a halo of flame." Why was it, I wondered, that on the rare occasions when Peter talked like that, he was always teasing?

The gold medallion glittered in the light, and I traced the spiral pattern with my fingers, staring at the misty reflection in the mirror. How could we decipher the secret message? And what would be waiting for us when we did? Smiling, I thought: Even if we found nothing, I was having an exciting adventure, some of which I would tell Peter about.

After a quick shower, I got dressed, tied back my hair, and walked briskly out of the bathroom.

Jack looked me up and down and whistled appreciatively. "You look fantastic."

I started to protest and he laughed. " I'm giving you a compliment, and you want to argue."

He had a point.

We went down to the breakfast buffet. Damask-draped tables lined one wall of the dining room. They were covered with mounds of fresh fruit, baskets filled with breads, platters of cold cuts and cheese, sealed plastic containers of marmalade, trays of bland cookies, assorted sweet rolls, and cream-filled pastries, and plates heaped with crisp hot *churros*, a kind of funnel cake. Jack took a large serving of *churros* and a cup of hot chocolate, as thick as pea soup, to dip them in. I selected several slices of thick, crusty bread and ordered a *café doble*.

The waiter brought the double-sized cup of steaming espresso, which I gulped down. Then I ordered another. I had a feeling I would need all the caffeine I could get.

Jack watched, amused. "Do you usually start your day this way?"

"Hardly," I laughed, "But these are not normal times, are they?"

"It's good to hear you laugh. I don't want you to be angry with me."

"I'm not angry," I replied quickly. Too quickly.

"Good. It's not my fault I can't keep my hands off you."

I stared out the window in exasperation.

He raised his hands in mock surrender. "Okay, okay. Enough said. What's the plan for today?"

"First we go to Roncesvalles. Then I don't know what we do."

"I hope you have the letter with you." I nodded. "Can I see it?"

I took the Xeroxed letter out of my bag and handed it to him.

He stared at the faint, blurred print, then tossed it back. "But this is illegible!"

"I know it's illegible. I know what it says because I read the original—which, by the way, wasn't much better." I translated the letter slowly, more from memory than from sight. "'. . . the path begins where our comrades in faith and battle, the Knights of Charlemagne, lie resting. Only the true pilgrim who follows the Milky Way will reach the treasure, and only if St. James the Apostle guides him. I have made a key to the treasure—.' It ends abruptly. Something must have happened to make the writer stop in the middle of a sentence. And then he hid the letter. Or somebody did. If it's real," I added. "It could be an elaborate fake."

"The letter's real, all right. I've got an unfailing instinct about these things." Jack chewed thoughtfully on a *churro*. "But I'm puzzled by something you read. A pilgrim can find the treasure 'only if St. James the Apostle guides him'?"

"That's right."

"What does that mean?"

"Maybe it refers to a figure of St. James. There are lots of statues of Santiago along the pilgrimage road."

Jack drummed his manicured fingers on the damask tablecloth and looked off into space. "'I have made a key to the treasure.'" He turned back to me. "But what is it?"

I folded the letter and put it in my bag. "The key or the treasure?"

"Both."

"The key is the medallion."

""But how do we use it? And what's the treasure?"

"Gold? Jewels?"

Abruptly standing up, Jack said, "Let's quit wasting time and find out!"

We packed our bags quickly and checked out. When we got into the car, Jack took the road map out of the glove compartment and handed it to me. "You navigate while I drive."

"Tell you what," I suggested, "Why don't I drive for a change?"

"No way. It's my car and I drive," he snapped.

Seeing my surprise, he said, "I'm sure you're a fine driver, Noa, but I can't stand to be in a car that someone else is driving." He smiled disarmingly. "Just another bad habit, I guess. One of many. I hope you don't mind too much."

Mollified, I found myself smiling back. His arrogance made me angry, but his apologies were charming. I unfolded the map.

"How far is it to Roncesvalles?"

"According to the map, it's 27 miles to Pamplona, then another 30 miles or so to Roncesvalles."

He settled back, hands lightly caressing the wheel. "We should be there in an hour."

"I don't think so. These aren't American highways or the German Autobahn. Traffic moves a lot slower."

"Just watch." He pressed his foot on the accelerator, and I grabbed the hand strap as, tires squealing, we sped onto the main road.

We skirted Pamplona and headed northeast on the highway approximation of the old Camino de Santiago, or so the highway signs, decorated with the scallop shell emblem of Santiago, indicated. But we were heading away from Santiago de Compostela, not towards it. Soon we were speeding down a two-lane country road through the lush green valley of the Río Arga, past Zubiri and up to the Pass of Erro, down into another lush green valley and past the village of Burguete. We were deep in the province of the Navarra, deep in Hemingway country, where men were men and women were—women.

We drove through one small village after another, the tiny clumps of habitation separated by rolling hills. Three-story-tall stone houses lined the sides of the road, their deep-set windows framed with sturdy green shutters, their slate roofs steeply pitched. It must get awfully cold and snowy, I thought. I'd hate to be a pilgrim walking the Camino in winter. But maybe they didn't. Maybe they only went in summer. Offhandedly, I wondered whether you went on the pilgrimage when you wanted to, or when you were called.

The road wound through the foothills, getting ever closer to the Pyrenees. Traffic was light, but it was slow; local buses, diesel-spewing trucks, tiny old Renaults called "deux chevaux" because of their lack of horsepower, labored up the hills. Soon the hillsides were covered with tall pine trees and the fields lay far behind.

Suddenly through the tall evergreens we saw the corrugated tin roofs of the Royal Collegiate Church and monastery flashing in the sun. Jack pulled the car into a parking spot right in front and we got out. It was chilly in the early morning mountain air, and I started to shiver, so Jack took off his suede jacket and draped it around my shoulders. It smelled like musk and felt like velvet.

Looking around impatiently, he asked, "Where should we start?"

I pointed at an open door in the huge stone monastery. "Let's start there. There's probably a guide or priest in the main build-ing."

We walked past a large boulder, and I paused to read the brass plaque in front. It was a monument to Roland. On August 15, 778, during the retreat following their defeat at Zaragoza, Charlemagne's famous knight Roland had been attacked at a nearby mountain pass. He had blown his magic horn Olifant to warn the rest of the army; mortally wounded, as were the twelve other paladins of Charlemagne, he eventually succumbed and died. He and the other knights were buried here, the plaque claimed, but I was learning to be skeptical of such claims.

We entered the monastery and were greeted by a short, slen-der man dressed in a long black habit. He identified himself as Canon Eugenio, the archivist, and assured us he would be happy to show us around. We followed him down a dark, echoing corri-dor.

Shaking his head sadly, Canon Eugenio said, "Centuries ago the monastery was filled with Augustinian monks, but now there are only six of us. The monastery was originally established to pro-vide hospitality to pilgrims traveling the Camino de Santiago."

"And today?" Jack asked.

A smile broke through his heavily lined face. "After centuries of decline, pilgrims in increasing numbers are walking the Camino. Many of them stop here for the night."

Surprised, Jack asked, "Pilgrims still walk this road?"

Canon Eugenio tucked his hands inside the wide black sleeves of his habit. "Yes, they still follow the Camino to Santiago, or, rather, they follow what's left of the authentic route."

"How far is it?" Jack asked.

"It's about 850 kilometers from here to Santiago," he replied. "Of course, many pilgrims start from France, and some from as far away as Germany or even Japan. For them the road is much, much longer."

I asked, "How do they know where the 'authentic' Camino is?"

"Some of them carry a copy of the original twelfth-century guidebook, the *Codex Calixtinus*. Others use modern guidebooks, including brochures published by the Ministry of Tourism and The Friends of the Camino. Some of these guidebooks still list the thirteen original stages of the Camino described in the *Codex*." He smiled. "Authenticity is very important."

"Where do these stages begin?" I inquired.

"In Saint Michel on the French side of the Pyrenees. The first stage passes through Roncesvalles and ends in Viscarret. If you came from France, you passed through Saint Michel."

Jack responded quickly, "Why, so we did."

Startled at this glib lie, I looked at Jack with surprise, but he motioned me to be silent and, uneasily, I acquiesced.

Canon Eugenio didn't notice our exchange. He continued, "A number of modern pilgrims, of course, travel by car, not on foot. And some even ride bicycles."

"Just how old is the Camino?" Jack asked.

"At least 1000 years old, since it was developed shortly after the discovery of the tomb of St. James in the early 800s. Parts of the Camino followed the Roman roads that were still in use, so I suppose you could say it was much older. But the Christian pilgrimage began in the 800s."

We arrived at the treasure room of the monastery, a large room lined with exhibit cases displaying medieval manuscripts, jewel-inlaid gold reliquaries that held bits of saints' bones, ornate caskets, and gilt-framed religious paintings. We walked carefully around the room but saw no sign of Santiago. On the way out, I noticed a table with books for sale, so I bought a brochure describing Roncesvalles. After thanking the priest, we left.

Turning to Jack, I demanded, "Why did you tell Canon Eugenio we started in France?"

"Because I don't want anyone to know where we came from. It's safer that way, believe me."

"Why?"

"Trust me."

"Why should I?" I retorted. "I want an explanation."

"We've got to cover our tracks. Remember: someone else is hunting for the treasure—and undoubtedly hunting for us as well. We don't want to make it too easy for them, now, do we?"

"If you say so," I muttered grudgingly. He had a point. He always had a point. Nonetheless, or maybe because of that, I felt deeply troubled about his behavior and my own. My instinctive responses—being helpful and honest—were obviously inadvisable, if not actually dangerous, on a treasure hunt. But they were my natural responses. I glanced at Jack, methodically scanning the countryside. I began to wonder if some of the danger wasn't standing right next to me.

Uneasy, I paged through the brochure. It described in detail the twelfth-century Chapel of Sancti Spiritus and the thirteenth-century Church of Santiago.

Jack asked impatiently, "Any idea where to start?"

"Let's try the Chapel of Sancti Spiritus, where Charlemagne's knights are supposed to be buried."

He started up the cobblestone path towards the small stone chapel and I followed quickly behind. We entered through the open door and waited a moment for our eyes to adjust to the gloom.

He looked around, at a loss. "Now what?"

Thoughtfully, I said, "Some phrase in the letter, combined with the medallion, must tell us what to look for. After all, whoever wrote the letter wanted his 'Honored Master' to find the treasure."

"So whatever we're looking for was here in the late 1400s. And it had to be something permanent, permanent enough that if the 'Honored Master' couldn't get here for a few months—or even a few years—it would still be here."

"Right. And it had to be something that was not obvious—or was meaningless—to someone who didn't know what to look for."

"Right."

We walked around but saw nothing even remotely related to the medallion or the Knights of Santiago.

"Let's try somewhere else, like the Church of Santiago," Jack said, impatiently.

"It has to be here," I replied stubbornly.

"But what is it?"

"The clue." I stroked the medallion around my neck, my fingers tracing the raised design. On one side was a labyrinth inscribed inside the scallop-shell emblem of Santiago. On the other were thirteen Roman numerals, each followed by a different symbol.

Excited, I grabbed his arm. "I've got it! It's the Camino!"

He looked at me blankly. "What's the Camino?"

"The medallion. The thirteen numerals stand for the thirteen stages of the Camino." My voice was hoarse. It always gets hoarse when I'm excited.

"Are you sure?"

"Absolutely. The first stage of the Camino starts at St. Michel, in France, in the middle of the Pyrenees. But whoever hid the treasure was in a hurry. He didn't have time to climb the Pyrenees. That's why he specifically states that 'the path begins where our comrades in faith and battle, the Knights of Charlemagne, lie resting.'" I touched the glittering medallion again. "The symbol after each number stands for that stage of the Camino. I'm sure of it."

Jack reached for the medallion. "You're right. I'm sure you're right. Whoever hid the treasure marked the trail with symbols so if someone stole the letter, but not the medallion, he couldn't find the treasure. Which is just what happened. Someone stole the letter. But we have a copy and the medallion. So all we have to do is to find the symbol that corresponds to the stage on the Camino where the treasure is hidden."

"But to do that, we have to follow each symbol to the next one."

"Right. The treasure could be hidden at Santiago, the end of stage 13, but we don't know that. It might be hidden at the end of stage 9, or 11 or—"

"And if we miss a clue, we won't know where to look next."

"Right." He looked around. "But we still have to find the symbol."

"St. James the Apostle will lead the way."

"Where is he when we need him?" Jack asked wryly.

We turned and walked in opposite directions around the small stone chapel, scanning the floor and walls. When we met by the front door, we looked at each other with disappointment. Nothing. So we continued around in the opposite direction, meeting in the middle, under the cupola.

"It's got to be here!" I exclaimed in frustration. "Let's look again."

"You look. I'm going outside," Jack said, exasperated.

I circled the chapel again. No luck. I walked over to the sarcophagus of the paladins and leaned against it, staring at the intricate vines, flowers, and figures carved deeply into the stone, staring without seeing. Suddenly my eyes focused on a tiny figure in a wide-brimmed hat, holding a staff with a gourd. His cloak was covered with scallop shells. At the bottom of his staff was a crudely scratched diamond with a dot in it.

With trembling hands, I unfastened the chain around my neck and examined the medallion. After Roman numeral III was a diamond with a dot in the middle.

I called for Jack, but he couldn't hear me, so I ran out of the chapel to find him. He was leaning against the wall, smoking a cigarette.

"I've found it!"

"What?" He dropped the cigarette, leaving it burning in the grass, and hustled me inside. Leading him over to the sarcophagus, I pointed at the figure of Santiago.

He looked at the faint, scratched marking. "Is that symbol on the medallion?"

"It is indeed. Right after numeral III."

"Great! But what's that mean?"

"It means we go to the end of the third stage, wherever that is."

We looked at each other.

I said, "Maybe Canon Eugenio will know."

Impatiently, Jack retorted, "Noa, we can't ask him. We don't want anyone to know what we're doing. Too many people know already."

Fastening the chain around my neck, I asked, "Do you have a better suggestion?"

"Eugenio said something about a twelfth-century guidebook to the Camino."

"There are modern ones, too," I said, excited. "Maybe we can buy one here. After all, this is a popular pilgrimage stop."

"It's worth a try, Noa, but we'd better be careful. Let me do the talking."

"Why you?"

"I'm more used to this kind of thing."

"What kind of thing?" I asked suspiciously.

"Well . . ."

"Deception?"

"Only in a manner of speaking."

I looked at him sharply, but he looked away.

We started to leave the chapel but stopped abruptly. Just inside the doorway, obscured by shadows, a tall, white-robed man leaned on a gnarled oak staff. His hood shrouded his face. Involuntarily, I shivered.

Jack turned to me and whispered, "Where did that guy come from?"

"How should I know," I whispered back.

The faceless monk made the sign of the cross as we hurried past him and headed back to the main building. I looked over my shoulder and saw him enter the nearby Church of Santiago. At least he wasn't following us.

Nervously, I asked Jack, "Do you think he heard us? Or saw the medallion?"

Voice grim, he replied, "Let's hope not. But what could he have heard, anyway? All we did was talk about the number three. I don't like it, though. Too many monks in white are showing up. First the one in Mateo's office, and now this one."

"First Mateo. He wore white, too." I thought a moment. "We've seen so many monks in white, we probably don't have to worry. They must be members of some popular religious order."

"Come to think of it, the Cistercians wear white robes."

"Mateo wasn't a Cistercian. I don't think they can marry, and Mateo was married. He even has—had—a son."

We found the priest still in the treasury. Jack smiled what I took to be his most charming smile. This time, I noticed it didn't reach past his mouth.

"We'd like to know more about the Camino de Santiago. Perhaps you have a guidebook that we could buy?"

Canon Eugenio sorted through the stack of brochures on the table and found one with a glossy red cover. Handing it to Jack, he explained, "This is published by the Spanish Tourist Office for car tourists, such as yourselves."

Jack took the brochure and opened it. In the centerfold was a sketchy map of the Camino. Disappointed, he asked, "Don't you have one that shows the thirteen stages of the Camino?"

The priest looked surprised.

Jack explained, with deep sincerity, "Even though we're traveling by car, we would like to follow the authentic route, you know, to sort of 'relive' the medieval experience."

Nodding with pleasure, Canon Eugenio led us down another long, dark corridor. Using a large iron key hanging from his belt, he unlocked the heavy wooden door. "This is my office," he said as he ushered us inside.

Scattered on top of a battered wooden desk were numerous papers and maps. In one corner were a covered container of yellow paint and a stiff, paint-covered brush stuck in a bucket. There was a faint odor of turpentine. The priest saw my nose twitching and smiled. "I have mapped the authentic old Camino in Navarra, and I paint arrows on the side of the road, or on tree trunks or walls, to guide foot pilgrims on their way."

Going over to a rickety card table, he started rummaging through a stack of papers, magazines, and books. After a few minutes, he pulled out a book and dusted it off. "This was published when the Pope visited Spain in 1982. Now it's available in a paperback edition." He handed the hardbound copy to Jack. "This version is too big and heavy for pilgrims walking the Camino, but that shouldn't be a problem for you."

Jack started paging through it. Soon he found a map of the Camino, stretching from the French Pyrenees to Santiago, divided into thirteen stages. He reached for his wallet. "What do I owe you?"

"Whatever you want to pay. I don't remember the cost."

Handing the priest a $20 dollar bill, he said, "Use the extra to feed the 'real' pilgrims."

The priest thanked him and escorted us out the door. As we stepped into the dimly lit corridor, I gave an involuntary gasp: a tall, thin, white-robed man was waiting in the hall, his face hidden by his hood. We brushed quickly by him, walked rapidly down the hall, out the main door, and over to the Mercedes. Before I had the car door closed, Jack had pulled out of the parking place.

Jack snarled, "I don't like it. I don't like it one bit!" Then he tossed me the guidebook. "You take it. Your Spanish is better than mine, and we don't want to miss anything. Where does stage III end?"

"Estella," I said, my voice shaking just a little.

"Estella it is. How far?"

I looked at the numbers on the side of the map. "About 55 miles."

Jack's eyes kept darting to the rear view mirror.

"What are you looking for?"

"I don't like the way those monks in white keep showing up."

"I thought we agreed it was just a coincidence."

"I don't trust coincidences. Not when they keep happening."

I looked at him solemnly. "My finding the letter was a coincidence. My meeting you in the library was a coincidence."

He laughed abruptly and patted my knee. "No, my dear, that was good fortune. Let me put it this way: I don't trust too *many* coincidences."

He settled back into the driver's seat, and I started reading the guidebook, trying to quell my growing anxiety with a heavy dose of pretentious verbiage.

Although we only had to travel 55 miles, the roads were narrow and winding. Jack hunched tensely over the wheel, unwilling to slow down. Eventually, he leaned back and said, "If we can't get there any faster, neither can they."

"Who's they?"

"Whoever is following us."

I looked behind. "Nobody's following us."

"I don't mean now. But somebody will be. Just think about it. Someone stole the letter in the library. The letter talks about a key. We show up at Roncesvalles and start looking around."

"So what? Even if they find the symbol, they won't know what it means without the medallion."

"What if someone, that monk in the chapel, for instance, overheard us mention the number three? And what if he talks with Canon 'what's-his-name' and finds out we were curious, very curious, about the stages of the Camino?" Jack stomped on the accelerator and the car surged forward, pushing me back into the soft leather seat. "We've got to be more careful what we say and to whom." Frowning, he glanced at me. "One man may already have died for the treasure. And who knows how many more? After all, what happened to the man who wrote the letter?"

I shifted nervously on the seat, thinking about the investigation into Mateo's death. I wondered what they had discovered.

Jack eyes flicked over my face, then back to the road. "Want out? If so, just let me know."

With false confidence, I declared, "I'm in this till the end, Jack. I was just thinking about Mateo."

"If you change your mind—"

"What—and let you have all the fun?"

His mouth curved in a sensuous smile. "I told you, you were meant for adventure. Besides, I'm selfish. The treasure hunt wouldn't be nearly as exciting without you. But I am worried about your safety."

"What about yours?"

"I can take care of myself," he said grimly.

We drove past Pamplona, past the small town of Puente la Reina, named after an eleventh-century bridge that they could see from the road, and arrived in Estella. I translated from the guidebook.

"According to Aymeric Picaud, author of the twelfth-century *Codex*, Estella was a place with 'good bread, fine wine, meat, and fish, and full of all kinds of happiness.' The water of the river Ega, which we just crossed, was 'sweet, healthy, and very good.'"

"Great. But what about Santiago? Where do we find him?"

"Unfortunately, there are a number of choices. The Church of San Pedro de Lizarra, San Pedro de la Rúa, the Palace of the Kings of Navarra, the church of Santo Sepulcro, the Convent of Santo Domingo, the Hermitage of Rocamador, the Hermitage of Our Lady of Puy—"

"These were all here in the late fifteenth century?"

"That's right."

"Any of them dedicated to Santiago?"

"Doesn't look like it. But one of them has a frieze of the apostles on the front."

"Let's head for that one. Which is it?"

"The thirteenth-century Church of Santo Sepulcro."

After driving by several churches, none the right one, we stopped and asked for directions. But we kept getting lost in the twisting streets and had to ask again. Each time, Jack got increasingly irritable. Several wrong turns later, we arrived at a derelict stone church on the bank of the River Ega. Lined up in niches on the front were life-size statues.

I started to get out of the car, but Jack grabbed my arm. "Don't get out! It's too conspicuous. Damn! We need binoculars."

"I brought a camera with a telephoto lens. Will that help?"

He grabbed me and kissed me hard. "You're a genius!"

Slightly stunned from the impact, I retrieved the camera from the back seat. I focused the lens and pointed it at the church.

"What do you see?" he asked, eagerly.

"Not much." I handed him the camera.

He peered through it, then shook his head. "We'll have to get closer." Tensely, he added, "I don't want anyone to see what we're doing."

Keeping a careful watch for passersby, we nonchalantly strolled up to the church. After identifying the statue of Santiago, which was standing guard at the side of the doorway, we searched the area around it for symbols.

"Got it!" Jack exclaimed. "At least I think so—"

"What is it?"

He pointed to some faint scratches hidden at the back of the statue. "Three wavy lines."

I held up the medallion dangling from my neck. I was just able to make out the symbols without taking it off. "End of stage V."

Back in the car, I checked the guidebook. "Burgos."

"How far is Burgos?"

"100 miles, more or less."

"Piece of cake."

As we drove away, I thought I saw a hooded, white-robed figure holding a gnarled staff walk up the side of the riverbank. When I turned around to look, he was gone—if he had ever been there. I started to shake, and it wasn't from Jack's driving.

Six

We sped past the small town of Los Arcos and the large city of Logroño. On either side of the road were seemingly endless fields of low, bushy grapevines; billboards invited us to visit private bodegas and buy local wines. I watched, hypnotized, as the fields and hills rolled by. Unexpectedly the road forked, and both road signs pointed towards Burgos. Jack pulled over abruptly onto the dirt shoulder; I put out my hands to avoid hitting the dashboard.

Fuming, he snapped, "You're supposed to be the navigator, remember? I do the driving, you tell me where to go."

"Don't tempt me, Jack, or I might!" Flushed with anger, I compared the road map and the guidebook to the Camino. Voice shaking, I said, "The 'authentic' route goes almost straight west, through Nájera, Santo Domingo de La Calzada, Villafranca Montes de Oca— but it looks like a narrow, winding road, worse than what we've been on. A much better highway goes northwest, up to Miranda de Ebro, and joins with the superhighway N I, then heads southwest to Burgos."

"It doesn't matter if the route's authentic," he said caustically. "This is a treasure hunt, not a pilgrimage."

"I know that," I replied coldly, "but we want to get to Burgos the fastest way possible."

Jack grabbed the map. "It looks like a toss-up. The route through Miranda de Ebro is a lot longer, even if the road is better.

We'll follow the shorter route. The Camino. I should still be able to make good time." He checked the highway for traffic and pulled out quickly, heading straight west.

Staring out the window, I refused to acknowledge Jack's brooding presence. He was rude, mercurial, and infuriating, I stormed silently. Mercurial? More like a chameleon! But, I admitted grudgingly, he was also charming, attractive, and, occasionally, exceedingly attentive. So who's perfect?

We passed a group of three pilgrims dressed in khaki shorts, T-shirts, and hiking boots. Dangling from the back of each of their backpacks was a scallop shell, symbol of the pilgrimage to Santiago. The hikers glanced back when they heard the Mercedes coming and automatically stepped off onto the narrow gravel shoulder of the road and kept on walking. I realized it would probably take them two or three days to reach Burgos, but it would only take us a couple of hours. Talk about delayed gratification.

The patchwork countryside of grapevines, olive trees, and asparagus mounds was gradually replaced with a hot, dusty plateau. In the distance was Santo Domingo de la Calzada, silhouetted against the horizon. At the outskirts I saw a verse painted on the side of a building. Translated, it read: "Santo Domingo de la Calzada, where the cock crowed after being cooked."

Uncomfortable with the tense silence, I started reading aloud from the guidebook. "A family of pilgrims going to Santiago stayed at an inn here, and the innkeeper's daughter grew infatuated with the son. He spurned her advances. In retribution, she hid a silver serving piece in his pack and then accused him of theft. He was hanged, and the parents continued on to Santiago, where they were promised a miracle. They returned to Santo Domingo and, lo and behold, their son was still alive—still dangling from the scaffolds. So they went to tell the mayor who was eating dinner. Naturally enough, he didn't believe them. He said he'd believe their story if the baked chickens he was about to eat would stand up and crow. Miraculously, they did just that, so the young man was set free. In commemoration, they keep a live hen and rooster in the cathedral, and pilgrims collect their white feathers for good luck.'"

Jack laughed unpleasantly. "Nice story, but it just confirms my belief. People are incredibly gullible."

"Why do you say that?"

"Look at that priest in Roncesvalles. We told him we had come from France and he believed us. We told him we were interested in 'reliving' the authentic pilgrimage experience and he believed us."

"You told him, I didn't," I pointed out.

"That's right. You're honest."

"And you're dishonest?" I shot back, feeling like I was baiting a bear.

"Let's put it this way. I'm just more experienced."

Tactfully, I changed the subject. "I'm getting hungry."

"So am I. Let's stop and eat."

"But do you think that's wise? After all, somebody may be following us."

"You know," he chuckled, "You sound just like a business partner of mine. He tells me I get sidetracked too easily. He says I've got to learn to keep my eye on the main chance. But the way I figure it, you only go around once in life. Besides, nobody saw us at Estella, and even if they did, they wouldn't know where to go next."

For a fleeting moment, I remembered the dreamlike apparition I thought I had seen in the rearview mirror. But I hadn't been sure, so I said nothing.

Following signs to the local *parador*, Jack parked the car behind the cathedral, hiding it between a large white bus and a small van. We got out and stretched in the hot afternoon sun; within a minute, my T-shirt was clinging to my back. When we walked around the bus, I saw a sign on the back: "Pélerinage à Compostele."

I commented, "A French pilgrimage tour to Santiago. I guess the pilgrimage really is popular again."

Jack just snorted.

We walked into the *parador* and stepped, as at Olite, into the Middle Ages. The bare stone walls were decorated with medieval shields, weapons, and armor. Gothic stone arches crisscrossed the vaulted ceiling, and blue-green light poured through the stained glass skylight, tinting the tile floor.

Following the tinkle of glasses, we found the dining room. Most of the tables were filled with French pilgrims wearing matching scallop-shell designs block-printed on their T-shirts. After choosing an unobtrusive table at the back of the room, we ordered the day's special, *conejo a la cazador*. The spicy, wine-and-tomato-drenched rabbit arrived, along with a bottle of red Rioja wine, French fries, and a large salad of lettuce, white asparagus, tuna fish, and sliced hard-boiled eggs.

Jack lifted his glass. "A glass of wine, a loaf of bread, and thou—"

"Jack—"

"Okay. To the hunt—" He clinked his glass against mine and smiled a half-smile, "and to us!"

"To the hunt," I repeated. I looked away, then looked back, unobserved for a moment. His eyes narrowed, his smile turned thin, and his lips tightened. Apprehensively I wondered: just who was hunting whom? And what was being hunted? Jack was watching me again, so I lifted my glass and took a deep drink of the velvety, oak-tinged wine.

After a leisurely meal, we started back on the road. Soon we were driving slowly up a winding road through the forest-covered Montes de Oca. I rolled down my window and breathed deeply, filling my lungs with the cool air.

"Do you mind if we turn off the air conditioning?" I asked.

"For you, anything."

"Oh?" I said archly.

He glanced at me. "Something bothering you?"

"Why do you ask?"

"You've been awfully quiet. I guess I should apologize. I was short-tempered earlier, about the map."

"You were."

"I'm sorry," he said, contritely. "I have a very quick temper. I know it gets me into trouble. If anything could reform me, it would be my love for you—"

I replied, "My God, Jack, we hardly know each other—"

"I knew the moment I saw you—"

"I bet you say that to every woman you meet."

He did not reply.

While Jack sulked, a mood I chose to ignore, I read the guidebook. "Guess what, Jack? We're traveling on the Milky Way. Any place name that includes the word *oca* or *ganso*—the Spanish words mean goose or gander—is on the old, pre-Christian initiation route called the Milky Way."

Grumpily, he responded, "You told me the Camino de Santiago was the same as the Milky Way, remember? So which is it?"

"It's both. The Camino de Santiago is also called the Milky Way. It officially ends, naturally enough, in Santiago de Compostela. The 'other' Milky Way, which is more or less the same, but not entirely, continues to Padrón, where the boat carrying Santiago's body landed, and to Noia and Finisterre."

"I think I've missed something. Wasn't St. James buried in Santiago de Compostela?"

"Close by. But first he was beheaded in Palestine in 42 AD or so by Herod Agrippa. Then, according to the legend, his body—and head—and two disciples were miraculously transported back to Spain, where he had supposedly been a missionary. They landed at Padrón. Are you interested in all the details?"

"Not really."

"I'll summarize," I said eagerly, relieved to feel the tension between us lessen. "After many miracles, his body was buried and eventually forgotten. Years later, in 814 or so, a shepherd or a hermit, named Pelayo, saw stars falling over a weed-covered hillside and heard angels' voices."

He snorted. "A likely story. He'd probably had too much wine."

"Anyway, he told someone and they found the tomb. Then, with the help of another miracle, they identified the bones and built a church over the remains. In the Middle Ages, Santiago, Rome, and Jerusalem were the three most important Christian pilgrimage shrines."

"It was that important? But where do the Knights of Santiago come in?"

"I'm not sure. The guidebook says that Santiago appeared on a white charger, waving a flag and brandishing a sword, at the probably imaginary battle of Clavijo in 843 or 844. He slaughtered Moors by the tens of thousands and led the Christians to victory."

"Another likely story."

"That's not all. Santiago Matamoros appeared again on various occasions, and even traveled with the conquistadores to the New World, where he helped kill the native heathens, instead of Moors."

Jack looked thoughtful. "What was the date on our letter?"

Our letter? Since when was it *our* letter? "1493. Why?"

"I just wondered. It couldn't have been 1593, by any chance?"

"Not a chance. Why?"

"I was just thinking of all the gold the Spanish took from the Incas."

"Off by a century."

We drove through the evergreen-covered hills in silence, passing a pair of pilgrims walking their bikes single-file up the steep incline. A little further we passed a straggly group of pilgrims walking slowly by the side of the road; while I watched, two of them limped off the road, shrugged off their backpacks, and collapsed, using the heavy packs as back rests. We climbed effortlessly up the hill in the sleek, powerful Mercedes, leaving them far behind.

Soon we saw a large plain spread out before us; in the distance was the sprawling city of Burgos.

"Any ideas where we should stay, Noa?"

"I've never been in Burgos. Sahagún's only 80 miles to the west, but when I was doing my fieldwork I never had any time to go sightseeing." Except once, with Peter, I remembered wistfully.

"All work and no play makes Noa a dull girl—not that you are, my dear. Life is an adventure. You have to learn to live a little." He glanced at me. "I'd love to teach you how."

I looked out the window.

We arrived in Burgos and parked alongside a shaded alameda. The pale lacy spires of the cathedral were just visible over the trees.

"Where to?" he asked, expectantly.

"The guidebook says there are half a dozen monuments worth visiting—the cathedral, the Royal Monastery of Las Huelgas, the Cartuja de Miraflores, the Hospital del Rey, the churches of San Nicolás, San Gil, San Lesmes, Santa Gaeda—the home of El Cid—"

He held up his hands in surrender. "Any specific suggestions? After all, you've got the guidebook."

"But you're the art historian, aren't you? By the way, just what is your specialty?" I asked curiously.

Jack replied blithely, "Originally it was Italian Renaissance, but that's changed a bit. Antiquities of various sorts, you might say. Old manuscripts. That kind of thing. But we're wasting time. Let's start at the cathedral. And don't forget the camera."

We walked through the imposing Gateway of Santa María and into the cathedral. Once our eyes adjusted to the gloom, I could see the enormous central nave, filled with baroque statuary and ornate carvings. A faint smell of incense and burnt wax tainted the air.

"Where do we start?" He asked.

"Maybe there's a chapel of Santiago or something." I scanned the guidebook. "Apparently not."

"Okay. You go one way, I'll go the other." He looked at his watch. "Let's meet back here in an hour."

Walking slowly down the central aisle, I paused directly under the ornate central dome to read the words engraved on a stone slab in the floor. As I deciphered the deeply cut letters, I realized with a shock that El Cid and his wife Jimena were buried under that slab of polished stone.

It seemed incredible to me that the noble swashbuckling hero of *The Song of El Cid* was actually buried beneath my feet, buried and decayed, his bones and those of his beloved wife, crumbling slowly together. I knew with absolute certainty that if I pried up the paving stone I would see his casket, and inside it would be several gently rounded mounds of dust. Faintly, as if at a great distance, I heard the muffled chanting of prayers.

I stood absolutely still, confronted for a moment with the undeniable reality of a legend that was 900 years old. Not daring to breathe, I felt suspended in time and place, as if the past had reached out and gently touched my hand.

In that still, silent moment, the treasure hunt changed irrevocably.

I realized that I had been acting with a "suspension of disbelief," the same way I went to the movies or watched a play. I had been pretending the treasure might be real but not really, truly, believing it. But El Cid had actually existed and fought the Moors, as had the Knights of Santiago, and he was buried right there, beneath my feet. Maybe the treasure of the Knights of Santiago had really existed too and could still be discovered. Maybe it was just as real as El Cid's body and Mateo's death.

Abruptly, I noticed that men and women were shuffling around me and sliding onto the wooden benches on either side of the aisle. Some of them were kneeling, clasped hands resting on the benches in front of them, rapidly whispering prayers while they waited for Mass to begin.

I walked quickly over to one of the chapels that lined the edges of the nave. The first one I entered was the Capilla del Santísimo Cristo. Hanging on one wall was the life-size carving called the Cristo de Burgos, a thirteenth-century, buffalo-hide figure of Christ. Life-like blood dripped from the wounds on its articulated limbs, barely missing the delicate linen and lace cloth that modestly covered the figure below the waist. Dismayed by the gruesome display, I fled.

There were numerous small chapels scattered irregularly around the perimeter of the cathedral. Most had name plates on the wall outside the entry, along with an alms box and, occasionally, a metal stand full of squat, sputtering white candles or, on occasion, electric lights in the shape of candles, like the ones used at Christmas back home. They seemed a shabby, though convenient, substitute for a flickering, burning flame.

While I watched, an old lady dressed in threadbare black dropped a coin in a box on the side of one stand of candles; muttering prayers, she took a burnt wooden match from a pile and lit one candle from the flame of another. The faint smell of melting wax wafted through the air.

At last I came to a chapel identified by a plaque on the wall as the Capilla de Santiago; oddly enough, it had not been mentioned in the guidebook. An equestrian statue of Santiago Matamoros, cape flying in the nonexistent breeze, bloody sword outstretched, was located on the upper part of the metal grillwork at the entry to the chapel, and the *retablo* or painted altarpiece displayed another image of the Moorslayer. Using the telephoto lens on the camera, I scanned the grill for scratched symbols but found none. I looked at my watch. It was time to meet Jack.

He was pacing impatiently by the entry.

I asked, "Find anything?"

He shook his head in frustration. "I found the head of a pilgrim carved into a capitol in the cloisters and a statue of Santiago in the cathedral museum. Neither the pilgrim's head nor the statue had symbols carved on them, as far as I could tell. And I couldn't find out where the statue came from. If we knew that, we could go there and look."

"I found the chapel of Santiago—"

"I thought you said there wasn't one!" He exclaimed, accusingly.

"Relax, Jack. The guidebook didn't mention it, that's all. The chapel has several statues of Santiago on horseback, but no symbols."

"Let's look together."

He followed me to the chapel and looked around. Nothing. The air smelled of damp stone and stale incense.

"Damn!" He struck a fist into his hand. "The clue's got to be here somewhere."

"One would think so," I said calmly. "What are our other options?"

"Too many. As you said earlier, there are a half-dozen other places we could look."

"'St. James will show the way.'"

"Where is he when we need him?" Jack complained again, then took the camera from me. "I'm going to look some more. The clue must be here somewhere."

I paged through the guidebook and talked to his retreating back. "There's a walnut doorway with an elaborate carving of Santiago leading a group of pilgrims at the Hospital del Rey, and there's a thirteenth-century statue of Santiago seated on a throne and holding a sword at the Monastery of Las Huelgas."

"Where are they?"

"Both are on the way out of town."

"Let's go."

When we were near the car, Jack suddenly started running.

I followed close behind. Breathless, I asked, "What's the matter?"

"I thought I saw someone lurking near the car. Did you see anyone?"

"No."

"I must be getting jumpy."

Remembering the white-cloaked man I might have seen at Estella, I wasn't so sure.

Following signs, we drove down a maze of streets to the Monastery of Las Huelgas. It was closed for the rest of the day. Frustrated, we drove to the Hospital del Rey and looked for the elaborately carved wooden doorway. It was gone, replaced by a sign, "*En restauración.*" A plain wood door stood in its place.

Jack slammed his fist into the wood, startling me with the violence of the blow. "Damn! What do we do now?" He shook his hand up and down, trying to ease the pain of his bashed knuckles.

With a nonchalance I didn't feel, I replied, "Wait till tomorrow."

"Wait till tomorrow," Jack spat out the words. "Easy for you to say!" He climbed angrily into the car and jammed the car into gear. "Let's find a hotel."

Retracing our way, we drove by the Hotel El Cid. Jack waited, double-parked, while I went in to see if there were any rooms. There were. He parked the car while I waited in the lobby. Then we checked in, leaving our passports behind the polished wood counter. The clerk handed each of us a room key, and a bellboy picked up our bags and led us to an antique metal-cage elevator. It creaked and swayed ominously as it slowly rose to the fifth floor.

The bellboy showed us our adjoining rooms, then left, whistling as he went. I noticed he bypassed the elevator for the stairs.

Now that we were alone, Jack turned to me, amused. "Two rooms?"

"Of course. I wouldn't want to tempt fate—or your resolve. Would you?"

"That's exactly what I like to do."

Wearily, I said, "Jack, I'm tired, and I'd like to rest a while."

"I can take a hint. Let's meet downstairs in half an hour."

"See you then."

I locked the door behind me and looked at the room. It was furnished with Castilian country-style furniture: heavy wooden chairs with leather seats and backs, velvet-upholstered lounge chairs, dark, ornately carved tables and chests, gilded mirrors, brocaded bedspreads. The bathroom was Castilian modern: a gleaming white porcelain douche and a half-bath with a seat in one corner, a showerhead on a flexible hose, and no shower curtain. Not the elegant *parador* of the night before, I thought, disappointedly. How quickly I had gotten used to luxury. It was easy to have one's expectations raised, I realized, but much harder to lower them once again.

After removing the hard, cylindrical pillow from beneath the green brocade bedspread and tossing it to one side, I took off my sandals and stretched out on the swaybacked bed.

A few minutes later someone knocked on the door, and I got up and opened it. Jack quickly stepped inside and slammed the door behind him. Furious, he turned on me.

"You have to be more careful. How did you know it was me?"

"Who else would it be, except the maid?" I replied, defiantly.

"You've got the letter and the medallion. Where would we be if they got stolen?" He reached towards me and took hold of the medallion dangling from the chain around my neck. "I think I should take care of this."

I pried his fingers loose and said coldly, "I don't think that's necessary."

Looking around, Jack noted the narrow door that connected our two rooms. He walked over and tried to open it. It was locked, and it locked from my side. Then he sat down on the bed, pulled out a cigarette, and lit it with a gold lighter.

I made no move to hand him an ashtray. Instead, I sat down in a nearby chair. "You're in a foul mood, aren't you?"

"Why shouldn't I be," he growled. "We can't figure out what to do next."

"I'm sure we'll think of something," I said soothingly. "After all, whoever hid the treasure wanted it to be found—by the right person, of course."

"Maybe that's it. We're not the right people."

I looked at him in surprise. "I didn't know you were superstitious."

"I'm not."

He lay down on the bed, one hand behind his head, staring at the ceiling. After a minute I said, pointedly, "I really do want to rest awhile."

He got up abruptly. "Sorry. I'll be back in half an hour."

After locking the door behind him, I stretched out on the bed and rubbed one bare foot against the other. Then I unpinned my coiled hair and massaged my head, my mind spinning.

Was someone following us or were we being paranoid? Of course, we *were* on a treasure hunt that had begun abruptly when Mateo died and a white-robed man fled the scene, so maybe we weren't paranoid, after all.

Talk about paranoid, I was even beginning to have my doubts about Jack. He was much too wealthy for an art history professor. He did consulting on the side, but I doubted that sideline could be so lucrative. Something didn't ring true. Maybe it was because he lied so easily. Or maybe it was because his charm was only skin deep, and I had seen him shed his skin more often than a snake.

I massaged my scalp some more, trying to ease the tension. There was a streak of violence in him that frightened me. Sue Ellen had said he had an aura of danger, but I didn't think she had meant violence. She might be an infuriating little gold-digger, but she didn't associate with criminals. Or did she? But why did I think of "criminal" in connection with Jack? I really was overwrought. After all, the worst he was guilty of was a violent temper, minor prevarications, and outright flattery. I hated violence, was compulsively honest, and, being compulsively honest, I had to admit that I was exceedingly—but ambivalently—attracted to him. Maybe I was just trying to build a case against Jack to protect my fragile relationship with Peter.

Suddenly, I wanted very much to talk to Peter. It was early afternoon in New York; maybe I could catch him between classes. Locking the door behind me, I went to the reception desk to make the long distance phone call, but Jack, standing with his back towards the lobby, was already using the phone, so I sat down in a nearby chair and waited for him to finish. Suddenly, his voice rose.

"I tell you it was a 'big zero.' A complete waste of time." There was a pause. "Why would I lie to you, 'Santa Claus'? Trust me." He slammed down the receiver and, turning around, saw me sitting there. He strode over to me, hands clenched.

"Been sitting there long?"

"No, I just got here. What was all that about?" I asked curiously.

"All what?"

"Who is 'Santa Claus,' for instance?"

"Oh, that." He unclenched his hands. "He's my business partner. We have some mutual investments, and I promised to keep in
touch while I was in Europe."

"But why do you call him 'Santa Claus'?"

Laughing, he said, "Sometimes I don't. Sometimes, I call him
St. Nick."

I waited for him to continue.

He took out a cigarette, lit it, then continued. "We've made a
lot of money since we started working together. One day I told
him it always seemed like Christmas when he's around, and he
said, 'Just call me Santa Claus.'"

"So that's how you live so well on an art professor's salary."

"You got it."

"So what's the 'waste of time'?"

"Just an investment lead that turned out to be nothing. Buy
you a drink?"

"No, I'm going to call Peter."

"Call him later. Let's get out of here. I feel like I've been cooped
up all day long, either inside the car or inside churches." He put
his arm through mine and led me out the door.

It was a pleasant summer evening, and the city was full of
people of all ages strolling slowly down the tree-lined alameda.
Little girls dressed in frilly pastel dresses and little boys wearing
navy blue sailor suits were playing in the park; slender, high-heeled
matrons in elegant dresses and their more casually attired hus-
bands were pushing elaborate baby carriages, complete with sun
umbrellas and ruffled upholstery, down the concrete walkways.
Plump grandmothers dressed in black, their feet encased in black
felt slippers, sat gossiping on the park benches. The air was fragrant with flowers.

We left the alameda and headed into the old part of town
through the Gateway of Santa María. Stores were still open, and
the bars were overflowing.

"Hungry, Noa?"

"Not really. Just tired."

He put his arm around my waist. I moved away.

In a husky voice, he said, "You know, you intrigue me."

"Me?"

"You're intelligent, charming, gorgeous—"

I started laughing but he refused to be put off.

"You're the kind of woman I find irresistible. But I can't get to first base with you." He turned me towards him. "Tell me: what am I doing wrong?"

"Not a thing. It's just that—"

"Is it Peter?"

"I suppose so." At least, that was part of the reason.

"But you two can't be that close. After all, you're in Spain for the summer, he's in New York."

Defensively, I replied, "I have my research and he has his."

"That's not what I mean. If we were involved, I wouldn't let you out of my sight. How can Peter even look at another woman?"

"How do you know he does?" I asked angrily.

He gave me a meaningful look.

In strained silence, we strolled down the street, looking in the store windows. Prominently displayed in a fancy hat shop was a wide-brimmed, black felt hat; the front of the brim was fastened to the crown with a large scallop shell.

Pointing to it, I commented, "They don't miss a trick, do they? Everything gets commercialized, even the pilgrimage.

"Why not? Everybody wants to make money, and if they see a way to make a fast buck, they do it."

"Well, I don't," I replied righteously.

"Come on, Noa," he scoffed. "You want to get rich quick. Otherwise, why are you on this treasure hunt?"

"Mateo's death—"

"Don't kid yourself."

Furious, I stomped off.

He caught up with me and grabbed my arm. "I'm sorry I offended you."

I shook his hand loose. "Just because you don't care about anybody but yourself doesn't mean everybody is like you."

"I said I was sorry," he protested. "You're right. I'm not used to being with somebody like you. Kind, considerate—"

"Just what kind of people do you hang out with?"

He looked at me silently for a moment, took out a cigarette, and lit it. "Oh hell, Noa. I'm always saying the wrong things to you. You're so touchy. Don't you let anybody close, anybody but Peter? Or do you keep him at a distance, too?"

I took a deep breath. Maybe I was touchy. Maybe I was try-ing to keep him at a distance by inventing all kinds of imaginary complaints: violent temper, pathological lying, criminal tenden-cies . . . What a tangled thicket of conflicting emotions I had constructed. How would I ever find my way through?

One thing was clear, however. We were on a treasure hunt. That's what had started the journey, and that's what would end it. Finding the treasure. For whatever reasons. The rest, the entire emotional mess, could get sorted out later.

I took another deep breath and let it out. "Let's call a truce, okay?"

"Okay."

Jack tried to talk me into drinking a glass of sherry at the hotel bar, but I excused myself.

"I just want to be alone."

"Let me see you to your room."

"Don't bother."

"I insist." He smiled disarmingly. "Don't worry, you can trust me. I just want to make sure you're safe."

I looked at him dubiously.

The elevator wouldn't come when we pushed the button, so we walked slowly up the four flights of stairs. When we arrived at my room, I noticed the door was unlatched. Silently, I pointed. Jack kicked the door open and it slammed against the wall. He reached inside with his left hand and groped for the light switch.

Warily, he entered the ransacked room. I followed close behind. The connecting door was open. Cautiously, we crept over and peered inside.

"They've been here, too!" He exclaimed, looking at the clothes strewn on the floor, the sheets and pillowcase torn off the bed. Quickly, he flung open the door to the bathroom. It, too, had been torn apart. Whoever had been there had been thorough—and was gone.

We walked back to my room, and I sat down on the disheveled bed.

Suddenly I jumped up, knelt down, and checked under the bed. Nothing. I sat down again.

Frightened, I looked at him. "Who could it have been?"

"Who else but the men in white."

"But how could they know we'd be here?"

"Maybe they know more than we thought."

"Or maybe there are more of them than we think," I said, thoughtfully.

"Just what do you mean?"

"Maybe there's a whole bunch of them, a brotherhood or something, and they're keeping watch at all the stops on the pilgrimage road. After all, Mateo's note said, 'beware the Brotherhood.'"

"Could be." Taking out a cigarette, he lit it and inhaled deeply. "What do we do now?"

"You tell me. You've obviously had more experience with this sort of thing than I have."He nodded absently. "We've got to be extra careful. I mean it. I'm not going to let you sleep alone."

"Come on, Jack," I protested, nervously. "They've been here and gone. They won't come back."

"But they didn't find what they were looking for."

"Which is?"

"The letter."

"I thought they *already* had the letter. Aren't they the ones who ransacked Mateo's desk?"

"Maybe there's more than one group, or maybe there's been a falling out among thieves. At any rate, they don't have the medallion."

My hand went to my throat and I rubbed the warm golden disk. "Maybe they don't know about it."

"Maybe they don't. But maybe they do." Jack turned to me. "I think you should give me the medallion."

"For the 'nth' time, no." I moved away, feeling vaguely threatened. "I'm tired. Let's go to bed."

"Don't forget, we're sleeping together."

I looked at him pointedly. "There's only one bed per room."

"So?"

"You don't give up, do you?" I said in disgust.

"Can't blame me for trying."

I looked around at the mess. "Well, we'd better start picking this up, I suppose, unless we want to explain things to the hotel management."

Fortunately, whoever had ransacked the rooms had been oddly careful; nothing was broken. Half an hour later, the rooms resembled hotel rooms for respectable guests. Little would they know.

Jack slept on the floor. I slept, or rather tried to sleep, fully dressed, on the bed.

Seven

I jerked awake, arm raised to fend off the white-robed priest who was about to bash me in the face with a huge, blood-red cross. Startled, I looked around the room. No priest. No cross. No Jack. Instinctively, I put my hand to my neck. The medallion was still there, nestling against my throat. But then, why wouldn't it be? Jack wouldn't steal it while I slept, would he?

Lying in bed, I heard the faint sound of running water. Jack must be washing up. Whatever else I thought about him, I knew he was clean. So much for a clean mind in a clean body—or how did that expression go? Still groggy, I got up, pulled open the heavy curtains and was temporarily blinded by the brilliant sunlight.

Squinting from the glare, I groped for a change of clothes and headed to the other bathroom. Ten minutes later, wearing a wrinkled green gauze skirt and matching top, I sat down in front of the large dresser mirror and started pinning up my still-wet hair.

While I watched in the mirror, Jack approached me from behind. He started to put his hands on my shoulders, then paused when he saw the look I gave him.

"Sleep well?" He asked, his voice husky.

I kept pinning up my hair. "Not really."

He reached down and pulled out the pins. "You have such gorgeous hair, Noa." He fanned it around my shoulders; the damp tendrils tickled as they spread halfway down my back. "It's such a waste to keep it pinned up and out of sight."

I started pinning it up again.

He sighed. "I can tell I am not getting anywhere with you. Maybe it's the time of day. Are you always like this in the morning?"

"Like what?"

"Unresponsive. Or maybe it's because of what happened yesterday."

"You mean our rooms being ransacked?"

"What else?"

What else indeed. I shook my head. "I didn't sleep well, but I really am all right."

"You know, Noa, we're wasting a wonderful opportunity—"

"Oh, Jack, come off it!"

We packed our suitcases in silence, then took the creaking elevator downstairs and walked through the deserted lobby to the dining room. The waiter took our orders for two *café doble* and directed us to a sunlit table for two. A napkin-draped bowl, painted with frolicking blue rabbits, was placed between us. The aroma of fresh-baked bread wafted through the air. Salivating, I selected a crusty roll and looked around for butter but, as usual, there was jam but no butter. The waiter brought our coffee.

Jack took a large gulp of steaming espresso and promptly dropped the cup. "Damn!" he swore, rubbing his lip gently.

I watched the brown stain spread across the white cloth. "Burglary making you jittery?"

"You don't know me very well, Noa," he replied angrily. "The burglary was a nuisance, that's all. But I am puzzled by the burglars. Why don't they wait for us to find the treasure and then move in? That's what I'd do."

"I'm getting to know you better all the time, Jack," I murmured.

"Just what do you mean by that?" he asked.

"Oh, nothing."

"Surely you don't think I'd do anything like that to you, do you?"

"And why not?" I asked, defiantly.

Jack reached out to touch my hand. "We're in this together. That's a completely different thing."

"Ah. I see. Loyalty among thieves?"

"You don't have to put it that way," he responded, sounding hurt.

I decided not to pursue that line of conversation. After all, it was possible that he believed what he said, and I could trust him not to double-cross me in the end. Maybe he saw himself as a gentleman thief or Robin Hood. Somehow, I doubted it.

I realized suddenly that he was watching me appraisingly, his eyes narrowed, his lips tight. Hiding my misgivings, I asked, "So why did they break into our rooms?"

"Maybe they're afraid they'll lose track of us. Or maybe they want the medallion for themselves." He looked at me intently. "Something else is bothering me. How did they find out we were in Burgos?"

"If they know about the stages of the Camino, they might have lookouts posted along the way."

After a moment, Jack shook his head. "No, it doesn't make sense. What thief would have so many partners?"

"They're thieves, Jack? And we're not?" I said, with a brittle little laugh.

"We're treasure hunters, Noa," he replied, patiently. "There's a difference. A big difference. We found the letter and the medallion; they're trying to take it away from us. We're treasure hunters, they're thieves." He finished his espresso and signaled the waiter for more. "In the meantime, we can't leave Burgos until we find the next clue, and we don't know where to look."

Thoughtfully, I said, "Our first clue was a statue of Santiago the Apostle. Our second clue was a statue of Santiago the Apostle. The letter says Santiago the Apostle will show the way to the true pilgrim, or words to that effect, right?"

He waited for me to continue.

Suddenly, I realized the import of what I had just said. "I've got it!"

"Got what?"

"Something so obvious you don't see it until it hits you on the head. The letter says Santiago the Apostle, not Santiago Matamoros, the Moor Slayer—"

"Santiago the Apostle will lead the way. Right." Jack took out a cigarette and lit it. "So we ignore the statues of Santiago on horseback. So where do we look next?"

"The clue must be in the cathedral. That was the most obvious church to go to. After all, the place could be obvious as long as the symbol wasn't. Actually, even an obvious symbol wouldn't be noticed, not unless you were looking for it." I sipped my espresso slowly. "How about the statue you saw in the cathedral museum? Maybe it came from somewhere in the cathedral. Or maybe the markings are on the statue and you just didn't see them."

"Not likely." He leaned back in the chair, looking thoughtfully at me.

Automatically, my hand went up to smooth my hair. "Is something the matter?"

"You haven't said much about last night."

"Last night? What about last night?"

"The fact that someone searched our rooms. Aren't you worried?"

I realized with a shock that I was more worried about what Jack was planning than about the burglars. "Of course I'm worried. But what can I do about it? We'll just have to be very careful. And we'll have to find the treasure before they do. The sooner the better."

Jack grinned. "A woman after my own heart. You really are enjoying this."

"Why not? As you said, 'you only live once!'" I said with false bravado.

We checked out of the hotel, leaving our suitcases in the car but taking the camera. The morning air was fresh and cool, lightly scented with the fragrance of the yellow and purple flowers planted on the banks of the river. Ignoring the beauty of the day, we strode rapidly to the cathedral and entered the slightly damp, dim interior.

We went directly to the museum. A faded label on the statue of Santiago informed us it had come from a church in a nearby village.

Jack said patronizingly, "Any more bright ideas?"

"Nobody said it would be easy," I replied angrily. "The clue has got to be here somewhere." I thought for a moment. "I know. We haven't looked outside."

So we left the cathedral and walked around the exterior. At the end of the north transept was a richly decorated doorway carved with sculptures of the apostles. Jack grabbed the camera and focused it on the scallop-shell-adorned figure of Santiago.

"Bulls-eye."

"What's the symbol?"

"A square with a cross in it.'"

I looked at my medallion. "Numeral VIII." I checked the guidebook. "León."

He glanced around nervously. "See anybody?"

"Nobody but that priest over there," I said, pointing.

The white-robed priest had just strolled into view, intently fingering his rosary. We walked the other way and then, once out of sight, doubled back to the car. With a squeal of tires, we left town.

Trucks, buses, cars, groups of bicycle-riding pilgrims all fought for space on the narrow two-lane road leading to and from Burgos. The air was hazy with pollution, and I was glad we had air conditioning. Even so, I felt queasy from the fumes. Or maybe it was from nerves.

We drove past a short, fat pilgrim dressed in a brown cloak, carrying a walking stick with a gourd swinging from the top.

Jack asked, "Why is he walking on the highway? Didn't the monk in Roncesvalles say he had marked the 'real' Camino?"

I read the guidebook. "According to this, the 'real' Camino follows the highway for a short distance outside of Burgos." We drove by a yellow arrow painted on a stone post. "Look—the route has been marked."

Jack didn't respond. He was hunched over the wheel, taking advantage of every gap in the traffic to dart in front of one vehicle after another. But even Jack could not pass them all.

"How far to León?" He asked.

"About 110 miles on bad roads."

"Any other way to go?"

"We can follow this route, Highway 120, until it links up with Highway 601 to León. Or, we can follow even worse roads on the 'authentic' Camino, through Castrojeriz and Frómista to Carrión de los Condes. That's where the Camino rejoins Highway 120. Or we can swing down to Palencia and pick up Highway 601. But that would take a lot longer and there might be even more traffic, since that road goes to Valladolid."

"They wouldn't look for us on that road, would they?"

"How should I know. I'm not used to thinking deviously."

"Better get used to it, my dear," he said with a quirky half smile. "That's part of the adventure."

When the traffic thinned out, Jack floored the accelerator, whipping around the remaining cars. Soon we left the fertile green fields behind. Small villages dotted the arid landscape. Each village had at least one church. The fortress-like buildings and tall square bell towers were silhouetted against the sky, reminding me of grain elevators in the Kansas countryside. The villages themselves were composed of red-tiled roofs and block after block of windowless, brown adobe walls.

I knew from experience that behind the featureless walls were living quarters and carefully tended gardens. Just like Jack, only in reverse. He, too, presented a certain façade to the public: charming instead of bland, but just as misleading. And behind the façade lurked—I wasn't sure.

The unrelieved drabness was broken by stands of blackish-green cypresses casting long, pointed shadows over the graveyards on the outskirts of town. Flocks of sheep grazed over the rocky fields. From the tops of the hills, the crumbling remains of castles established during the Reconquest kept silent watch.

We passed through Carrión de los Condes, where El Cid's infamous sons-in-law, the Beni Gómez brothers, had lived.

With awe in my voice, I said, "Nearly 1000 years ago El Cid rode through this country fighting Moors."

Jack grunted.

"And so did the Knights of Santiago, a few centuries later. We're literally traveling in their footsteps. Isn't that incredible?"

"You're so refreshingly enthusiastic, Noa," he replied. "You're right. It is incredible. And just as incredible is the fact that we're hunting their treasure, 500 years later." A hint of excitement in his voice, he added, "Maybe the treasure of the Brotherhood is precious jewels and gold taken from the Moors."

"I'm not so sure," I said, skeptically. "Would a group of military-priests think 'their greatest treasure' was something as mundane as gold and jewels?"

"Believe me, Noa," Jack replied with a knowing smile, "It would be gold and jewels." He trounced on the accelerator and the car surged forward.

On the outskirts of one of the villages we saw heavy wooden doors set into the side of small embankments; ventilator pipes stuck out of the ground above.

"What are those?" Jack asked, pointing at the unusual constructions.

"They're underground wine cellars, called *bodegas*."

"I thought a bodega was a winery."

"It's that also," I explained, relieved to have something neutral to talk about. "This is a wine-growing region, although a lot of the grapevines have been torn up in the past few years because they were poor quality. Some people still make their own wine or buy it from the local cooperative. They store it in their bodegas, far underground, where it stays cool, even in the hot summer months. Behind the door is a steep stairway leading to one or more underground storage and dining rooms."

Only half-listening, Jack nodded absently.

Looking at the villages passing by, I commented wistfully, "When I lived here before I wanted, but couldn't afford, to rent a car and visit these towns. I wanted to explore the marketplaces, take pictures of the churches, drink espresso at the sidewalk cafés, visit with the locals." I shook my head in disbelief. "I never thought I'd see these towns this way."

"What way?"

"As a treasure hunter. A hunted treasure hunter."

Jack didn't reply. He was lost in thought. That worried me.

About an hour and a half after we had left Burgos, we reached Sahagún, the town where I had lived for a year while doing my fieldwork. I caught a quick glimpse of the red brick towers of the three medieval churches, the tile-roofed adobe homes of friends, and the cement apartment building where I had lived.

I saw someone I knew walking down the street, so I started to roll down the window and call out, but she disappeared into a shop. It was probably just as well, I consoled myself. After all, what could I have said? "Hello—good-bye—no time to stop—I'm late! I'm late for a very important date!" I felt like the white rabbit, or maybe the March Hare. I had always wanted to return, but not like this. With a shiver, I wondered if I could ever return, here or anywhere. Would I always be hunted?

We drove by the ruined Franciscan monastery on the hill. It was a favorite picnic spot for villagers, who enjoyed the shade and the cool breeze at the summit. I thought I saw several people sitting in the shadows.

Soon we crossed the one-lane Roman bridge at the edge of town and passed the grove of swaying green poplars planted on the other side, next to the municipal swimming pool.

Nostalgically, I said, "I spent a wonderful year doing research in Sahagún."

"Looks like a dreary town."

"Funny you should say that. Someone else said the same thing recently."

"Who was that?"

"Sue Ellen."

"Who?"

"Sue Ellen. You remember, the blonde in the café in Madrid? The one who wanted to come along?"

"Oh, her."

I glanced uneasily at Jack. "You know what she said about you?"

"No idea."

"She said you had a 'look of danger' to you. I guess she was right."

He changed the subject. "How much further to León?"

"Another hour or so."

"Any idea where we should go when we get there?"

"As a matter of fact, yes," I said, laughing. "I've been in León several times."

He chuckled. "I knew you had to have been somewhere other than Sahagún. Where do we begin our search?"

"There's a beautiful medieval cathedral, a twelfth-century church, San Isidoro, with incredible frescoes, and, of course, the five-star Hotel San Marcos. That was the headquarters of the Knights of Santiago. It's been converted into a luxury hotel."

"Whoever hid the treasure was hiding it from whoever had taken over the Order, right? So the old headquarters is probably the last place he'd leave a clue. Let's start at the cathedral."

The road wound its way down from the dry plains of the meseta into the fertile valley of the Esla. Soon we passed the ugly factories, warehouses, and huge tracts of cement apartment blocks that spread like a blight around León. Following color-coded signs, we drove through the bustling downtown area, past a medieval church, past a turreted stone castle that was actually a modern savings bank, past a plaza lined with medieval buildings and filled with pigeons, tourists, and vendors. The car windows were closed, but I could imagine the babble of noise and profusion of smells.

Jack parked the car across the street from the cathedral in front of an ancient, arcaded building that housed the tourist office and a number of souvenir shops, all of which were closed.

He looked at the closed shops, surprised. "What time is it?"

"1:30."

"The cathedral will be closed, too. Damn!" He got out of the car and slammed the door hard.

We crossed the street to the locked cathedral, parts of which were surrounded by scaffolds and a high fence. It was *en obras*—under repair. While Jack started to look around, I wandered off to explore the shaded north side. I strolled around for a few minutes, staring up at the numerous grimy statues of saints and apostles. Pollution was taking its toll, eating away like leprosy at the fine stone carvings.

Suddenly a white-hooded figure jumped out from behind a buttress and lunged at me. I screamed and stepped back, but the man grabbed me by the shoulder, throwing me off balance. We fell down together and rolled over and over on the rough stone pavement, locked in a painful embrace. He tried to break the chain around my neck by grabbing the medallion; I struggled desperately to push him away.

Jack came running. Seizing the hood of my assailant's robe, he pulled him off me, half strangling him. As I rolled out from under, Jack abruptly let go and the man fell back. His head made a loud cracking sound—like a watermelon splitting open—when he hit the pavement. Jack stood over him and kicked him twice in the kidneys. The man moaned, then lay still.

Dazed, I looked at my attacker, lying unmoving on the ground.

"My God, Jack—"

Jack was flushed and breathing hard. "What the hell did you expect me to do? Ask him politely to let you go?"

"No—but—"

He looked around quickly. No one was in sight. "Let's get out of here before the cops come." Grabbing me by the hand, he jerked me up from the pavement, dragged me to the car, and shoved me in. Before I could close the car door, he was speeding away.

"Where are we going?" I asked, my voice quavery.

"We're going to that five-star hotel and act like innocent tourists."

I sat rigid in the seat, staring straight ahead. Jack glanced at me, but I refused to acknowledge his look.

After a few minutes, he broke the silence. His sounded almost apologetic. "There's a lot you don't know about me, Noa."

I sat silent.

"I grew up in a tough part of Oakland. You didn't survive if you didn't learn to protect yourself."

I replied angrily, "Did you have to hit him so hard? Twice? My God, Jack—"

"Reflex action. I'm sorry you had to see it, but I was so worried about you—"

"Hah!"

His voice was thick. "Noa, you're the best thing that's ever happened to me. You're not like the other women I've known."

"Come off it, Jack!" I exploded.

"I know you don't believe me—"

"You're damn right."

We rode in silence. Jack followed magenta-colored signs to San Marcos and parked in the large lot in front of the *parador*. When we got out of the car, I suddenly felt like a giant Gumby doll: I had to lean against the car to keep my rubbery legs from collapsing. Jack rushed over to my side and held me up. Grabbing me tightly around the waist, he helped me across the street to the hotel.

We entered the enormous lobby and walked over to the registration desk. Jack asked for one room. I started to protest, but he squeezed me hard and whispered to me to shut up. I was too shaken to argue. He registered for both of us, then marched me up the carpeted stone staircase to the room.

Once inside, I shook off his arm and glanced around. The limestone-walled room was furnished with antique tables, chairs, bureaus, and two canopied beds. Two beds, not one. I was grateful it wasn't the same room Peter and I had shared.

"At least there are two beds. I thought I'd made it clear—"

Jack retorted, "After what's been happening, do you think I would let you sleep alone?"

My legs started to wobble, and I sat down abruptly on one of the beds. "Just leave me alone," I said, my voice shaking.

Jack was suddenly apologetic. "I'm sorry, Noa. I know this has been a great shock to you. It's not every day you get mugged." He looked at me, sympathetically. "First time?"

I nodded numbly.

"I've been jumped a couple of times. You never get used to it, but you do learn to protect yourself." He continued contritely. "I'm sorry I told you to shut up, but we want to be unobtrusive, and you can be damn sure the desk clerk would remember us if we had had an argument."

I took a deep breath. "Fine."

"Can I get you something?"

I thought a moment. "How about a nice cold Coke? And the guidebook? I think I left it in the car."

"No problem. I'll get it for you. Don't open the door for anyone but me."

I bolted the door, kicked off my sandals, lay down on the green velveteen bedspread, and stared up at the matching canopy and its dangling gold fringe. The fringe swayed in time with my heartbeat.

I practiced deep breathing, trying to slow the pounding of my heart. After a few minutes, the fringe quit swaying.

Calmer, I reviewed what had just happened. I was much more shaken by Jack's violence than by the attack itself. Of course it was frightening to be mugged. Very frightening. Nothing like that had ever happened to me. But I had halfway expected an attempt on the medallion. What I had not expected was the practiced viciousness of Jack's response. His unleashed brutality made the white-robed man's attack seem positively gentle.

Who and what was Jack? He was clearly not just an art history professor, and clearly not some romantic gentleman thief. He was a dangerous, brutal man, and I was alone with him in Spain. And it was all my fault. After all, I had wanted to have an adventure!

The canopy fringe started to sway again, and I forced myself to breathe rhythmically. In for five, out for five. Soon my heartbeat was back to normal and I could think more clearly.

Objectively, I knew that the reasonable thing to do was to give Jack the medallion and run away. Fast. But I refused to consider that possibility. After all, it was *my* medallion and it was *my* adventure, even if it was more than I had bargained for. Besides, I admitted to myself, Jack probably wouldn't let me get away. I knew too much.

I wondered why Jack didn't just take the medallion and leave. He could have done so while I slept—or at any other time, I now realized. My feeble attempts to stop him would have been totally ineffective. Maybe he figured he couldn't find the clues by himself. I'd noticed that his track record so far had not been very good, and his knowledge of Spanish was limited. Or so he claimed. Maybe he was afraid I would go to the police. Maybe he really did care about me.

Ruefully, I shook my head. Scratch that last thought. That only happened in fairy tales. And this was no fairy tale. It was more like a nightmare. I wondered how badly injured my attacker was. I was very grateful that Jack had saved me from him, but I still hoped the mugger hadn't been badly injured—and not just because I was concerned about the police. I didn't want anybody to get hurt, including me, including the attacker. How unrealistic, I realized. This wasn't a kid's game of hide and seek. It was a treasure hunt.

I took a deep breath and exhaled. I knew what I really wanted to do. Crazy at it seemed, what I really wanted to do was run away with the medallion and find the treasure myself. But leaving Jack behind would be much too dangerous: I'd have the men in white *and* Jack after me. As long as I played along with Jack and didn't let him know how much I mistrusted him, he would protect me. At least from them. At least until we found the treasure.

Finding the treasure on my own would be impossible for purely practical reasons, I acknowledged. I didn't have the money to rent a car, and I couldn't rely on a bus or train to travel to a specific village on the Camino de Santiago—especially when everyone else seemed to have cars, if not wings. I sighed. I might as well take advantage of the fact that I was stuck with Jack and travel as conveniently, and luxuriously, as possible.

I stroked the softly gleaming medallion. It made me both valuable and vulnerable, as I had learned at the cathedral. The medallion. That was the key. Whoever had it could find the treasure. Abruptly, I got up from the bed and took a notebook and pencil from my purse. I placed a page of the notebook over the deeply engraved gold disk and rubbed the pencil across the paper. Then I turned the medallion over and did the same on the other side. Satisfied with the results, I put the notebook back in my bag, next to the guidebook.

There was a loud knock on the door and Jack called my name. For a moment I toyed with the idea of not opening the door, but I knew I really had no choice.

Jack looked me over, then handed me a glass and poured an open can of Coke into it. "I hope you're feeling better," he said, a worried frown on his face. "By the way, I couldn't find the guidebook. Sure you don't have it with you?"

"Maybe it's in my bag. I'll check in a minute." My hands trembling, I lifted the glass to my mouth and drank it quickly.

He refilled the glass and sat down beside me on the bed.

Suddenly there was another loud knock on the door.

Jack turned to me, threateningly, "Expecting company?"

"I was about to ask you the same thing," I said, my voice shaking slightly.

He strode over to the door and growled, "Who is it?"

A familiar, honeyed voice replied, "It's me, Sue Ellen."

Slowly, Jack opened the door. There stood Sue Ellen, cool and relaxed in a pale pink dress, her hair tied back with a matching scarf. She held a drink in one red-tipped hand.

"Mind if I come in?"

Eight

Jack dragged Sue Ellen into the room and slammed the door closed with his foot.

"You're hurting me," she whimpered, plucking at his fingers.

He held on tight. "What the hell are you doing here?" He glared accusingly at me. "Did you tell her we were coming here?"

Indignant, I replied, "How could I? I didn't even know."

"Jack, dear, please let go of my arm, " Sue Ellen pleaded as she started to stroke Jack's arm with her long, red fingernails. Suddenly she dug her nails into the back of his hand; he yelped and let go.

Rubbing his bleeding hand, he demanded, "Tell me how you got here!"

Sue Ellen strolled over to a one of the green-leather-covered chairs and sat down, crossing her ankles gracefully. "Why, by train."

"That's not what I meant and you know it." He loomed over her, clenching and unclenching his fists.

"I knew you were following the Camino de Santiago. I figured you'd probably stop in León, so I just took my chances." She stirred her drink with a red-tipped finger, then licked it. "Nothing ventured, nothing gained, I always say. And I was right, wasn't I?" she said, smugly.

I was impressed. "But why the Hotel San Marcos?"

"Honey, I'm no fool. This used to be the monastery of the Knights of Santiago, and you told me you'd stayed here with Pe-

108

ter. So where else would you go? Besides, it's the best hotel in town, and I had a feeling Jack wouldn't settle for anything less. Right, Jack?"

I burst out laughing.

Jack glared at me. "What's so funny?"

Wiping tears of laughter from my eyes, I gasped, "We must be carrying a homing signal. Everybody knows where we're going, even before we do."

Ignoring me, Jack turned to Sue Ellen. Grimly, he said, "You were taking quite a chance, Sue Ellen."

"I like taking chances." She glanced around the room. "One room, hmm? My, how quickly things have progressed. I'm surprised at you, Noa. What would Peter say?"

Before I could reply, Jack responded angrily, "Just what do you plan to do, now that you've found us?"

Sue Ellen looked at him ingenuously. "Why, come with you, of course. I just love treasure hunts!"

There was a moment of silence; then I started to laugh again. "If you can't beat 'em, join 'em, right, Jack?"

He stood scowling at us. Gradually his threatening stance softened, and he slouched down in a leather-covered chair. Sue Ellen smiled coyly and twirled a long blond tendril of hair around her red-tipped finger.

From the bed, I watched the two of them watch each other. I wondered how the treasure hunt would change, now that Sue Ellen was here. Would Jack double-cross me and run off with her? He knew I had begun to distrust him. Besides, if what he wanted was sex, he'd obviously have better luck with Sue Ellen.

But if they teamed up, what would happen to me? I knew too much. They would have to get rid of me, either temporarily or permanently. A cold chill crept slowly up my spine.

Of course, there was another possibility. Jack could decide to bring both Sue Ellen and me along. We'd be the three musketeers— or the three stooges—or two stooges and one stoolie. Or the good, the bad, the ugly. And who was which?

Or would Jack try to get rid of Sue Ellen? Just how smart *was* he? Smart enough to realize he was better off with me? After all, I was more trustworthy, and I'd proven I could figure out the clues to the treasure.

Suddenly, I realized I was thinking only in terms of what Jack wanted. What did *I* want? At first I had wanted Sue Ellen gone. Immediately. But her presence had certain advantages. I knew Sue Ellen was a gold-digger, but that didn't make her a would-be murderer. I was worried about what Jack would do to me after we found the treasure. But if Sue Ellen were with us, he would have to get rid not just of me but also of her, which would obviously be twice as difficult. Unless, of course, they used me to find the treasure and then they discarded me. Permanently.

I watched Sue Ellen take a cigarette out of her purse. Jack got up from his chair, pulled out his gold lighter, and lit it for her, steadying her hand with his other hand. She smiled up at him and inhaled deeply. Pale wisps of smoke spread like mist through the room.

With a start, I realized I ached all over. I needed a massage or a hot shower. But was it wise to leave the two of them alone? Mentally, I shrugged. Better they should get to know each other sooner rather than later.

Getting up slowly from the bed, I said wearily, "I need to wash up."

Sue Ellen nodded disinterestedly and blew smoke in Jack's general direction. He took out a cigarette, absentmindedly tapped it on the back of his hand, lit it, and stared at her pensively.

Ignored by all, I opened my suitcase, took out jeans and a brightly colored Hawaiian-fish-decorated T-shirt, and headed to the bathroom.

The bathroom reminded me of the idyllic time I had spent with Peter. The same black marble counter tops, black tile walls, white porcelain double sinks, huge tub, toilet, and bidet; the same expanse of gleaming mirrors and chrome. There was even a generous supply of black Magno soap, shampoo, and *gel de baño*, the Spanish version of liquid bath soap. It was all strangely comforting.

After setting the adjustable showerhead to pulse-massage, I turned on the hot water full blast. As soon as the spray hit my skin, I felt as if I was being flayed. Only then did I realize that my neck was raw, and my arms and legs had been badly scraped in the mugging. Soberly, I realized that I was still much better off than my attacker, who had been left motionless on the ground.

Trying not to wince at the pain, I washed off the dried blood. The color reminded me of Sue Ellen's nail polish. The Magno bath gel formed rich, soothing bubbles on my skin. I rinsed, very gently blotted myself dry, got dressed, and, taking a deep breath, rejoined Jack and Sue Ellen.

When they saw me they stopped talking. Sue Ellen had the bad taste to look extremely pleased with herself; Jack still looked wary.

Since the room was now hazy with smoke, I walked over to the large double doors at the far end of the room and opened them, stepping out onto a foot-deep balcony that overlooked the gardens and the street below. The afternoon sun was blazing hot, turning the air into a blast furnace, but at least it didn't reek of tobacco smoke. Instead, it stank of diesel fuel.

I turned to face Jack and Sue Ellen. "It's almost 3:00. Let's go eat."

Jack looked at me, concerned. "You sure you feel up to it?"

"Why wouldn't she?" Sue Ellen asked.

He replied quickly, "Noa had a minor accident. She slipped and fell, about an hour ago."

"Poor dear," Sue Ellen purred.

"Spare me, Sue Ellen," I remarked dryly, my mind churning. So Jack didn't want Sue Ellen to know about the mugging. Because he didn't want to frighten her? Or because he didn't want her to know about the medallion? My head was muzzy from trying to think deviously, but I knew I was going to have to get used to it. As Jack had so accurately pointed out, thinking deviously was part of the adventure.

They were both watching me intently. I feigned impatience and said, "Well, are you coming with me or do I go alone?"

They looked at each other and stood up in unison.

Side by side—the staircase was quite wide—we went down to the dining room located off the lobby. The waiter led us to a table for four, and Sue Ellen slid into the red-velvet upholstered chair next to Jack's. I sat down across from them. The waiter handed us elaborately printed menus and began reciting the specialties of the day.

Jack and Sue Ellen ordered *entremeses* and frog legs. Although I wasn't hungry, I wanted to appear normal, so I ordered the same. At the suggestion of the waiter, Jack ordered a bottle of Vega Sicilia Fourth Year.

Soon the waiter returned and, with a flourish, deposited a large ceramic platter of *entremeses* in the middle of the table, presented the open bottle of wine to Jack, and poured a bit into his glass. He sniffed the rich oaky perfume approvingly, rolled the wine around in his mouth, and got a far-off look in his eyes. To the waiter, he said, "Excellent suggestion."

The waiter poured wine into the our glasses, then left.

Jack grinned at us and said, "To treasure and the hunt!"

We clinked our glasses together. "To treasure and the hunt."

We helped ourselves to the assorted cheeses, sausages, salamis, and fat white asparagus. While I sat in silence, Sue Ellen and Jack exchanged superficial inquiries and replies about each other's lives.

Watching the three of us, I felt as if I was in a play—not a tragedy, at least not yet, but certainly a surreal melodrama. Here we sat, distrusting conspirators on a race to find a hidden treasure, acting like friends on a holiday, sampling fine wine, toasting each other as if we meant it, exchanging idle chitchat.

After half an hour, the waiter reappeared with the main course: tiny frog legs sautéed in oil and garlic, then baked with green and red peppers in an earthenware casserole. The pungent aroma of garlic filled the air.

While Jack and Sue Ellen made every effort to charm each other, I grew increasingly nervous. The more I thought about how viciously Jack had attacked the white-robed figure, the more anxious I became. Jack had been awfully vague about his background— and about a lot of other things. The one thing he wasn't vague about was brutal assault.

In the middle of a mouthful of tender frog legs, I abruptly stopped chewing. I had just had a terrible thought: was it possible that Jack had something to do with Mateo's death? Had he gotten into a violent argument with Mateo and either brought on his heart attack or actually killed him? True, a white-robed man had run out of the room, but maybe he was just an innocent, frightened witness.

I tried to tell myself I was letting my imagination run away with me. After all, I was basing this fantastic scenario on the fact that Jack had gallantly jumped to my defense and saved me from the mugger. I shouldn't hold that against him, should I?

I watched Sue Ellen ooze Southern charm all over Jack. Soon, he was almost eating out of her red-nailed hand. Disgusted, I wondered if he was stupider than I had thought.

I found it increasingly hard to swallow as I contemplated what might happen to me if Jack and Sue Ellen became too chummy. Should I try to out-charm Sue Ellen? I tried to visualize myself competing with her and gagged. Not even the treasure was worth such debasement.

Suddenly I held the white linen napkin over my mouth and coughed delicately. In a faint voice I murmured, "I'm not feeling very well."

Jack started to stand up, but I motioned to him to sit down. "Thanks, Jack, but you can't help."

I looked pointedly at Sue Ellen, who had made no effort to move. "Don't bother to get up. I'll be fine. I'm just a little shaky, that's all."

I stood up and ran from the room, but instead of heading for the ladies' lounge I rushed over to the registration desk.

"I need to make an international call right away," I whispered to the desk clerk. "In private." Seeing him hesitate, I handed him a $20 bill. He glanced around, ushered me into the cramped, paper-strewn office, and closed the door. Then he dialed the number. After a moment he hung up the phone and shook his head. All lines were busy.

I pleaded, "Please try again."

He promised to try in a few minutes and left the room. I looked at my watch. It was nearly 9 A.M. in New York. With any luck, I could still reach Peter before he went to the office. Then I remembered it was Saturday. Hopefully he had spent the night at home.

I paced the crowded office, worrying that Sue Ellen would come looking for me in the ladies' lounge. Not likely, I reassured myself. I kept looking at my watch: one minute, two minutes, three minutes . . .

Five minutes later the desk clerk returned and redialed the number. This time I heard Peter's sleepy voice on the other end. I grabbed the phone from the clerk. He left the room, shutting the door behind him.

"Peter—thank God you're there!"

He was instantly awake. "Noa? I'm so glad you called! Are you all right?"

"Well, for the time being, I think so."

"What do you mean?"

"I just got mugged."

"By Jack?"

"No. It was some guy in a white robe."

"You sure it wasn't Jack?"

"Of course I'm sure. In fact, Jack may even have murdered the guy in his effort to protect me. If he didn't, it wasn't for lack of trying."

"Noa, you've got to be very careful. I called Nicholson again, and he says Jack has a very unsavory reputation. Something about smuggling drugs."

"Smuggling drugs? Mateo said something about an international smuggling ring, but he was talking about art, not drugs."

"Nicholson was pretty vague about the details, but I know he said drugs, and I know he was upset when I told him you were on a treasure hunt with Jack."

"You mentioned the treasure hunt?"

"Of course."

"And the medallion?"

"Sure. Why not?"

"I guess it can't hurt, " I said, uneasily. "After all, Nicholson is a highly respected historian."

"By the way, he thinks the medallion is a hoax." There was a pause, then Peter said lightly, "Now, Noa, I told you to have fun, but don't you think this is getting out of hand?" He paused again. "Where are you?"

"We've checked into the Hotel San Marcos. In León. We're sharing a room—that's Jack's idea—he thinks I'll be safer that way."

Peter snorted. "I bet!" He thought a moment. "I tell you what: Stay where you are."

"What do you mean, stay where I am?"

"Stay where you are so I can find you when I get there."

"What do you mean, 'when you get there'?"

"My dear, you sound like a talking parrot. What I mean is that I'm going to Spain. I just realized I am sorely in need of a vacation."

"Are you serious?"

"Dead serious. Sorry. That was a poor choice of words."

"Peter—"

"Now, Noa, don't be selfish. You can't have all the fun."

I took a deep breath and let it out slowly. "When will you get here?"

"How long is the flight to Madrid?"

"About seven hours, but don't forget it's six hours later here."

"I'll catch a plane this afternoon or early tonight, fly to Madrid, and rent a car. How far is it to León?"

"About four hours by car."

"I should be able to get there by tomorrow afternoon at the latest. I'll look for you at the Hotel San Marcos. Stall any way you can."

"I'd better hang up before they find me—"

"They?"

"I forgot to tell you. Sue Ellen showed up."

"Who?"

"The conniving blonde I've told you about."

"How'd she get there?"

"It's a long story. I'll tell you when you get here."

"You sure you'll be all right?" He asked, not bothering to hide his concern.

I found that wonderfully comforting. "Sure. No problem. I'm 'made for adventure,'" I said, with false bravado. "At least that's what Jack says. See you tomorrow."

"Righto."

Feeling oddly cheerful, I hung up the phone and left the office, checking first to see if either Sue Ellen or Jack was in the lobby. There was no sign of them, nor of anyone in a white robe.

After a brief stop in the ladies' lounge I returned to the restaurant, just in time to see Sue Ellen place her hand around the back of Jack's neck and whisper in his ear. He laughed, a low, sensuous laugh, and inclined his head towards hers. I walked over to the table and cleared my throat loudly. They looked up, startled.

"Are you feeling better?" asked Jack.

"Much better, thank you," I replied, and, with a newly restored appetite, sat down to finish eating. Unfortunately, the once-bubbling casserole had cooled, and the frog legs and peppers now poked out of a covering of congealed oil and tomato sauce. I pushed it away.

After we ordered espresso and cognac, Sue Ellen pulled a cigarette out of her purse. Pointedly, she looked at Jack. He pulled out his gold lighter. She steadied his wrist with her hand as he lit her cigarette.

Still holding onto his wrist, she looked into his eyes. "Well, Jack, what should we do now?"

He looked meaningfully at her. She smirked and looked away.

I asked dryly, "Am I in the way?"

Jack released his wrist abruptly. "Why, Noa, of course not. Whatever gave you that idea?" He moved his chair closer to mine and put his hand on the back of my neck. I winced in pain and jerked away.

"My neck is still raw from the mugging," I explained, glancing at Sue Ellen. "Jack *has* told you about the mugging, hasn't he?"

Eyes wide, she shook her head.

"He didn't?" Looking innocently at Jack, I asked, "Why didn't you tell her?"

Sue Ellen glared at him. "You promised you'd tell me everything. Just remember, I know about Mateo."

Jack and I both gave a start. I wondered what she meant. Then I realized that she knew we had found him dead. After all, that's what I'd told her.

Sue Ellen continued, threateningly, "I'm along for the ride whether you like it or not."

Trying to sound offhanded, Jack said, "I gave Noa a pretty gold coin, and somebody saw it around her neck and grabbed it. I warned her not to wear it, but you know how ladies are."

"You gave Noa a gold coin?" She said incredulously.

"Why not?"

Jack wasn't telling Sue Ellen anything he could avoid telling. Maybe I didn't have to worry about the two of them ganging up on me after all. In which case, if he wanted her to come along, that was fine. Even better. She would divert his attention from me—me and Peter. My breath caught: What would Jack do when he found out that Peter was joining our cozy little trio?

Sue Ellen interrupted my thoughts. "I'd be happy to take care of your coin, Noa, and spare you the discomfort of another mugging."

"I really think you should let me take care of it," Jack urged.

"I thank you both for your concern," I said, wryly, "but I wouldn't dream of giving it to either of you. Think of the guilt I'd feel if anything happened to you." My hand went to my throat and I started to stroke the medallion.

When Sue Ellen reached over to look more closely at the medallion, I tucked it inside my T-shirt.

Jack leaned back, swirling the amber-colored cognac in the large snifter, inhaling the bouquet. "Let's get down to business. Remember, we're here on a treasure hunt."

I replied briskly, "Right you are. What do you propose we do next?"

"How about looking at the cathedral?" He suggested.

I shook my head vehemently. "I think we should stay close to the hotel today. After all, Jack, if the guy who mugged me was badly hurt, the police might be looking for you."

Sue Ellen gulped. "How'd he get hurt?"

"When he jumped Noa, I knocked him out," Jack replied.

Sue Ellen looked at him with admiration. "Why, Jack, I am so relieved to know I am in such capable hands. I like a man who can protect himself and his companions. I had no idea—"

"There's a lot you don't know, Sue Ellen," he said coolly, examining his manicured fingernails.

I continued, "We don't want to get involved with the police, correct?" Both Sue Ellen and Jack nodded. "So we'd better 'lie low' for a while, agreed?" I looked pointedly at Jack, who nodded again. "Besides, there are lots of statues and carvings to look at in the hotel."

"I thought we agreed that the monastery of the Knights of Santiago was the last place they'd hide a clue," Jack protested.

"Jack, Jack, come on. Think deviously! That might be just what whoever hid the treasure would want you to think."

"You may be right," he admitted. "So where do we start?"

I took the guidebook out of my bag and began to translate. "Let's see. Ferdinand and Isabella founded the Convent of San Marcos in gratitude for the Knights of Santiago's help in wrestling Spain back from the Moors. The site had been occupied by a twelfth-century hospital for pilgrims, founded by the Order." I skipped a bit. "The east wing of the hotel is joined to the unfinished church of San Marcos, the front of which is decorated with innumerable carved scallop shells. San Marcos has beautiful choir stalls. The sacristy, cloister, and adjoining chapter rooms house the Provincial Archeological Museum. Etcetera."

Sue Ellen tapped her high-heeled sandal impatiently against the thick oak table leg.

I turned the page. "During the last 100 years, the one-time monastery has been used as a veterinary college, a barracks, and a storehouse. In the 1960s the government remodeled the decrepit old building, along with a number of others in Spain, to encourage tourism.

"Ah, here we are. The two-story limestone façade is covered with ornate carvings, and the 328-foot Plateresque façade is unsurpassed in richness and delicacy . . . filled with busts of famous people and friezes of biblical scenes. Mounted over the elaborate entry way is the horseback-riding figure of Santiago Matamoros." I glanced up from the guidebook. "Let's start there."

Jack protested, "Noa, we decided to ignore the Matamoros figures, remember?"

Sue Ellen interrupted, "Just what are you two talking about?"

I looked pointedly at Jack. "If she's going to come along, and I gather she is, she might as well help."

Jack gave an exaggerated sigh and whispered, "We've deciphered the code in the letter."

"And just what is this code?" Sue Ellen took a deep drag on her cigarette and crushed it out in a saucer.

"A symbol carved next to a statue of Santiago tells us where to go. The trick is to find the right statue."

"There must be more to it than that," she said suspiciously.

To my amusement, Jack seemed at a loss for words, so I helped him out. "How astute of you, Sue Ellen. Of course there's more to it than that. We look for a figure of Santiago that seems to be pointing somewhere. We look where the figure is pointing, and that's how we find a directional indicator."

"But how do you know where to go?"

"We've agreed to let you come along," Jack snarled, "but don't expect us to tell you everything we know. If we did, you wouldn't stick around for very long, now, would you?"

She batted her big blue eyes at him and said, in a voice like syrup, "Why, Jack, how could you misjudge me so?"

Disgusted, I stood up. "Let's go."

We left the restaurant and started across the spacious lobby to the main entry. Abruptly, I held up my hand and we all stopped. "It's too conspicuous if we all go. Sue Ellen, why don't you take my camera and look for a symbol, any symbol, next to a figure of Santiago."

"Why the camera?"

Patiently, I explained, "You can use the lens as a binoculars. Besides, it's protective coloration. Pretend you're taking pictures."

After Sue Ellen had walked past the two black-and-gold-uniformed doormen at the entryway, Jack turned to me with a conspiratorial smile. "Good thinking, Noa. Now we can look without her. We'd better make the best of it. At least the men in white won't connect her with us." He stared off into space and added softly, "Actually, she might come in useful. For a while."

I pretended not to hear.

We walked across the lobby and through a glass door into the archeological museum housed in one wing of the cloisters. Chunks of carved Roman inscriptions were hung on the beige limestone walls and mounted on pedestals arranged seemingly at random on the cobblestone pavement. A plaque on the wall explained that León was named after the VII Roman Legion; the carved tombstones and other markers had been unearthed during various excavations of the city. Fascinated, I examined several of the stele.

Turning to Jack, I commented, "You said your field was Italian Renaissance, so I suppose you can read these Latin inscriptions." He glanced at a tombstone from the third century. "Of course I can, but these stones don't interest me. They don't have any value, except to historians. Our treasure, on the other hand, has a great deal of value. So let's stop wasting time. Let's find Santiago." He took my arm and led me down the covered walkway.

Soon we came to an exhibit room lined with glass cases. I was drawn to the one that displayed an eleventh-century ivory carving called the Cristo de Carrizo. The pale ivory figure had a very large head and carefully braided hair and beard. Its eyes, made of white and black enamel with gold inserts, stared mournfully towards its feet, which, like its long, thin hands, were nailed to a large wooden cross. Its arms and legs were quite short in proportion to its body and head.

Jack came up behind me. "That's a real beauty, isn't it?"

Silently, I nodded, then looked in the guidebook. "It says here that at the end of the last century, the cross was owned by a lawyer for the nuns of Carrizo. He decapitated the figure and put the head on his walking cane. Someone recognized its value and reclaimed it for the museum." I was outraged. "How could someone *do* that?"

"I only wish I *could* do that. Think what it would feel like to own something so valuable and do whatever you want to with it. That's power, real power, power that only money can buy."

"But you're an art historian," I said, shocked. "Aren't you supposed to preserve things?"

"Noa, my dear, you are charming, delightful—and hopelessly naïve."

Before I could reply, he walked off into another room, past the museum guard who stood at the doorway. I followed close behind. On a small table stood a worm-eaten wooden figure of Santiago, complete with scallop shell and pilgrim's cloak. Jack strode over to it.

"Pay dirt."

We examined the figure under the watchful eye of the museum guard but could find no symbols.

I scanned the other displays. "Here's another figure of Santiago."

We examined it as well. Nothing.

"Damn it," Jack complained, "Maybe the symbol's on the wall next to where the statue was originally placed. But how can we find where these figures came from? Do you think the guard would know?"

"Too risky, don't you think?" Pulling out my guidebook, I read, "One of them came from San Miguel del Camino, a nearby town."

"Which one is it?"

"How should I know," I retorted, then pointed to a figure of Santiago Matamoros carved into a niche high in the wall of the sacristy. "How about that one?"

Jack objected, "I thought you said we should ignore Santiago on horseback."

Soothingly, I replied, "I know I did, but it's here, isn't it? And how do I know what the person who hid the treasure was thinking?" Actually, I was just trying to prolong the search any way I could. After all, Peter couldn't get here until the next day.

We walked over to the near-life-sized carving and looked up at it.

"We need the camera," Jack said. "I'll go get it."

I started to point out that if the symbol was carved too high for us to see without our "binoculars," it would have been too high for "the Master" to have seen unless he climbed a ladder, which probably wasn't available and would have been too conspicuous anyway. But then I realized that Jack's lack of perceptiveness would help me stall.

How, I wondered, had he earned a Ph.D. with such a sloppy, unsystematic approach? Maybe he was more patient and careful about his scholarly research, but I doubted it.

Lost in thought, I jumped when a hand touched my shoulder. With a sigh of relief, I saw it was Jack.

"Come on, Noa," he said, impatiently, "I'm not leaving you here alone."

As we walked quickly down the corridor, we heard the faint, light sound of sandals slapping on cobblestone. Turning in unison, we saw a tall, white-robed man behind us. Jack started towards him, but I grabbed his arm and held him back. When the hooded figure came up to us, he made the sign of a cross with pale, bony fingers and walked slowly by.

"I think that was one of them," Jack whispered.

"So what were you going to do, attack him? Talk about calling attention to yourself," I said angrily. "Besides, I think he was a Cistercian monk."

"Maybe."

Sue Ellen was no longer examining the carving on the front of the hotel; instead, she was drinking alone at a table for two in the smoke-filled bar.

Jack stalked over to her. "I thought I told you to check the façade!"

"I did," Sue Ellen said sulkily. "And there was nothing there. Anyway, you really haven't told me what to look for, so how would I know when I found it?" She brushed back her hair. "Besides, I could only pretend to take photos for so long. And it was terribly hot. I just about wilted."

Jack motioned to me to wait with Sue Ellen and, picking up the camera, went back to the museum. I sat down in the deeply cushioned leather chair across from her and ordered a Bitter Kas.

Sue Ellen watched me calculatingly. "Well, here we are. Just the two of us."

"Here we are," I replied, coolly.

"Noa, let's let bygones be bygones. I'm willing to forget that you left me standing on the sidewalk after you promised to take me with you."

I started to interrupt, but she continued. "I could have gone to the police and reported that you were present at the scene of a murder, but I didn't."

"Murdered? You're sure Mateo was murdered?"

"You didn't know?" She obviously didn't believe me.

"I thought he died of a heart attack. If he was murdered, I had nothing to do with it. Mateo was my friend."

"Try telling that to the police," Sue Ellen said smugly. "They think it's murder."

I didn't reply, unsure whether to believe her.

Sue Ellen reached over and rested her hand lightly on my arm. I lifted it off the way you would pluck off an unpleasant insect, but she didn't seem to notice. "Don't you worry, Noa. I won't say a word about it to anyone." She picked up her half-empty glass and took a gulp. "Like I said, let bygones be bygones. All I ask is that you take me with you."

"What's the matter?" I asked snidely, "Having trouble convincing Jack?"

"Not a bit. I told you he was my kind of guy. But it would be a lot nicer if we were friends, that's all."

"Why?" I asked, not expecting an answer. In silence, I nibbled on the salted almonds the waiter brought with my drink and tried to think calmly and objectively about Sue Ellen's offer. Admittedly, I didn't like Sue Ellen, and I was angry that she was determined to share the treasure hunt—and the treasure—with us. But it would be much better if we could trust each other. After all, I knew, even if she didn't, that neither of us could trust Jack. Besides, she would help keep Jack occupied once Peter showed up.

Grudgingly, I conceded, "Okay, Sue Ellen. Let's let bygones be bygones."

She smiled at me gratefully, but I noticed that her smile went no further than the edges of her mouth. I wondered whether her mother had warned her to avoid crease lines—or real feelings.

Just then Jack returned. "No symbol," he groused.

I took the camera from him. "I think we'd better check the façade again. Sue Ellen's right, you know. She didn't know what to look for."

Leaving Sue Ellen alone with her drink, Jack followed me outside. In the shimmering heat, we examined the numerous busts and friezes and pilasters and columns that decorated the front of the hotel. Then we examined the scallop-shell-studded façade of the attached church. Eventually the light started to fade, so we went back inside and rejoined Sue Ellen in the bar. Her glass was half-empty, but I had no way of knowing if this was the same drink or a subsequent one.

"Frankly," she said, examining her fingernails, "I find this all rather boring. If you don't object, I'll go upstairs and take a bath." She looked coquettishly at Jack. "Care to join me?"

Jack ignored her.

I asked, "What's your room number? We might need to get hold of you."

"Jack already knows." She got up and sauntered out of the bar.

Taking my cue from Sue Ellen, I stretched slowly and stood up. "I think I'll go upstairs too."

"I'll go with you."

"Why, Jack," I said, pretending to be jealous, "I thought you weren't interested, now that Sue Ellen's here."

He grinned broadly. "She has her uses, Noa, but she reminds me of a black widow spider. I've known a lot like her. You, on the other hand, are so refreshingly honest—and so naïve." He stood up. "I'll see you to our room for safety's sake."

We walked up the carpet-covered stone staircase and down the corridor to our room. I unlocked the door and Jack turned to go. Then he paused and looked at me intently.

"Don't open the door for anyone, Noa. I don't have to remind you that these guys mean business. I'll meet you in the lounge in an hour."

When I went downstairs I found Jack and Sue Ellen cozily ensconced in a plush maroon sofa. Together, we went into the dining room and ordered a light supper. As if by mutual agreement, nobody talked about the treasure. Instead, Sue Ellen told amusing stories about the South, Jack told amusing stories about art historians, and I sat there attempting to look amused, trying to disguise the deep discomfort that I felt in their presence.

Then we went back to the bar and seated ourselves in three high-backed green leather chairs arranged around a leather-topped, hobnailed-studded wooden table.

While we were waiting for our drinks to arrive, an attractive middle-aged man came in, his tie loose around his neck, his jacket thrown nonchalantly over his shoulder. He looked around expectantly, then, disappointed, went up to the orange-and-white-striped, canopy-covered bar. Sue Ellen got up and ran over to him. From where we sat, we could see the man kiss her warmly on both cheeks. They carried on an animated conversation, during which she gestured towards us. He looked displeased. After a while, she returned, looking smug.

"Who is that?" Jack asked.

Just then, the waiter brought our drinks and a bowl heaped with salted almonds. Sue Ellen ignored Jack's question.

As soon as the waiter left, Jack leaned threateningly towards her and repeated: "I said, who's that?"

"Why, honey, nobody you know, I'm sure."

"Where'd you meet him?"

"Here." Sue Ellen twirled the straw in her drink.

Jack grabbed her wrist and she dropped the straw. "I want to know who he is."

"His name is Juan." She looked defiantly at Jack. "Don't forget, I've been waiting here for days. I had to find *some* way to keep myself occupied."

"I don't like it." He said, his voice grating like chalk on a blackboard.

"What difference does that make?" Immediately reconsidering her reply, Sue Ellen looked at him through her long eyelashes and smiled coyly. "Why, Jack, I didn't think you cared."

He replied tightly, "Don't take it personally, Sue Ellen. I just don't want anybody knowing about my—our—business."

"Now Jack, I'm no fool. I wouldn't dream of mentioning a word to anybody." She reached over and stroked his arm slowly. "Trust me."

I stood up, disgusted. "I don't know about you two, but I'm tired. And I ache all over from the mugging. I'm going to bed."

Jack pushed back his chair. "I'll go with you."

Sue Ellen said sweetly, "My, my. Wonders never cease."

Jack dug his fingers painfully into her shoulder; she winced. "I think you'd better come too. It's not safe for you to get picked up by some stranger at the bar."

"Juan isn't just 'some stranger.' Besides, do you have a better suggestion?" She asked angrily.

"I'll think about it. Let's go."

"Jack, dear, you wouldn't want to make a scene, would you?" She said calmly, removing his hand from her shoulder. "I think I'll stay right here and finish my little drink, if you don't mind. See you around."

I intervened. "She's right, you know, Jack. You don't want to make a scene. Come on."

We left Sue Ellen swirling the straw in her drink. I glanced over my shoulder and saw Juan walk over to her table. Jack started to turn back, but I took his arm and led him quickly through the lobby, looking around to make sure no white-robed men were in sight.

Once in our room, we took turns washing up and getting ready for bed. Within a few minutes, I had crawled under the covers and turned off the reading light next to my bed. Jack turned his off soon afterwards.

At first I felt very uneasy. I was afraid that Jack would try to steal the medallion—or do something more deadly—while I slept. But then I realized he had had plenty of opportunities to do so and he would have more tomorrow, so I might as well quit worrying and get some rest. In a few minutes, I was asleep.

During the night, I heard Jack get dressed quietly and tiptoe out of the room. I looked at the clock on the bed stand. 12 A.M. I went back to sleep but woke up when he came in, just as it was getting light.

Nine

The sound of an alarm interrupted my dream of a glittering gold medallion floating like a giant balloon across a black velvet sky. While I watched in awe, it swelled larger and larger and turned into a blazing star, illuminating the night with burning light. Suddenly the glowing medallion exploded, showering the earth with razor-sharp shards and impaling me, bleeding, on the ground.

Eyes still closed but relieved to be awakened, I groped towards the jangling noise and turned off the alarm. Groaning, I covered my face with my pillow, trying to postpone the disruptive events that the day would surely bring. In the suffocating darkness, I wondered again why Jack didn't just steal the medallion and leave me—and possibly Sue Ellen—behind. Suddenly a new possibility occurred to me: maybe I provided protection for him. After all, I was the one who had gotten mugged. In that case, of course, Sue Ellen would do just as well. Gasping for air, I dragged the pillow off my face and stared up at the swaying fringe overhead.

Jack came out of the bathroom, humming.

I grumbled, "You seem remarkably ebullient."

"And why not?" He smiled cheerfully. "I'm on a treasure hunt with not one but two beautiful women. And I have a gut feeling that Lady Luck is with me."

"You sound like a gambler."

"I am indeed. But don't tempt fate, Noa. Get dressed and quit looking so inviting."

As he started towards me, I jumped out of bed, threw my robe over my nightgown, and headed towards the bathroom. Through the locked door I could still hear him humming. It was a most annoying sound.

On the way to breakfast, Jack picked up a copy of the local newspaper, *El Diario de León*. We walked into the dining room, sat down at a table for four, and ordered espresso and *churros con chocolate*.

I kept looking towards the doorway. "Did you tell Sue Ellen to meet us for breakfast?"

He glanced up from reading the paper. "I told her."

"Maybe I should check on her," I said nervously.

"Don't worry about her. She's just sleeping late." The left corner of his mouth twitched into a half-smile. "She didn't get much sleep last night."

The waiter brought two steaming mugs of espresso, two orders of *churros*, and one cup of thick hot chocolate, rich as melted candy bars.

Jack dunked the fried fritter into the chocolate, which coated it like frosting. I looked at it distastefully. I preferred salt on my *churros*, maybe because their shape reminded me of crinkly French fries, not crullers.

After finishing one *café doble* I signaled to the waiter for another. When he brought it, I ordered more *churros*. After all, I might as well start stalling over breakfast.

Jack finished the newspaper, folded it, and slapped it down on the table. I jumped at the sound.

"I was right," he chortled. "This is my lucky day."

I watched him, curious but reluctant to ask why.

"There's nothing in the paper about a dead man being found near the cathedral," he continued. "That's a relief. I'd hate to get involved with the cops."

His callousness shocked me, but I realized I was just being naïve. After all, I'd seen him in action, so why was I surprised? Pointing at the paper, I said, "I didn't know your Spanish was that good, Jack."

"There's a lot you don't know."

Sue Ellen strolled into the dining room, sat down next to us, and yawned fetchingly. She signaled to the waiter, who came over with a large mug of *café con leche* and a glass of orange juice. Toying with a gold coin dangling from a chain around her neck, she took a *churro* from Jack's plate and sprinkled sugar on it. Then she gulped down the coffee laced with milk. Soon she looked more alert.

"What's the plan for today?" She asked, looking at Jack.

"Since we've struck out here at San Marcos, we're going to have to go back to the cathedral."

"But that's where I got mugged," I protested.

"I don't think they'll try that again, now that they know what they're up against," He said. "Just stick with me, kid, and everything will be fine." He started to get up. "Let's go."

Sue Ellen took another *churro* from his plate, yawned again, and brushed back a strand of hair. "I haven't finished my breakfast yet."

"Watch it, Sue Ellen," Jack growled, "You're pushing your luck."

She gave a deep, throaty laugh. "Somehow I don't think so, Jack." Licking the sugar off her fingers, she stood up and smoothed the clinging skirt of her peach-colored sundress. "All right, I'm ready."

I felt my *churros* rise in my throat. How could I possibly pretend to be her friend? I tried to tell myself she was a product of her environment, but that didn't really help, so I told myself that although she pretended to be a bubble-headed, harmless flirt, she was actually one smart, devious cookie. That helped.

She slid her arm through Jack's, and I followed them out the main entry to the Mercedes. Jack unlocked the doors and motioned for us to get in, but I protested.

"I don't think we should take the car," I said.

He turned towards me, puzzled. "Why not?"

"You don't see many silver Mercedes around here, do you? They'll be watching for it."

Unconvinced, he started to get in.

"Remember, Jack," I pleaded, "You thought someone was looking at the car in Burgos, and then our rooms were searched."

"So?"

"And you wondered how they found us in León. If they see the Mercedes, they'll know we're nearby."

"But, Noa, it's easier to get mugged if we're walking."

"Didn't you just say they wouldn't try that again?" I reminded him.

Sue Ellen interrupted angrily, "I know Noa got mugged yesterday, but you didn't say anything about your rooms being ransacked!"

Jack turned to her. "You insisted on coming along for the ride, remember?" He smiled ominously. "Still want to come along?"

Without waiting for her reply, Jack and I started walking down the broad, tree-lined avenue, leaving Sue Ellen standing indecisively by the car.

After a moment she called out, "Wait for me!" and ran to join us. Within a block, however, she had fallen behind. We waited impatiently for her to catch up.

Pointing to her delicate, high-heeled sandals, she complained, "I just can't walk any faster in these shoes."

"So go back and change," Jack replied, irritated at the delay.

"I didn't bring any walking shoes," she complained. "I didn't know we'd be making the treasure hunt on foot."

I said soothingly, "We'll just have to walk more slowly, that's all."

Sue Ellen looked at me in surprise. "Why, that's downright considerate of you, Noa."

"What are friends for," I replied.

We walked slowly down the avenue, eventually reaching the commercial district. Every so often Jack and I would wait for Sue Ellen to catch up. While we waited, we looked at the sumptuous displays of Loewe leather goods, elegant shoes with stiletto heels, Hermes scarves, and expensive jewelry.

"This certainly is an upscale neighborhood," I commented, after seeing some of the price tags.

Jack laughed. "You ain't seen nothing, Noa. You should see Bern. Every shop in the covered arcades, which go on for blocks, is full of expensive goodies." He pointed to his watch. "That's where I got my Rollie."

I admired the sparkling gold and black band. "You really must have a good business partner."

"I can't complain. 'Santa Claus' has been good to me."

"What were you doing in Bern?" I asked.

"Oh, nothing much. Looking after investments, that kind of thing."

"The ones you made with 'Santa Claus'?"

"Some of them."

Sue Ellen caught up with us and we continued walking; soon we passed a large sand-colored stone church, and I took off towards the entry. Jack ran after me.

"Just where do you think you're going?" he asked angrily, grabbing me by the arm. It was a habit I was getting tired of, but I knew that in this case patience was a virtue.

Loosening his grasp, I said placatingly, "This is the other church I mentioned. It's called San Isidoro, the one with the twelfth-century frescoes."

"So? I thought we were going to the cathedral—"

"We are, but I think we should try here first. After all, the letter says Santiago will show the way to 'real' pilgrims, and according to the guidebook, 'real' pilgrims stopped at San Isidoro. So maybe our clue will be here, not in the cathedral."

Sue Ellen hobbled up beside us. "She's got a point, Jack. Besides, I need to rest my poor, aching feet for a while."

Grumbling, he followed us into the cool, dark interior. Sue Ellen tottered over to a low stone bench in the antechamber, sat down, and slipped off her sandals. Rubbing her feet, she sighed with relief. "I'll wait for you here."

A uniformed guide stood next to an open door, behind a counter covered with brochures. Jack and I started to walk past him into the main part of the church, but he stopped us.

"You'll have to wait a few minutes for the tour to start."

"But we just want to look inside for a minute—" Jack protested.

"I'm sorry, but you have to wait."

Jack wanted to argue, but I whispered, "Come on, Jack. The tour won't take long. And it's the only way we can look for clues."

Soon we and a dozen other tourists followed a guide down the hall while she rapidly recited the history of the main building, mentioning casually that El Cid and Jimena were married here almost 1000 years ago.

We walked down a narrow flight of stone stairs to the subterranean Pantheon of the Kings, a royal burial vault whose ceiling was covered with remarkably well-preserved frescoes showing life in the Middle Ages: a shepherd and his flock, a man feeding his dog, goats with locked horns fighting. Every section of the ceiling told a different story from the Bible, but none showed Santiago.

Soon our loquacious guide led us up a curving flight a stairs to the stone-walled treasury, where we admired an eleventh-century Scandinavian wood chest decorated with delicately carved ivory plaques, an eleventh-century chalice encrusted with golden filigree and carved precious stones, a twelfth-century blue, green, and gold enameled coffer from Limoges, and an assortment of ornate reliquaries. The guide lectured on.

Jack muttered, "Won't she ever stop?"

I looked at him in surprise. "I thought art history was your field."

"I hate museums. I like to hold things in my hands."

Passing through an elaborate wrought iron gate, we entered the archive/library, its walls lined with locked, glass-fronted cabinets. The guide pointed out a beautifully illuminated Mozarabic Bible from the tenth century and a fifteenth-century breviary decorated with elaborate miniatures.

Although the objects were old, rare, and beautiful, none had the same impact on me as the grave in Burgos of El Cid and his wife. When I had stood over their tombstone, the past had seemed palpably present. Maybe that was why I was an anthropologist, not an art historian. I was interested in people, not things. So why was I on this treasure hunt? Guilt about Mateo? Greed?

Jack brought me out of my reverie by hissing in my ear, "Let's get out of here. We haven't seen a single sign of Santiago."

I hissed back, "We can't leave. We have to stay with the guide." The group started to move forward. "It's almost over," I said reassuringly.

When we finally left San Isidoro, the contrast between the cool interior of the church and the hot, steamy outdoors made me gasp. Nonetheless, I insisted that we carefully inspect the outside of the building. We spent another half hour searching for Santiago, walking around the extensive walls, examining the biblical scenes carved over the doorways. Sue Ellen waited on a nearby bench, fanning herself with a newspaper, smoking one cigarette after another and grinding the butts out with the sole of her sandal.

Over one doorway we found an enormous sword-wielding figure on horseback. I pointed to it excitedly, and Jack looked at it through the camera. But it wasn't Santiago. I checked the guidebook. It was St. Isidore.

I wanted to keep searching, but Jack was getting impatient. Looking piercingly at me, he said, "If I didn't know better, I'd think you were stalling."

"Stalling?" I repeated, innocently. "Why would I be stalling?"

"I have no idea."

Motioning to Sue Ellen to get up, he started off. I followed behind. Suddenly he stopped and turned to me. "Which way is it to the cathedral?"

I pointed towards the east. Single-file, we followed the sidewalk past the crumbling stone remains of Roman walls, then turned down an alley that opened abruptly onto the elegant, graceful cathedral.

During our previous brief but eventful visit, the area around the cathedral had been deserted; now it was bustling with activity.

I looked around nervously but saw no white-robed men. Jack put his arm around me. Irritated, I tried to move away.

He held tight. "Just a safety precaution, Noa."

Sue Ellen looked miffed.

On the outside of the cathedral, clustered around the main doorway, was a group of life-size carved saints and apostles standing on pedestals. The Virgin Mary was in the middle; on her right was a statue of Santiago. He had a curly beard and what looked like a small sword-shaped cross around his neck. Jack pulled out the camera but found no symbols scratched on the figure or the wall behind it.

Frustrated, he turned to me. "Any other ideas?"

"Maybe we should look inside the building."

"Right."

He strode off, and Sue Ellen and I followed close behind.

When I entered the cathedral, it took a moment for my eyes to adapt to the dimness. But once I could see clearly, I was dazzled by the huge rose windows and the multi-colored stained glass windows that soared up to the distant ceiling. Light filtered through the glass, tinting the floor with jewel-like colors.

Jack looked around impatiently. "What does the guidebook say? Is there a chapel of Santiago?"

I paged slowly through the guidebook and found a description of the cathedral.

"I think it's off this way somewhere," I said, gesturing vaguely. Taking the camera out of the bag, I started walking slowly around the perimeter of the church, admiring the stained glass windows as I went. Jack and Sue Ellen trailed behind; she whispered something, and he stifled a laugh. Pausing for a moment next to one of the windows, I smiled to myself and walked on. Soon I moved to the center of the church and started a detailed examination of the enormous gold-framed altarpiece covered with oil paintings of unidentified saints and Virgins.

"Come on, Noa, quit admiring the altar," Jack demanded. "Where's the chapel?"

"It should be here somewhere." At last I led them to the chapel of Santiago. It smelled of stale incense and burnt wax. With a sigh of relief, Sue Ellen collapsed on a wooden bench while Jack and I looked for images of Santiago. We found the saint but no symbols.

Jack slumped down on the bench next to Sue Ellen, who had taken off her sandals and was rubbing her blistered right heel.

"It's nearly 1:30 P.M.," he snarled. "We've been in León for almost 24 hours. We've been in this damn cathedral for over two hours, and we still haven't found the clue."

I sat down at the other end of the bench and said helpfully, "Maybe we should try the cathedral museum. Unfortunately, it closed at 1:30."

"That's just great," Jack said, slamming his fists together in frustration.

"But I think it opens again after 5."

Sue Ellen had been watching both of us. Eyes narrowed, she asked tensely, "How do I know you haven't found the symbol already?"

I said slowly, "I don't follow you."

"How do I know you two aren't keeping something from me?"

Before I could protest, Jack replied, "We've agreed we're in this together. What's the matter, don't you trust us?"

"Not really."

"This is getting us nowhere." I said, wearily. "I don't know about you, but I'm beat. Let's go back to the hotel."

As we started walking back to San Marcos, it became obvious that Sue Ellen wouldn't be able to make it.

Wincing with pain, she stopped and leaned against the side of a building, rubbing one of her heels. "Noa, you may have the stamina of an Amazon but I don't. I just can't keep going. Besides, it's time for lunch, so why don't we stop at that restaurant over there?" She pointed at a restaurant that advertising its specialties of roast suckling pig and fresh shellfish in an enticing, still-life window display.

I shook my head. "I'm not hungry. Why don't you two eat lunch while I go back to the hotel alone?"

"I don't think that's safe, Noa. Not after what happened yesterday," Jack said.

"Then walk me back to the hotel."

Pointedly, he looked at Sue Ellen. "She'll never make it. I told you we should have brought the Mercedes."

"Obviously, I should have listened to you," I said, trying to sound sincere. "But what do we do now? It's like that brainteaser about the pumpkin, the fox, and the rabbit. Do you know the story?"

"No, and I don't want to hear it now, Noa."

I changed the topic. "I know. Why don't you walk me back to the hotel, pick up the car, and come back for Sue Ellen?"

Sue Ellen chimed in, "That sounds like a wonderful idea, Jack. I'll meet you in that restaurant over there." She hobbled to the restaurant, then turned and waved. "See you soon."

Jack and I walked quickly back to the Hotel San Marcos. When we entered the spacious lobby, I glanced around. There was Peter, sitting in a maroon velvet lounge chair in the corner, hidden behind an open newspaper. His face was hidden but I recognized his long-fingered hands, his faded blue shirt with the sleeves rolled up, beige corduroy pants, and battered Mephisto shoes.

Peter lowered the newspaper a fraction when we came in and, recognizing me, started to get up. Heart pounding, I shook my head. He settled back in the chair and raised the newspaper again. Jack was too preoccupied to notice the exchange.

Jack accompanied me to our room, and, after telling me not to open the door for anyone, he left. I waited a moment, then opened the door a crack and peered out. I watched impatiently until he was out of sight. Then I crept down the hall, my sandal-covered feet making no sound on the carpet-covered stone.

Without once looking back, Jack strode down the main staircase, across the lobby, and out the door. I followed surreptitiously. From the entrance to the hotel I saw him walk over to the Mercedes and start to unlock it. Before he could do so, however, a white-haired man approached him. Jack paused, appeared to be giving the man directions, gesturing in the direction of the cathedral. Then Jack got in the car, the man walked off, and Jack drove away.

As soon as he was gone, I ran over to where Peter sat, hidden behind the newspaper. My voice hoarse with emotion, I exclaimed, "Oh, Peter, I'm so glad you're here!"

Disentangling himself from the paper, Peter gave me a passionate embrace. Then he stood back, looked me up and down, and started to smile. His smile lit up his eyes. "You're looking great, Noa. Adventure becomes you."

Brushing back my long auburn hair, I batted my eyelashes at him. "Funny you should say that," I laughed, hooked my arm through his, and led him up the stairs.

Ten

An hour later, Peter and I walked arm in arm down the staircase and strolled obliviously across the lobby to the dining room. Sitting at a cozy table for two, we ordered *entremeses ahumados*—a selection of smoked hors d'oeuvres—and the house specialty, baked suckling pig, and a bottle of local red wine. My appetite had returned and I felt ravenous. So did Peter, but because of the time change, for him this feast was a substitute for breakfast.

The waiter soon returned with the *entremeses* and the bottle of wine, which he opened and poured. It looked like liquid rubies, glinting in the light.

Peter touched his glass to mine. "To shared adventure."

"I'll drink to that." I inhaled the rich cherry aroma and took a deep swallow. "It's delicious. You have wonderful taste."

"Couldn't you tell from that from the company I keep?"

"Why, Peter, you say the nicest things," I said, taken aback.

"You seem surprised."

"I suppose I am. Whatever happened to your sardonic detachment?"

"Ah, my dear," he said, with a mysterious smile, "It is but one of my many masks."

I looked at him, perplexed, but he ignored my scrutiny and raised his glass again.

While I finished bringing him up to date, we nibbled on the delicately smoked slivers of trout, salmon, and shellfish arranged on little wedges of toast.

In the middle of my description of the day before, he sputtered, "You mean you spent yesterday afternoon examining San Marcos? But Noa, don't you remember? I told you the monastery was built in the early 1500s—20 years after the letter was written. And the façade is even more recent."

"I knew that but they didn't," I chortled. "And I made sure I was the only one reading the guidebook."

"My dear, little did I suspect your knack for duplicity."

"Live and learn, as they say. But there is more to tell." I paused dramatically. "I know where the next stop on the treasure hunt is."

"What?" Peter exclaimed, knocking over his wineglass.

The blood-red stain spread rapidly over the white tablecloth. Unperturbed, I wiped it up with an enormous damask napkin.

"I know where we go next. When we were wandering around the cathedral, I noticed Santiago the Pilgrim in one of the stained glass windows. The spiral symbol for numeral XIII was scratched in the lead at the bottom of his staff. Naturally, I didn't point it out to anyone."

"Fantastic! So where is XIII?"

"The end of the Camino. Santiago."

Excitedly, Peter leaned over the table and kissed my palm. His lips tickled delectably. "Have clue, will travel," he said, refilling our glasses and raising his in salute.

I looked tenderly at his long, blunt-fingered hand. There was a faint ink stain on one of his fingers, and his nails were not well cared for—unlike Jack's—but they were well used. My eyes moved up to examine his face, so alive with enthusiasm. His steely blue-gray eyes reminded me of the North Sea, full of dangerous currents and high tides. Crows feet were deeply etched at the corners. His curly brown hair was beginning to be streaked with gray, and it was tousled from where he ran his hands through it, a nervous habit he couldn't, or wouldn't, break. His nose was aquiline, his cheekbones sharp, his mouth expressive. Not a handsome face, but an interesting one. It was flushed, now, with excitement.

Suddenly I realized that he was looking at me expectantly. "Did you say something?"

"Nothing important, my dear. All I said was I have a proposition to make."

"A proposition? What a disappointment. I was hoping for something more respectable."

"Hope springs eternal. But do be serious for a moment, and consider the following: Should we take off and leave Sue Ellen and Jack behind?"

"Now, why didn't I think of that." I thought a moment and shook my head sadly. "There is one serious drawback, of course."

"What is it?"

"It's a 'he,' not an 'it.' Jack. He'd follow us. And I have a feeling he's a dangerous man to cross."

"You're right." He contemplated his wineglass morosely. "And you were right to be worried about him. So is Nicholson."

"Professor Nicholson?"

"The same. He called me yesterday just before I left town. He wanted to know if there was any way to get in touch with you to warn you about Jack. He said he was going to be in Spain in a couple of days, and he wanted to help you out if he could." Peter frowned at his wineglass and swirled the ruby-colored liquid around and around. "Nicholson says Jack is very, very dangerous."

"That bad, huh?" I said with a shiver.

"That bad. Head of an international drug-smuggling ring." Peter stroked my hand gently. "Seriously, Noa, do you realize what you've gotten yourself mixed up in?"

With a nervous smile, I complained, "I just can't win. You're always telling me I should be more adventurous, but now that I am, all I get is criticism." Before he could reply, I patted his hand affectionately. "Really, Peter, I appreciate your concern and your riding to my rescue like a knight on a white charger—"

"Shades of Santiago, hmm? Actually, nobody ever accused me of being a saint before, though some have accused me of proselytizing—"

Just then the waiter returned with the main course. With a flourish, he placed half a suckling pig on a large white plate in front of each of us. The golden-brown body—thank goodness there was no head—was tiny, its hind legs the size of small drumsticks. Dubiously, I stared at it. Pork chops were one thing, but a baby pig, torn directly from its mother's tits? I hadn't expected it to be so little.

Peter had no such compunctions. He bit into the crispy skin with relish; a drop of grease slid down his chin. I twisted off the little limb and started to bite into it. The scent of garlic and baked pork filled the air.

I glanced up and thought I saw a gawky redhead standing hesitantly at the entrance of the dining room. He looked a lot like

Fred, but it couldn't be Fred, could it? He *had* seemed awfully intent on talking with me that last time I saw him, but surely he hadn't followed me to León. Or had he followed Sue Ellen?

Just as I was getting up to look, Sue Ellen rushed into the crowded dining room, stopped for a moment, and looked around. She was extremely pale, and she put her right hand against the doorframe to steady herself. The chiffon scarf that had tied her hair back now dangled from her limp hand; her peach-colored dress had slipped off one shoulder, but she hadn't bother to hitch it up.

When she spotted me, she came stumbling over. Behind her were two olive-green-uniformed policemen. They strode up to the table, shiny black hats on their heads, shiny black boots on their feet, shiny black holsters on wide, studded belts draped around their hips. I noticed their holsters were unsnapped.

Leaning on the table for support, she gasped, "Jack's been shot."

I had started to stand up but, stunned at her announcement, I slowly sank back into the chair. "What?" I whispered.

"Jack's dead."

Peter pulled another chair over to the table and Sue Ellen fell into it.

Stupefied, I asked, "Why would anyone want to shoot Jack?"

Sue Ellen sobbed, "How should I know!"

Hands shaking, she took a cigarette out of her purse and lit it with a gold lighter. She inhaled deeply, then exhaled. Her voice trembling, she said, "We were walking back to the Mercedes after lunch. Jack had parked it around the corner from the restaurant. Somebody bumped into us, and all of a sudden Jack sort of grunted and fell down. I looked, and there was blood all over the ground." She inhaled deeply, eyes closed. "I guess I just stood there in shock. Next thing I knew, someone led me back to the restaurant so I could sit down. Then the police came."

I put my hand on Sue Ellen's arm to comfort her. It felt clammy.

"Did you see who shot him?" I asked. "Was it someone in a white cloak?"

"I don't know. There were so many people around." She grabbed my hand. "I told the police I was too upset to talk and had to come back to the hotel for a moment. I told them I was with you. They're going to interrogate us! What should we tell them?"

I glanced at the two policemen. Sue Ellen said, reassuringly, "Don't worry, they don't speak a word of English."

Relieved, I said, "What do you mean, what should we tell them?"

Sue Ellen stubbed out her cigarette in the ashtray and said calmly, "About the treasure hunt, of course. What should we say?"

Coming out of my daze, I leaned forward and whispered intensely, "Don't say anything."

"What?"

"Don't say anything. We're three friends who agreed to meet in León and follow the Camino. That's it."

I handed Sue Ellen a glass of wine. She took a large swallow and put the glass down on the table with such force that some of the wine spilled. Reaching into her purse, she pulled out a gold compact and examined herself in the tiny mirror. Using my wine-soaked napkin, she delicately wiped beads of perspiration off of her neck, forehead, and upper lip. She got out her hairbrush and brushed her hair, tying it back with the chiffon scarf. She reapplied her lipstick and pinched her cheeks to give them some color. Then she took another drink of wine. Peter and I watched in fascinated silence.

Her reconstruction completed, she glared at me. "You should have warned me! I had no idea this treasure hunt would be so dangerous." Then she stared off into space and added, wistfully, toying with the gold coin around her neck, "I was just getting to know Jack, you know. He really was my kind of guy. And now—"

With a start, Sue Ellen realized Peter was sitting next to her. She turned towards him in bewilderment and asked, "Who are you?"

"Sue Ellen, meet Peter. Peter, meet Sue Ellen."

Sue Ellen turned to me in disbelief. "Where the hell did he come from?"

Courteously but firmly the police asked us to go back to headquarters with them. Without protest, we accompanied them out of the hotel. I looked around but saw no sign of Fred. I must have been imagining things. We got into the shiny black police car waiting at the curb. The air wavered in the mid-afternoon heat.

We were driven to the nearby police headquarters and ushered inside. Noisy overhead fans gently stirred the stifling air, ruffling the papers scattered on the tops of desks. The place smelled of stale cigarette smoke and sour sweat. We were shown to a windowless room and told to wait while an interpreter was found. Obediently we sat on the rickety oak chairs and waited in cautious silence. After ten minutes, we were separated.

About half an hour later, two policemen came in and, with the aid of the interpreter, questioned me politely and extensively. I concentrated on telling a coherent story and hardly noticed the policemen, except that one was young and looked serious and the other was old and looked bored.

I explained that I was traveling on the Camino de Santiago with Jack, an acquaintance from the U.S. whom I had happened to run into in Madrid. He was an art history professor at SUNY. I had no idea who could have shot him or why. The police wanted to know if I knew who his family was, who should be contacted in case of emergency. I had no idea, I replied, since I hardly knew him.

In that case, the older policeman asked, why were we sharing the same hotel room? It was more economical that way, I explained. Why was Sue Ellen there? She'd been waiting to meet us. And who was Peter? He was an old friend who had also arranged to meet me here. After all, the Camino de Santiago was of great historic and cultural interest, surely they realized that? They nodded their heads.

I suggested, tactfully, that although they might wonder about my morals, they could hardly accuse me of murder. After all, Peter and I had been eating dinner. The waiter could vouch for us.

Could I think of any motive for the shooting? Perplexed, I assured them I was at a loss. Suddenly I remembered something. I told them that just before Sue Ellen ran into the dining room with the shocking news, Peter had started to tell me that a mutual friend had told him that Jack was involved in a drug-smuggling ring. The police exchanged meaningful looks and left the room.

I was exhausted and soaked with sweat—not just because of the heat. I felt as if not only Jack had died, but so had something else, something much more important to me: my honesty. And I'd done it to myself.

The door creaked open, and the older policeman returned. He handed me a transcript of what I had said and told me to sign it. I did. My hands were damp, however, and I smeared the ink on my signature. Grimly, he examined the paper and signaled for me to follow him. My heart started to pound. I could see it thumping through my T-shirt. Where was he taking me? To jail? To confront me with the inconsistencies between my story and Peter and Sue Ellen's? With a tremendous effort, I smothered my desire to confess everything. And I wasn't even guilty. Dealing with the police just had that effect on me.

Following meekly behind, I entered another room. Peter and Sue Ellen were sitting there, waiting. When he saw me, Peter jumped up and gave me a warm, supportive hug. I buried my head against his neck, which smelled of cigarette smoke, roasted suckling pig, and perspiration. Regretfully, I moved away. Sue Ellen sat in her chair, tapping her feet nervously.

The police said we could go back to the hotel but should remain available for questioning. Hesitantly, I explained that we had planned to leave town that afternoon. Would that still be possible? Sue Ellen looked startled but said nothing. Peter offered to give them his rental-car license number, which they carefully took down.

After conferring together, they agreed we could leave, as long as they knew where we were going. After all, they had our passport numbers, and we would need our passports to register in any hotel in Spain. We would be easy to find.

The young policeman asked where we were going. I stalled a moment, then said, "Santiago de Compostela." I avoided looking at Sue Ellen.

Where would we stay? I explained that we hoped to stay at the Hotel de los Reyes Católicos, the luxury *parador* in Santiago located right beside the cathedral. But we wouldn't get there till the next day. The young policeman called the hotel for us, making a reservation for—one, two, or three rooms? Two rooms, I said, blushing. He made a whispered comment to his partner, and they both laughed.

When they brought us back to the hotel, I asked what would happen to Jack's rented Mercedes. They had me point it out them in the parking lot. They looked at the car with considerable interest and assured me they would take good care of it and of Jack's belongings. Then they followed us into the hotel lobby, which was full of interested bystanders, and indicated that we were free to go.

Without a word, we went into the dimly lit hotel bar and sat down in a corner. We all ordered cognac. It reminded me of the exquisite stuff I had been drinking with Jack—where was it—outside Pamplona?—just a few days before. How quickly time had passed. I was surprised at my reaction or, rather, my lack of reaction, to Jack's death. Part of me was relieved, part of me was terrified, but most of me was in shock.

Looking around to make sure no one was near, Sue Ellen whispered, "Well, well, well. Santiago de Compostela, is it?"

I shifted uncomfortably in the chair.

"So you were holding out on us. I knew it! Miss 'Goody-Two-Shoes'—"

"Come off it, Sue Ellen, and keep your voice down," I whispered angrily—a hard thing to do, believe me. "Look who's talking. Didn't you try to get Jack to leave me behind?"

Sue Ellen glanced away.

"I thought as much. So drop it, okay? We've got more important things to worry about. For example, why would anyone kill Jack?"

Peter stated confidently, "Because of the treasure, of course."

I shook my head. "That seems obvious, but actually it doesn't make sense. The men in white want the medallion, remember? Jack doesn't—didn't—have the medallion: I do. So there was no reason to kill him. And besides, the white-robed guy who mugged me was an amateur. Whoever killed Jack was a real professional."

"Why do you say that?" Peter asked.

"The man who mugged me just didn't seem very experienced, that's all."

"I didn't know you were an expert on muggings, Noa," Sue Ellen said, her voice reeking with condescension.

"I'm not. But if I were going to grab a medallion from someone's neck I'd have wire cutters with me."

Tapping her long red fingernails on the table, Sue Ellen replied, "That's beside the point. Jack's death must have something to do with the treasure. He must have been killed by the same men—the men in white—who mugged you." She took a gulp of cognac and a look of sudden comprehension spread across her face. "I know! It's their revenge on Jack for murdering Mateo!"

In unison, Peter and I said, "What?"

She repeated smugly, "It's their revenge on Jack for murdering Mateo. An eye for an eye. You know."

Exasperated, I replied, "We don't know that Jack, or anyone, killed Mateo. He probably died of a heart attack."

"Don't be so naïve. You know the police suspect foul play."

"But they haven't proved it, have they?" I continued, "Not that Jack couldn't have killed someone. I've seen him in action. I admit it's possible that Jack murdered Mateo. He had the opportunity. But so did the man in white who ran out of the room. What about *him*? And if *he* murdered Mateo, then the men in white would have no revenge motive for killing Jack."

"Well, if the men in white didn't kill Jack, who did?" Sue Ellen asked, bewildered.

We sat in silence for a moment.

"I told the police that Jack might be involved in smuggling drugs," Peter commented. "Do you think somebody could have been 'out to get him' for some crooked deal?"

"Drug smuggling? Jack?" Sue Ellen was stunned. After a moment, however, she gave a sigh of relief. "Well, if that's the case, we don't have anything to worry about, do we? We don't know anything about drug smuggling." Her hand went to the gold coin at her throat; then she turned to me and asked abruptly, "Now what's all this about a medallion?"

With a sigh, I realized I had, once again, said more than I meant to. I just wasn't used to thinking deviously.

"You didn't think I'd notice that little slip, did you?" She said, a nasty edge to her voice. "You and Jack told me the mugger wanted a gold coin Jack gave you, a gold coin like the one he gave me—"

"He gave you a gold coin?" I had seen the one dangling from her neck that she had been caressing, but I hadn't put two and two together. Mind racing, I wondered whether that meant Jack had planned to use her as a shield for me, or had he planned to steal my medallion and use her as a shield for himself? Of course, he simply could've been rewarding her for her sexual favors, but somehow I doubted it. He didn't seem like the kind who was used to paying.

"Don't be jealous, dear," she smirked, bringing me back to the conversation. "Let's not keep any more secrets, shall we? What's with the medallion?"

"My 'gold coin' is actually a medallion," I confessed, grudgingly. "Jack and I discovered it in the book where I found the letter."

"It's the key to the treasure, right?"

"Right."

"So how do you use it?" Seeing my unwillingness to explain, she threatened, "Don't forget. I can still tell the police about Jack and Mateo—and about everything else you haven't told them."

Reluctantly, I said, "The symbols on the medallion are paired up with Roman numerals, which stand for the stages on the Camino de Santiago. The trick is to find the symbols next to a statue of Santiago."

"I don't see why you couldn't have told me that before. Don't you trust me?"

I started to reply but changed my mind and stood up. "I think we'd better get out of here as soon as possible."

Peter agreed. "No point in waiting around like sitting ducks."

Sue Ellen looked around nervously. "Sitting ducks for whom?"

"For whoever killed Mateo or mugged me—"

"Or shot Jack—" Peter added.

"I get the point," Sue Ellen said, turning slightly gray.

I nodded. "Good. Let's get our things and check out."

The waiter came over and handed us the bill. Peter paid.

Sue Ellen insisted that we stay together, so we went upstairs to my room, only to discover that a policeman was investigating all of its contents. Under his watchful eye, I packed my belongings. He searched them carefully, then followed us to Sue Ellen's room and did the same.

Peter had brought a battered leather carry-on bag, which he had left at the main desk. He reclaimed it and waited while the we checked out of the hotel. After sorting through a stack of papers, the registration clerk presented each of us with a bill.

Ruefully, I pulled out my lone credit card. "It was Jack's idea that we stay here. I told him I didn't have much money, and he promised to pay the bill. Just goes to show you can't trust anybody these days."

Peter laughed. "He certainly went to unusual lengths to leave you in the lurch."

"Do you think we could get the police to pay the bill?" I asked, hopefully, "Or get Jack's estate to pay it posthumously?"

"You could try," Peter said with an amused smile.

I engaged in an intense conversation with the startled registration clerk, who ended up calling the manager. After much discussion they regretfully declined to honor Jack's credit card, even though he had originally been the one who was billed for the room. When I suggested that the police might pay, they looked at me with disbelief. Defeated, I handed them my credit card. I hoped there was enough credit left.

Sue Ellen paid her bill and watched me with condescending amusement. At last, we were ready to leave the hotel.

Sue Ellen accompanied us a few steps, hesitated, and abruptly turned back, saying, "I just remembered something. I was supposed to meet Juan this evening. I'd better leave him a note." She smiled ingenuously, "After all, it just wouldn't do to leave him without so much as a fare-thee-well. I'm just not that kind of girl."

Before we could say anything, she turned back to the reception desk, pulled a piece of hotel stationary and an envelope from her purse, and scribbled a note, signing it with a flourish. After licking the envelope and sealing it, she handed the letter to the clerk, giving him hurried, whispered instructions. I wished I knew what she was saying.

While we waited, Peter took me by the shoulders, turned me towards him, and looked into my eyes. "Are you okay?"

Tears started to roll down my face. "Not really."

"Is it Jack?"

"Of course it's Jack," I sniffed.

Peter started to turn away, but I touched his hand. "Peter, I didn't care for Jack—in fact, he was beginning to frighten me—you know that." He nodded slowly. "But it's not every day somebody I know gets shot down in cold blood."

He held me close for a moment. I was trembling.

I muttered into his shirt, "Two people I know have gotten murdered in just the last few days. Is it any wonder if I'm a bit upset? Nobody I knew ever died before. Except my great-aunt. And I hadn't seen her for a long time. And my grandfather, but he hadn't been himself for years. Even so, I cried when he died."

Stroking my hair gently, he made soothing noises and kissed my forehead.

Sniffling, I dug blindly into my bag for some Kleenex. I couldn't find any. "I'm sorry. I've dribbled on your shirt."

"Don't worry. It'll dry."

Sue Ellen walked up to us and said cattily, "What's the matter, Noa? Having second thoughts? If so, I'm sure Peter and I can continue without you."

I ignored her. Peter handed me his handkerchief and I dried my eyes. Then we walked over to the parking lot to find the car Peter had rented.

I took one look at the bright red Escort and started to giggle. "Peter—It's bright red! It'll stand out like beacon."

"It was all I could get on such short notice," He replied, defensively.

He got into the driver's seat. Sue Ellen headed for the front passenger's seat, but I headed her off and climbed in first. She got in back.

After starting the car, Peter hesitated. "Which way do I go?"

I took a map out of the glove compartment and compared it with the guidebook. I looked around for a moment, then pointed: "That-away, over the bridge."

With a grinding of gears, we started off to Santiago.

Eleven

The two-lane highway N 120 led west over the River Bernesga, then through the outskirts of León and past the modern sanctuary of the Virgin del Camino. Thirteen enormous Giacometti-like bronze figures were perched on the cement façade of the church, holding a mute conversation. In the middle of the lawn a cement cross soared hundreds of feet into the air.

As we drove by, a white-robed monk stepped out of the church and ran to his car. I watched, holding my breath, waiting to see if he would follow us. He drove the other way and I sighed with relief.

Peter looked at me curiously. "What was that about?"

"Noa's just jumpy, Peter," Sue Ellen said in a patronizing tone. "She keeps worrying about white-robed men, though what possible harm a monk could do—"

I interrupted angrily, "There's a lot you still don't know, Sue Ellen."

Peter reached over and rested his hand on my knee. The contact felt comforting.

"Didn't a guy in a white robe mug you?" He asked.

"Right. And Mateo wore a white robe. And a white-robed man ran out of the room where Mateo died—or was murdered. And there were several white-robed men at Roncesvalles." I swiveled around to face the back seat. "Sue Ellen, are you sure there wasn't a white-robed man around when Jack got shot?"

"I can't remember," she replied. "I was looking at Jack, not the crowd."

"What's the connection?" Peter asked.

"I wish I knew. Just before he died, Mateo left a scribbled note that said, 'beware . . . the Brotherhood'—or maybe it was ' . . . beware the Brotherhood." It was almost indecipherable. Mateo belonged to some kind of brotherhood. Maybe it had suddenly gone bad. Maybe that's who killed him. I just don't know."

Peter frowned. I could see the furrow between his eyebrows get deeper and the muscles in his jaw tighten, but he said nothing.

On the outskirts of Hospital de Orbigo we stopped for gas. I watched the cars speeding by, but no one slowed down at the sight of us.

After getting three cold cans of Coke from the vending machine, we started off again. A little further down the road we passed a dozen pilgrims walking in single file on the side of the road. They were all dressed in identical uniforms: heavy leather boots, gray socks, khaki shorts, white T-shirts, straw hats with a scallop shell sewn on the crown. Some carried walking sticks but none carried backpacks.

I waved at them, and several of them waved back. It was odd, but I felt a growing kinship with the pilgrims. After all, I told myself, I too was on a pilgrimage, of sorts, to Santiago.

A little further down the road we passed a parked Volkswagen van with a scallop shell painted on the side. Leaning against it was one of the identically dressed pilgrims. The group was using the van to transport luggage.

Some 30 miles from León we arrived at the outskirts of the city of Astorga. Solid Roman walls still encircled part the city, which was built on a small rise. Behind Astorga I saw the foothills that marked the beginning of the Maragatería region and the Mountains of León, part of the Cantabrican mountain range that lay between Santiago de Compostela and us.

Suddenly we came to a highway intersection, and I told Peter to pull over. While Peter and I examined the road map and the guidebook, Sue Ellen peered over our shoulders from the back seat.

Tracing the route with his finger, Peter said, "It looks like the quickest and easiest way to Santiago is to take the main highway through Bembibre, Ponferrada, Lugo, and on to Santiago. The 'authentic' Camino looks like it's barely a cart trail between Astorga and Ponferrada. In fact, that road is only shown on one of these maps."

"Normally it would make sense to follow the quickest and easiest route," I replied thoughtfully, "but what if we're being followed?"

"By whom?"

"By whoever killed Jack."

Sue Ellen asked, "You mean the guys in white?"

"Maybe. I'm not so sure."

"But why would whoever killed Jack want to follow us?" Sue Ellen asked. "If they were evening up a score, they've done it."

Peter cleared his throat. "'Sufficient unto the day . . .' Let's stick with the problem at hand, shall we?" He looked at me. "Which route do you suggest?"

"I don't know. I'm not used to being devious." Turning towards the back seat, I said sweetly, "Sue Ellen, dear, what route do you think we ought to take?"

"Why, that's obvious. The less obvious route."

I retorted, "But which is less obvious?"

"The one that isn't there, of course!" she said smugly. "Maybe it isn't marked on their map—whoever they are—either."

Peter put the car in gear. "She's got a point. Besides, it's only 30 miles. So here we go on 'the road less traveled,' to quote a famous poet, although I don't think this is quite what he had in mind. For one thing, there's no snow. For another—"

"There're no horses' hooves."

"But Noa, don't forget, our car has a certain amount of horse power beneath its hood."

"Neigh-h-h, forsooth, I had forgot."

Sue Ellen grumbled, "Do you two always carry on like this?"

I chuckled. I knew our silly repartee was a harmless way to relieve nervous tension, but it seemed to add to Sue Ellen's.

The road skirted Astorga and then headed straight toward the hills. Soon we began climbing slowly into the mountains on a twisted, bumpy, narrow strip of black asphalt spread on top of the old Camino de Santiago. We came up behind a tour bus that was also following the 'authentic' route and were stuck behind it for miles. Unpleasant fumes spewed from the bus and mingled with the hot, humid air.

Sue Ellen complained, "Can't you close the windows and turn on the air conditioning?"

"Sorry," Peter replied. "There isn't any air conditioning."

"No air conditioning?" she said in disbelief. "Jack's car had air conditioning."

"Jack's car was a Mercedes," I pointed out. "Most rental cars in Europe don't have air conditioning."

"Jack traveled in style."

"Jack's dead," I reminded her.

Winding our way into the mountains, we drove through the tiny village of Santa Catalina de Somoza. Low walls made of gray-brown stones partitioned the fields near the village into tiny parcels of land, divided and subdivided over centuries of inheritance. The houses themselves were constructed of the same irregularly shaped slabs wedged together to form walls. White-painted borders outlined the deep-set windows and the huge, green-painted doors of the houses. In each yard was a haystack with a pole through the middle, the top covered with a small plastic tarp. Low stone walls, piled with hay, connected the various outbuildings.

An old man dressed in black and wearing a faded black beret shuffled across the road, followed by a mangy old dog. Peter slammed on the brakes and swore, barely avoiding hitting the decrepit beast. Ignoring—or perhaps not hearing—the shriek of the brakes, the old man kept on walking until he joined a group of men tossing stone balls at cone-shaped targets arranged in a pattern on an earthen field.

In just a few minutes we had traveled through the entire village. Soon we passed a wooden-wheeled cart pulled by a lumbering ox, returning with a full load of hay from the fields. An old woman and a young boy walked beside the beast, switching off flies. They moved to the side of the narrow road to let us pass by.

According to the map, the collection of gray-brown stone buildings was called El Ganso. I felt something tickling the edges of my memory. I looked in the guidebook.

Turning to Peter, I said , "This part of the Camino de Santiago follows an old Roman road through the mountains. It's known as the Milky Way."

"Tell me more."

"Some people believe the Camino de Santiago is really an ancient, pre-Christian initiation route. For them the Camino ends not at Santiago but at Padrón, where the boat carrying Santiago's body and two disciples landed, or at *Noia*, where Noah's ark supposedly landed, or at Finisterre, the 'End of the Earth'—the farthest western point known to the Romans." I gestured at the guidebook, "It says here that this ancient route passes through places with certain names, such as *oca* or *ganso*, words that mean goose or gander."

"Do people really believe that?" Peter asked.

"They do indeed," I said. "When I was doing my fieldwork in Sahagún, I met some pilgrims who were following the Milky Way. They walked a route that kept them within a certain latitude, and they made sure they passed through the right towns— Villafranca Monte de Oca, El Ganso, for example. They also looked for ancient Celtic symbols and arcane carvings hidden in churches. It was fascinating. Just imagine: they're recreating—or re-enacting—rituals that have been in existence for thousands of years."

"You are really naïve, Noa," Sue Ellen commented. "It's just a bunch of superstitious mumbo-jumbo, that's all."

Ignoring her, Peter said, "Now that I think about it, I remember reading about something similar in England. Modern-day Englishmen and women dress up like Druid priests and celebrate the summer solstice at Stonehenge. And modern pilgrims follow Chaucer's Pilgrim's Way to Canterbury."

Sue Ellen snorted a most unladylike snort.

"Well, it doesn't hurt anybody," I replied, defensively. "And who knows, maybe there's something to be learned from 'walking in the footsteps of one's ancestors.'" I paused a moment. "Actually, some of the pilgrims talk about their journey just that way. They're 'following the footsteps of their ancestors.' But which ancestors? Pre-Christian ones?"

"Why not," Peter said.

The road climbed past Rabanal and up to Foncebadón. Judging by the size of the name on the map, I had expected Foncebadón to be a large, thriving town, but instead it was nearly abandoned, its gray-brown stone buildings in ruins, their slate roofs fallen in, exposing the skeletal remains of worm-eaten rafters. A few of the dozen or so houses that remained habitable had cars parked in front with Madrid or León license tags. Perhaps relatives of previous inhabitants had come to reclaim what was left for a weekend retreat.

Swinging over the top of the mountain pass, we saw a cross on top of a tall stake on top of a huge mound of pebbles and rocks. Nearby was a small stone sanctuary with evergreen fronds tied to the grillwork door.

"This cross must be the Cruz de Ferro, the 'Iron Cross,'" I said. "The pile of rocks is supposed to have existed since Roman times or even before. The tradition was—and still is—that travelers carry a stone to the pile for good luck."

Peter pulled over to the side of the road, stopped the car, and turned to me. With a smile, he said, "We could use some good luck, don't you think? Or does this go against your anthropological training?"

"To tell the truth, Peter, I like rituals. I guess I'm a closet believer." I turned towards the back seat. "Coming, Sue Ellen?"

"Hardly."

Peter and I got out of the car, picked up some pebbles from the side of the road, and tossed them on the pile. Then we scrambled up the side of the mound, rocks and pebbles sliding out from under our feet. The mound was much higher than it looked, extending at least 20 feet above the level of the ground. From that height we could see the road we followed winding its circuitous way back into the hills. No cars were visible. It looked as if we were not being followed.

We started off again. A few miles further on we reached the deserted village of Manjarín, built one house deep on one side of the Camino. The other side of the Camino was a steep, impenetrable mass of tangled bushes.

Abruptly, Peter pulled the car over to the side of the narrow road.

I looked at him, puzzled. "Engine trouble?"

"Not exactly. Nature calls."

"You're hearing things, I presume."

"Hah. I was simply trying to spare your delicate ears the harsh reality of biological necessity."

"Don't bother. I've got to go, too." I glanced at the rearview mirror. "How about you, Sue Ellen?"

"Unlike you, I was taught the proper way for a lady to behave."

"Your Southern upbringing obviously dealt more with propriety than with physiology. It'll be a while till we reach the next gas station."

"I can wait."

"Suit yourself."

When we got out, Peter took the car keys with him. Together we walked down the road, peering into the abandoned, shattered houses. In one, we saw the remains of someone's lunch; in another, a pile of broken bottles and trash. Peter went behind one building. I walked a bit further down the road and disappeared behind another.

While waiting for Peter to return, I explored the remains of the village. which was perched on the side of a steep hill. A herd of cattle grazed on the steeply canted fields below. Sitting patiently on a rock next to a spring, a dark-haired, dark-skinned woman wearing a multi-colored printed skirt and clashing blouse kept watch over her charges. She looked like a Gypsy—or rather like my idea of what a Gypsy would look like.

We started talking and she explained, in a barely understandable dialect, that she came from the south of Spain. A huge truck carried her and others like her, and their cattle, up to the cooler hills of the Maragatería for the summer months. Cooler than what, I wondered, as sweat dripped down my back.

Peter stepped out from behind a tumbled-down wall, and I waved to him to join us.

He smiled politely at the woman, then looked longingly at the spring and asked, "Do you think the water is safe to drink?"

I shrugged. Polluted water was the least of our worries.

The herdswoman nodded encouragingly, so we cupped our hands and drank the cool, mineral-tasting water from the mountain spring. Then we walked up the road. Sue Ellen was leaning against the car, fanning herself with the map.

We started off again, windows rolled down. The breeze generated by the speed of the car cooled the air—not much, but even one degree helped.

When we reached El Acebo the bumpy asphalt pavement ended abruptly and the road changed to cobblestone left over from the Middle Ages. We drove between dark stone houses with overhanging wood balconies leaning towards each other across the narrow road. Old ladies dressed in black sat knitting in chairs pulled up alongside doorways. A group of villagers sat fanning themselves on the porch of El Acebo's bar. They watched us, following the car with their eyes.

Outside the village the asphalt pavement began again. Soon the road started to descend and we passed through Riego and, then, Molinaseca. The villages became more populated and prosperous the further we traveled out of the mountains. Some of the houses even had imposing coats of arms displayed over massive, iron-barred doorways.

It was after 8 P.M. when we finally reached Ponferrada. Perched on a hill between the Río Sil and the Río Boeza, it overlooked the Bierzo region and several large iron and coal mining operations. Our road meandered up to the center of town and we started looking for a hotel.

Soon we saw one, so Peter waited in the car, double-parked, while I hopped out and went in. It was full. We drove down the street a block and saw another one. I tried again but got the same response. There was a line of cars behind us, honking impatiently.

"I suppose I should park the car somewhere and we could all get out and look," Peter said, "But I am a bit fagged. After all, I didn't get any sleep last night on the airplane."

With a start, I realized it was only that afternoon that Peter had arrived in León, Jack had been killed, and we had started off, the three of us, to Santiago.

Pointing out the window, I said, "Look, Peter, there's a parking place. Why don't you park the car, and I'll walk around and find a hotel."

"Sounds good. But is it safe for you to walk around alone?"

"Don't worry, I won't be alone." I got out of the car and motioned towards Sue Ellen. "Come on, Sue Ellen."

She showed no signs of coming. Languidly, she replied, "What's the matter, Noa? Afraid to leave me alone with Peter?"

"Hardly. He has better taste than that, at least I think he does. But it's safer if we stick together."

Grumbling, she got out of the car, and we walked down the block and around the corner. On the wall next to a doorway we saw a metal plaque with the letters "Hs," with one star over the s and the number 2 next to it, indicating there was a one-star hostel two floors up. We climbed the creaking stairs to the second floor and rang the doorbell.

A heavy-set woman dressed in black came to the door and peered out. When we asked for a room, she motioned for us to follow her inside. She shuffled over to a large wooden counter and opened a dog-eared registration book.

Gazing at us through smudged half-frame glasses, she said, "You're in luck. I still have two rooms, one with a bath, one without."

Relieved, I said, "We'll take them." Then I turned to Sue Ellen and, with a shock, realized how bedraggled she looked. I said, sympathetically, "Why don't you wait here while I get Peter? You must be exhausted, after all you've been through today."

Sue Ellen put her arm through mine. "Why Noa, you don't think I'm that gullible, do you? How do I know you won't just leave me behind?"

"That's what I get for trying to be nice." I turned away and headed down the stairs. Then, a little embarrassed, I remembered she had a point: Jack and I *had* left her behind in Madrid.

Sue Ellen caught up with me at the street and followed me silently down to the car. There was Peter, asleep at the wheel. I tapped gently on the window, and he woke up with a start. He unlocked the trunk, we grabbed our suitcases and returned to the hostel.

Leaving our passports at the desk, we walked down the dismal, stale-smelling corridor to our rooms. The torn linoleum-tiled floor crackled under our feet.

"At least we'll know if anybody's following us," Peter said, wearily.

We entered the first room and looked around. The walls were covered with faded, water-stained wallpaper. Perhaps that accounted for the faint smell of mildew. In one corner were a half-bath and a sink. A sagging bed, covered with a threadbare chenille spread of indeterminate color, nearly filled the rest of the tiny room. Heavy wooden shutters opened onto a small iron balcony overlooking the street. Through the cracks, we heard trucks rumbling up and down the road, the voices of people walking on the sidewalk, and the putt-putt-putt of motorscooters.

"Do you think they put us in the Bridal Suite by mistake?" Peter asked.

Before I could reply, Sue Ellen asked, "And just who is going to sleep with who?"

Peter corrected her: "You mean, 'with whom.'"

"Just what *do* you mean, Sue Ellen?" I said frostily.

Crossing her arms across her ample chest, she asserted, "I mean there is no way I am going to let you both out of my sight at the same time. So you have a choice. Either you sleep with me, Noa, or, if you prefer, I'll sleep with Peter."

"No way!"

Peter stood by, looking amused.

Sue Ellen continued. "Of course, there is another option."

"And just what is that?" I asked distrustfully.

"We can all sleep together." Sue Ellen looked Peter up and down slowly. "That could be rather interesting."

Peter started to laugh.

I glared at him. "Just what's so funny?"

"The look on your face."

Furious, I headed out the door.

"Where are you going?" Peter called after me.

"To check out the other room," I snarled.

That room was equally dismal and equally noisy. In addition, it had no shower, and the bed was even more sway-backed than the other.

"I was right," Peter said, coming up behind me. "The other room was the Bridal Suite. This one's the Servant's Quarters."

"Well, what'll it be?" Sue Ellen smiled coyly at him.

I said sarcastically, "Don't you mean who'll it be?"

"I'm overwhelmed to be in such great demand, ladies," he interjected, "but I'm afraid that in my present state I would be of little use to either of you—let alone both of you. You two take the other room and I will sleep alone, unaccustomed to that though I may be."

"I refuse to share a bed with Sue Ellen," I said angrily.

She replied, "Really, Noa, if I don't object, why should you?"

Peter laughed. "Let's go get something to eat."

"That's a wonderful idea, Peter," Sue Ellen said. "I'm so glad you thought of it."

"I would have thought Jack's death would spoil your appetite, Sue Ellen," I said with disgust.

Chewing on the chipped polish on her thumbnail, she retorted, "No use crying over spilt milk, my mother always said. Besides, what about you? You spent more time with Jack than I did."

"We were never that close," I replied archly.

"Ladies, ladies," Peter said, "I need to wash up. It's been a long day—or is it two?"

"Ta, ta," I said, and left. Sue Ellen trailed behind.

Sue Ellen took "washing up" literally, beginning with a shower and shampoo and ending with a manicure.

While she monopolized the shower, I stretched out on the creaking bed, staring at the peeling, yellowed paint on the ceiling, wondering why she irritated me so. I prided myself on my non-judgmental approach to people, but she triggered an automatic hostile response. Instead of finding her behavior ludicrous, I found it threatening.

A friend of mine would have said that Sue Ellen was "jerking my chain"—but what chain? Was I really worried that she would "steal" Peter away, just as she had started to do with Jack? Of course, it didn't take much to capture Jack's attention. Besides, I had never really thought I had it, despite his frequent, charming assertions. Peter was a very, very different kind of person—at least I thought he was.

Did I really know Peter? Uncharacteristically, he had come running to Spain to save me from danger. Or had he come running for the treasure? After all, he had made that disconcerting comment about his "many masks."

I shook my head in frustration. I really was starting to think deviously, and I didn't like it at all.

Watching a large spider crawl across the ceiling, I realized I was very angry. Angry with Sue Ellen for perpetuating and encouraging the sexist stereotypes that I found so despicable. Angry with Peter for not making a commitment to me and for finding Sue Ellen amusing. I tried to turn my anger into pity—or, at least, into understanding. Poor Sue Ellen was a product of her environment. Poor Sue Ellen? Hah! What had Jack called her? A black widow spider.

Abruptly, I sat up on the squeaking bed. What a waste of emotional energy. I couldn't control Sue Ellen, but I could control myself. And I was determined not to give Sue Ellen any power over me. I'd try to look at her as an interesting kind of creature, one worthy of observation and analysis, but not of anger.

"Want to wash up?" Sue Ellen asked, drying herself off on the one large towel.

"Thanks. I will," I said calmly, and took a shower to rinse off the dirt and sweat of the afternoon. I dried myself ineffectually with the remaining stiff hand towel. I made a mental note to ask the landlady for another large towel.

It was too early for dinner, so we decided to stroll around town. The air was still warm but no longer blazing hot, and a light breeze brought relief. In the distance we could see the towers of the thirteenth-century Castle of the Templars. Dusk had fallen, and the fading light softened the edges of the massive fortress. Following a narrow dirt trail around the high, rough stone walls, we reached the long causeway that led to the entry. Spotlighted green and red pennants flapped noisily overhead.

I grabbed Peter's arm, suddenly enthusiastic. "This is just what a castle should look like! Look at those tall round towers, with their saw-toothed balconies on top. They look just like the paper crowns I used to cut out in grade school."

"It's obvious you know nothing about architecture," Sue Ellen remarked. "Those 'saw-toothed balconies' are called crenellated parapets."

I replied cheerfully, "I don't care what you call them, they're marvelous."

I practically skipped over the creaking drawbridge and through the raised iron gate. But instead of a dark, deserted castle, we were greeted with blinding spotlights and deafening applause: a medieval pageant was being performed in the central courtyard. Bright lights illuminated the wooden stage erected on the open, grass-covered field, and a large, raucous audience cheered now one, now another, white-cloaked Templar as they fought the dark-faced Moors, resplendent in red-and-gold-brocade robes.

Swords clashed, trumpets sounded, banners waved, and at least one Templar lay writhing in mock death on the stage. We watched the action from the edge of the crowd, caught up in the dramatic recreation of an ancient battle. I cheered for the Moors, since no one else did.

After a few minutes, Sue Ellen complained, "I can't see much from here and my feet hurt."

Peter and I ignored her.

"My feet hurt. Let's find somewhere to sit down."

Peter turned to me. "Let's look at the rest of the castle."

We started off without Sue Ellen, but she tagged along. As we walked past crumbling walls into another courtyard, the battle sounds and applause faded.

The medieval castle was actually a fortress made up of several layers of walls and towers built one inside the other. Designed in the shape of a large, uneven rectangle, most of the interior was open space. We walked through one grass-covered field into another, past towers, archways, and staircases that led to partly collapsed walls, all that remained of the medieval living and storage areas. As usual, Sue Ellen lagged behind.

It was nearly 10 P.M. A full moon had risen, and a gentle breeze rustled the grass in the field. The moonlight shone softly on the castle walls.

Peter whispered, "I wouldn't miss this for anything."

I lifted my face towards him and smiled in the dark. "What wouldn't you miss? The moonlight?"

"You're being remarkably obtuse. I only hope it's intentional. What I was trying ever so subtly to say was that I'm glad I'm here with you. I wouldn't miss it for anything."

"You really mean it?"

He held me close, running his hands through my hair, pulling out the hairpins and letting it cascade around my shoulders. "Of course I do, though you certainly could have found a more straightforward way to get me here."

"Really? Like what?" I murmured.

He nuzzled my ear. "If you couldn't bear to be without me, you should have just asked me to come, instead of arranging this elaborate treasure hunt to lure me to your side—"

"Peter, you're tickling my ear! Stop it!" I drew away and tried to see the expression on his face in the dim moonlight. "And just what do you mean, I 'should have just asked,' after you made it clear we should go our own ways this summer, etcetera, etcetera, etcetera?"

"Ah, my dear, you sound like the King of Siam."

"And just why do you think I couldn't bear to be without you? I was doing just fine! Really, the incredible arrogance of—"

Suddenly a scream tore through the night air.

A white-robed form had jumped out from behind a ruined wall and grabbed Sue Ellen, who had paused to rest on the steps of a staircase at the base of a nearby tower. While we stood frozen in shock, she stomped her high heels into her attacker's foot. He howled in pain but still managed to grab her around the neck. We started towards them, but the man got what he wanted and pushed Sue Ellen away. She fell to the ground and he fled, white robe flapping in the breeze. Peter took off after him while I ran over to Sue Ellen.

"Are you all right?" I asked as I helped her sit down on the steps and brushed off her dress.

She struggled for breath. "I'm fine, no thanks to you!"

"What on earth do you mean?" I said, taken aback.

"This whole thing is your fault!"

"My fault? You're the one who insisted on coming along."

"It's still your fault! Whoever attacked me must have thought I was you. Though how they could have made such a mistake is beyond me."

"What are you talking about?" I asked, bewildered.

"Somebody mugged you in León because they wanted the gold coin hanging from around your neck, right? Somebody just mugged me because he wanted the gold coin hanging from *my* neck. He must have thought I was you." Sue Ellen rubbed her neck and winced.

"You may be right," I said, looking around nervously, "And if so, they'll be back when they discover their mistake. We'd better get out of here."

Staying far away from shadow-filled ruins and treacherous overhangs, we hurried back to the pageant. Peter was standing on the outskirts of the crowd, looking frustrated.

"Nobody in a white robe?" I asked.

Peter gestured towards the crowd and the stage. "Actually, there are plenty of people in white robes. Approximately half the performers are dressed in white robes, as well as some of the audience." He turned towards Sue Ellen and asked wryly, "See anyone you know?"

She looked at the dozens of white-robed forms and shook her head. "They all look the same."

"Some of them have sandals on," I pointed out. "Did your attacker wear shoes or sandals?"

Peter smiled approvingly. "How observant you are, my dear. The makings of a true sleuth. Sue Ellen, do any of the sandals look familiar?"

She shook her head again.

"I was afraid of that. All cats look black at night, that sort of thing." He looked around nervously. "Let's get out of here."

We race-walked down the causeway to the street, then stood breathless and indecisive on the sidewalk, looking both ways and behind us.

"I need a drink," Sue Ellen gasped. "And I'm hungry."

Peter pointed towards a grape-vine-covered café at the foot of the castle. "Let's eat over there."

"Is that wise, Peter?" I asked, "We'll be so visible."

"Even better. Besides, they think they've got the medallion, so we should be safe for a while," he said soothingly.

We chose a table in the middle of the open-air café and sat down on green metal folding chairs. Through the dangling bunches of grapes, I could see bits of the night sky. Bats chittered from the nearby trees, and the light breeze ruffled the red-and-white checked tablecloth on the rickety wooden table.

The waiter came over and recited the menu. I had no appetite, but I ordered for the others since Sue Ellen was lost in thought and Peter was too tired. The main course arrived, an earthenware casserole filled with garlic-scented, dark, bubbling liquid. Round, smooth-fleshed lumps floated to the surface.

Peter looked at it distrustfully. "Now, I know that 'one man's meat is another man's poison' but—"

"It's *sepia en su tinta*—tiny stuffed squid in a sauce of their own ink," I explained, laughing, "But be careful, the ink stains."

Sue Ellen looked up from spearing one of the sepia on her fork. "Noa's right. In fact, sepia was used in early Roman times to make permanent ink. I think it still is." She popped one in her mouth.

Peter took a bite and chewed it for a moment. A look of surprise came over his face. He swallowed, then took another piece. "This really is quite good. Unlike anything I've had before. One might even say it's made an indelible impression."

I groaned.

Peter raised his glass. "A toast."

Sourly, Sue Ellen responded, "What on earth for? My gold coin's gone."

"Better that than a jewel of greater value, which nothing could replace," He said solemnly.

"Maybe you'll get it back when they discover their mistake," I said, stifling a laugh.

"A toast to moonlight and adventure."

Peter and I clinked our glasses together. Sue Ellen refused to join in. Instead, she sat nervously smoking one cigarette after another, ordering one cognac after another. Peter and I sat silently also, but our silence was companionable and strangely soothing. After a while, Peter reached out and took my hand, entwining my fingers with his.

Sue Ellen said abruptly, "It's getting rather late, don't you think? Time for bed." She stood up to go.

The waiter brought the check, and Peter and I started to pay.

I looked pointedly at Sue Ellen. "Aren't you going to pay your share? You insisted on coming along for the ride, but that doesn't mean it's free."

She gave me a venomous look, took out her wallet, and threw some money on the table. Then she stalked out. The waiter, hovering nearby, quickly took the money. We stood up and left.

Sue Ellen was waiting for us outside the café. Together we walked warily back to the hostel. The sidewalks were crowded with families strolling in the mild night air. Several men in white robes strode rapidly by, but since they were carrying plastic swords and foil-covered shields, they presumably were performers from the pageant.

When we reached the doorway to the hostel, we ran quickly up the stairs, rang the doorbell, and waited impatiently for the landlady to let us in.

Our footsteps crackled on the broken linoleum tiles as we walked down the hall to our rooms. We arrived first at the room Sue Ellen and I were sharing. After I unlocked the door, Peter stepped inside and looked around quickly, then walked over to the bed and peered beneath it. Nobody was there. He motioned for us to come in, then turned to leave.

In a throaty whisper, Sue Ellen said, "It's not too late to change your mind, Peter."

"Well, they do say that 'consistency is the hobgoblin of small minds'—"

I interrupted, "Don't forget, Peter, they also say 'you're known by the company you keep.'"

"Right. Thanks for reminding me. Sorry, Sue Ellen, I think I'd better pass. After all, 'Discretion is the better part of valor.'"

Laughing, I quipped, "'Fools jump in where angels fear to tread—'"

"Oh, shut up you two," she snarled. "You sound like a cheap vaudeville routine."

"Better that than a burlesque show," I replied.

As Peter left, he kissed me gently on the forehead.

"Don't open the door for anyone," he cautioned. With a laugh, he added, "Not even for me!"

Twelve

Once again I woke up to the sound of water, only this time it was splattering right next to the bed. Sue Ellen was taking a long, noisy shower, oblivious to the water spraying on the floor—and to me, trying to sleep.

After she had finished I started to shower, but the hot water gave out when I was partly lathered. The Swedes—or is the Russians?—say that ice bathing is invigorating, but it must lose something in the translation. Shivering, I dried off with the small face towel, still damp from yesterday. It was not an auspicious beginning.

I quickly got dressed in jeans, T-shirt, concha belt, and sandals, brushed my hair, and put on mascara. Then I waited impatiently while Sue Ellen blow-dried her hair, put on her makeup, and sprayed herself liberally with perfume. The scent wafted across the room.

"What's the perfume?" I asked idly.

"'Tabu.' Why? Interested in learning my secrets for attracting men?"

"Not really. I just figured you'd wear 'Indiscreet.' or 'Poison.'"

"Really, dear, you shouldn't try to be catty," she said, glancing at me in the mirror. "You haven't had enough practice to do it well."

She, of course, had had a lifetime. Why was I raised to be a puppy dog, rolling over on my back at the first sign of attack, while she was raised to be a cat, purring softly but with claws always ready to strike?

We packed our suitcases in hostile silence, a silence soon broken by a knock on the door.

"Who is it?" I asked cautiously.

"'Tis I, your Knight of Santiago, come to spirit you away in my bright red charger," replied a deep, English-tinged voice.

Laughing, I opened the door and ushered Peter in. He gave me a warm hug and kissed my cheek.

"I hope you slept well," he said softly.

"Not really. I'm not used to sleeping with someone."

"Poor dear," Sue Ellen purred. "Just think what you've been missing."

"Let me rephrase that," I said. "I prefer to choose my companions carefully—and I prefer them to be men."

"Like Jack?" she asked innocently.

Peter looked startled, and she laughed. "Bet you didn't tell him about that, did you, Noa."

"It wasn't like that!" I protested.

"Oh really? We only have your word for that."

I looked pleadingly at Peter. "For heaven sakes, Peter, you don't believe her, do you?"

"It doesn't matter, really," he said, sounding detached. "I've always said we both were free to do whatever we choose."

"I don't know what you've chosen to do," I replied bitterly, "but I chose not to."

After a moment, he said, "Of course I believe you. You're the most honest person I know."

"Oh really?" interjected Sue Ellen. "Remember, she lied about finding the clue in the cathedral in León. And she lied to the police."

"That was different," I asserted.

"Why was it different? Either you're honest or you aren't."

The trouble was, I agreed with her. Unable to respond, I picked up my suitcase and left the room. Sue Ellen and Peter followed. We checked out of the hostel, reclaiming our passports from the black-dressed landlady.

When we stepped outside, I realized that the heat wave had broken and the morning air was fresh and damp. I shivered; Peter put his arms around me, and I leaned back against him, feeling reassured. At least he was on my side. I wasn't sure I was.

"Let's get some breakfast," Sue Ellen said.

"I think not," Peter replied. "Let's get out of town. We can have breakfast further down the road."

We walked quickly down the block to the red Escort, tossed our luggage in the trunk, and attempted to leave town, but the narrow, winding, one-way streets all seemed to lead in circles or into cul-de-sacs. Frustrated, Peter leaned out the window and asked two motor-scooter-riding teenagers wearing tight blue jeans and Grateful Dead T-shirts for directions to Santiago. One rider told him to follow the street until it split, then take the middle fork, and then the lower one, and then—but it was obvious that Peter was lost. Finding one's way in a hilly town built up over a thousand years is not an easy task.

One of the motor-scooter riders gestured to us to follow them, and we did. Twisting and turning in a corkscrew careen, we spiraled down the hill to the outskirts of Ponferrada and a highway. With a friendly wave, our guides putt-putted back up the hill.

"It's that time again, folks," I said, trying to make light-hearted conversation. "We have to decide whether to follow the authentic Camino de Santiago or one of two modern four-lane highways."

"The men in white must have followed us yesterday on the old Camino," Peter said, looking pointedly at Sue Ellen. "So much for your devious thinking. I recommend we change our game plan and follow one of the highways to Santiago instead. Agreed?"

Stroking her neck where the gold chain had hung, she replied, "That's just what they'd expect us to do."

"Are you sure?" I asked suspiciously.

"Of course I'm sure." She ran her fingers over her neck again, then shrugged. "But what do I care? It's your neck they're after, not mine."

"She has a point, Noa," Peter replied.

"I suppose if we can't out-guess them—and so far we haven't—we might as well do as we please. So let's stay on the old Camino. I've always wanted to follow the real Camino de Santiago," I mused, "But I wanted to do it on foot."

"On foot?" he said in surprise, "I didn't know you enjoyed that kind of thing."

"What kind of thing?"

"Pain. Deprivation. Physical exercise."

I attempted to laugh mysteriously, but it sounded like I was clearing my throat. "There's a lot you don't know about me."

"Let's get going, shall we?" Sue Ellen grumbled.

Peter looked at me and nodded. "The old road it is."

I smiled and put my hand on his thigh. He took one hand off the steering wheel and patted my hand.

The narrow two-lane country road wound its leisurely way through the fertile Bierzo region. Soaring overhead was *autopista* N VI, a wonder of modern highway construction, its elevated concrete spans hanging suspended for miles, high above the curving hills. N VI ignored the dips and rises of the hills and valleys. The Camino de Santiago, on the other hand, meandered slowly through the valley, following the sinuous course of the river.

We drove through Cacabelos, then through Villafranca del Bierzo, with its impressive, shield-emblazoned houses and numerous churches, then through Trabadelo. We drove past groves of chestnut, cherry, and acacia trees, past lush fields of grain. Slowly, our road climbed out of the valley, following a serpentine route around one hill, then around another.

Stone houses huddled together on either side of the Camino, which was now just a bumpy strip of asphalt laid down over a narrow trail sliced into the steep hillside. Peasants in blue overalls labored in the fields, cutting the grain with scythes. The slopes were so steep that it looked as if they needed mountain-climbing gear to stay upright.

A lone pilgrim was leaning on his staff by the side of the road. He wore traditional medieval regalia: thick leather sandals; brown, coarsely woven tunic fastened with a crude leather belt; long, brown, woolen cloak; leather food bag on his belt; and a broad-brimmed hat decorated with scallop shells. A water gourd dangled from his tall, gnarled staff. I watched him in the rearview mirror but he stood as still as if he were carved out of wood. Soon he was out of sight.

As we rounded a curve, we came up behind four pilgrims on horseback. We were forced to slow our pace to the plodding walk of the horses until the riders reached a driveway. They led their horses off the road and waited until the car passed by. I waved; they waved back. Their horses switched their tails, but not at us. They were switching away flies.

Sue Ellen commented, "Isn't that just the most romantic thing, riding horses to Santiago."

"I know it looks like fun," I said, "But when I lived in Sahagún I talked to several horse-riding pilgrims, and they said it was a lot of hassle. They have trouble finding fodder and shelter; they can't visit the big cities because the horses get upset in traffic. And on some stretches of the road—like here—there is nowhere for them to ride except on the highway, which is bad for the horses' hooves."

"Oh."

"Ah, my dear," Peter said, "How cruelly you have burst the bubble of illusion. Have you no pity?"

"Surely you won't tell me that walking is better?" Sue Ellen responded.

"Believe it or not, I have it on good authority that walking has its advantages. You really experience the journey, for one thing."

"Give me a Mercedes anytime," she said, settling back in the seat.

"Jack drove a Mercedes, and Jack's dead," I observed.

In the silence that followed, I reflected aloud, "Why aren't we talking about Jack's death?"

Sue Ellen responded immediately, "Really, Noa, how could you. It's so unpleasant. And in such bad taste."

"Come on, Sue Ellen, be honest for a change. Somebody killed Jack, but we're avoiding the topic like the plague."

Peter asked, "What is there to say? Got any new ideas?"

I shook my head.

"You're right, it is like the plague," he continued. "We hope we don't catch it but we aren't sure how to avoid it except by not mentioning it."

"A kind of reverse magic, I suppose," I replied. "Instead of getting something to happen, we're trying to get it not to. Only it already has."

The weather had been damp and hazy when we started, but instead of burning off with the morning sun, the mist had congealed into fog. As we drove higher and higher into the mountains, following the winding road up the side of the narrow valley of the Valcarcel to the pass of Piedrafita, the fog seemed to come after us, gathering opacity as it came.

Some 30 miles from Ponferrada we reached the town of Piedrafita and entered the province of Galicia. Because of the thick fog, we almost missed the turnoff that led to the Pass of O Cebreiro.

Peter turned the lights on and the windshield wipers to high speed. It didn't help. Trying unsuccessfully to peer through the murk, he said tensely, "At least no one can follow us in this pea-soup fog."

I looked back down the road and could see nothing except a fast-approaching sea of white. "If they were following us, how would we know? We can't see them either."

Nobody replied.

Although we couldn't see beyond the side of the road, we knew by the way the car engine labored that we were climbing slowly to the top of the mountain pass. The road leveled out for a few meters and a road sign, "O Cebreiro," suddenly loomed out of the fog. Abruptly, Peter headed up what appeared to be a narrow driveway.

Sue Ellen was dozing in the back of the car, but she sat up when we turned off the road. Looking around, she asked nervously, "Why are we pulling off?"

"I can't see the road any more," Peter explained. "We'll have to wait here until the fog lifts."

He pulled the car up to a low stone wall in a courtyard and we got out and looked around.

I whispered, "It's like being inside a cloud."

Peter pointed across the courtyard, where we could just make out pale, yellow light emanating from the windows of a barely visible building on the other side. As we walked over to it, wisps of fog wrapped around our legs and muffled our footsteps. Next to the door was a sign, partly visible through the drifting mist: "Mesón O Cebreiro." We pushed open the moisture-beaded door and went in.

Warmth, noise, light, and the smell of hot coffee and fresh-baked bread greeted us. A group of six or seven pilgrims sat at one long trestle table in the dining room. Several black-robed monks and a group of tourists sat at another. They made room at one end of a bench for us, and we squeezed in together.

The jolly, red-faced innkeeper came over and cheerfully asked us what we wanted for breakfast. Espresso. He shook his head. No espresso: the machine was broken. All he had was Nescafé. So we ordered instant coffee and bread, which he brought in just a few minutes.

While we waited for the coffee to cool, the innkeeper pulled up a chair and, wiping his large hands on his soiled white apron, asked, "Been here before?"

We shook their heads.

With an expansive gesture, he bellowed, "Welcome to Galicia, famous for its Celtic music, witchcraft, and sorcery. You must have come to see our *pallozas* and our miraculous chalice."

"Tell us more," Peter said.

"My pleasure." The innkeeper got up and went over to the far corner of the room to talk to one of the black-robed priests. The priest looked in our direction, nodded, and came over.

"I'm Father Raimundo," he said warmly. "Do you mind if I join you?"

Peter and I smiled in welcome, and he sat down in the chair vacated by the innkeeper. "You're interested in the *pallozas?*"

"If we knew what they were, we might be," Peter said.

"They're stone huts, dating back to the ninth century. The Celts used to live in houses just like them. People still lived in some of our pallozas until ten years ago. Then one was turned into an ethnographic museum and another became a shelter for pilgrims to Santiago. The Hospital—that's this building—was founded in the eleventh century as a refuge for pilgrims and other travelers stranded on the high mountain pass. The church dates back to the ninth or tenth century." He paused.

I smiled encouragingly.

"Have you heard the story of our miraculous chalice?"

Peter and I shook our heads. Sue Ellen looked bored and started drumming her fingernails on the wooden tabletop.

Unfazed, the priest continued, "In the church there is a miraculous chalice. Sometime in the Middle Ages, a faithful soul hiked up from his village to the church here to hear Mass. It was an awful, stormy day. When he got here, the monk, who had little faith, ridiculed the man for venturing out in such bad weather just for a bit of bread and wine. But at the moment of communion, the Host was miraculously converted into flesh and the wine into blood, much to the amazement of the priest. Pilgrims soon spread the word of the miracle throughout the world. It just goes to show what faith can do."

Sue Ellen commented cynically, "You can fool some of the people all of the time."

A chill ran up and down my spine and I shivered, once, all over. Jack had made that same remark.

Another black-robed priest came over and stood patiently beside Father Raimundo. He glanced up at him and said regretfully, "I must go. I promised my friends a guided tour."

"Thank you for telling us about O Cebreiro," I said.

"Of course. Perhaps we will meet again."

Peter stood up. "I think I'll go sight-seeing, too. Coming, Noa?"

"Sure."

Sue Ellen held up a red-tipped hand. "Wait a minute. You're not leaving without me." She quickly drained her coffee cup and followed us out the door.

Thirty feet away, fading in and out of the fog, was a square church bell tower. We walked through the swirling mist to the lichen-covered stone portico and entered what appeared to be one large room with several small alcoves. A dozen crude wooden benches were placed in rows in the middle of the room.

At the far end, candles on a wrought-iron stand flickered in front of the twelfth-century polychrome statue of the Virgin and child. Perched on his mother's lap, the solemn Christ figure had his left hand raised in the sign of peace. A faint smell of burning wax and dampness permeated the room. Nearby was a six-foot-tall glass display case containing the miraculous golden chalice, covered with crudely set cabochon jewels and carved agates.

I pulled out the guidebook. "According to this, Wagner used the miracle of the chalice for his version of Parsifal."

Peter said, surprised, "I suppose this might be related to the Parsifal legend, but there are many legends. There's also the one about King Arthur and his knights, and Gawain's quest for the Holy Grail . . . ."

"Our quest is for the treasure, right?" I said, looking intently at him.

He returned my look and replied thoughtfully, "Right."

"What else would it be for?" Sue Ellen asked, bewildered.

"How about a search for love? You know, something trivial."

"Give me treasure any time! At least you know what you've got and when you've got it."

Shaking his head, Peter said, "You really are single minded, aren't you?"

"I just know what I want. Do you?" she challenged.

He turned away abruptly. "I think I'll go look at the *pallozas*. Coming, Noa?"

"You go ahead. I'll wait here till you come back."

"Sure you'll be safe?"

"Why not? You said nobody could have followed us here in the fog. Besides, Sue Ellen will wait here with me." I looked pointedly at her. "Won't you, Sue Ellen?"

She nodded curtly.

Apparently reassured, Peter said, "I'll be back in a few minutes." He strode quickly down the aisle and out of the church.

Sue Ellen tapped her foot impatiently for awhile, then sat down on a nearby bench and examined her fingernails. I remained standing, lost in thought, contemplating the chalice and thinking about treasure hunts and holy quests. And about getting what you think you want.

Coming out of a daze, I gradually realized Sue Ellen was nowhere to be seen and Peter had not yet returned. I was alone except for a tall man in a white robe, his face hidden behind a cowl. He was strolling slowly around the church, apparently examining the ancient stonework.

As he slowly circling the room, I kept a uniform distance between us. Just when he appeared to have decided to cut across the room towards me, a group of tourists accompanied by Father Raimundo walked in. I slipped behind them and fled out the door.

The thick fog had thinned into wispy sheets of gauze, and now I could see the low, conical-shaped thatched roofs of the *pallozas* poking up through the mist. Dug partway into the ground, the squat stone huts huddled against the hillside for protection from the fierce winter storms. They resembled a patch of mushrooms sprouting from the side of the mountain. Peter and Sue Ellen were nowhere to be seen.

Going over to the nearest *palloza*, I saw several tired-looking pilgrims warming their hands at a smoky campfire built just outside the doorway. I asked them if they had seen a brown-haired man or an attractive blond woman and they said no. Beginning to feel nervous, I went over to the next hut, an ethnographic exhibit, according to the sign on the door. I walked in, bending slightly to get through the low doorway.

The *palloza* was filled with a rank smell, absorbed from the animals—and humans—that had inhabited it for centuries. In the dim light that filtered through the doorway and the tiny opaque windows, I saw a large oval room with a hard-packed earth floor and unadorned stone walls.

Suspended from the thatched roof was a huge metal drying rack from which bladder-like shapes dangled. Sausages, I decided, after my eyes adjusted to the gloom. In one part of the room was a crude wooden loom. A partially woven, striped blanket was suspended from the crossbars. Nearby was a table with a washbasin and a rough wooden bench beside it. A few stools and wooden chests were arranged along the wall.

Walking slowly around the dimly lit room, I came to an alcove raised one step above the rest of the floor. A low moan emanated from the shadows.

"Peter?" I whispered.

The only response was a groan. The sound came from the darkest corner, where I could barely make out a blanket-covered heap on the floor. Cautiously, I started creeping over to the shrouded form.

It moved. A familiar hand appeared. Peter's.

I ran over and pulled off the blanket. "Are you all right?" I asked, my voice trembling.

"I don't know. I think so." He tried to sit up but couldn't.

I cradled his head in my lap. "What happened?"

"Somebody must have slugged me," he said weakly.

I examined his head; despite my efforts to be gentle, he winced.

"Nothing seems broken," I said reassuringly.

He put his hand to his head, withdrew it and looked. No blood. With a sigh, he said, "Fortunately, as you have often told me, I have a thick skull." He stood up gingerly and sat down abruptly.

Suddenly I realized someone was still missing. "Where's Sue Ellen?" I asked.

"Isn't she with you?" he said in surprise.

"No. She left the church when I wasn't looking. I thought maybe she was with you."

"I haven't seen her. I heard a muffled cry and went to investigate."

"Was it Sue Ellen?"

"I don't know. Somebody knocked me out before I could find out."

He tried again to stand, and this time he succeeded. With his arm draped across my shoulder for support, we searched the *palloza* but found no sign of her, not even a scrap of fabric torn from her dress, not even a faint whiff of her perfume. Peter looked haggard.

"Let's get you some fresh air," I suggested, guiding him to the entryway.

With a show of spirit, he squeezed my shoulder and stepped away. He swayed for a moment but then stood on his own. We walked slowly toward the next *palloza*. I walked beside him to steady him as needed.

The pilgrims I had seen earlier were still warming themselves by the sputtering fire. I asked them if they had seen Sue Ellen, but they said they had seen no one except me. We went back to the church and asked the group of tourists, but their answer was the same. The man in the white robe had also disappeared.

With growing concern, we returned to the inn. The innkeeper remembered our attractive blond companion but had not seen her since we left. As a last resort, we looked in the car, but Sue Ellen wasn't there either.

Peter's head was throbbing painfully, so we went back to the inn and sat down at the far end of one of the trestle tables. I ordered coffee for myself and a cup of *manzanilla* for Peter.

He looked distrustfully at the fragrant, tan-colored liquid.

"It's chamomile tea. It's good for upset stomachs and nerves," I explained.

"I don't have nerves."

"Obviously."

"Why my dear, this is a common, everyday occurrence," he said, dismissively. "I frequently get bashed on the head, but usually it's by irate students."

"Or jealous boyfriends." I touched his hand gently. "Seriously, Peter, what do you think happened to Sue Ellen? I'm worried."

"Maybe the guy who slugged me slugged her," he suggested.

"But why? She didn't have the medallion or even a gold coin."

"Got me."

"So what happened to her?" I asked, my voice becoming shrill.

"Got me." He winced. "My brain feels like mush."

"How distinctly un-British. If you had said oatmeal—"

"Noa, I know you're trying to cheer me up, but don't."

"Sorry," I said contritely, staring into my coffee. "So where is Sue Ellen? Knowing her, I could imagine that she could have slugged me, stolen the medallion, and taken off."

"Would she know what to do with the medallion?"

"I told her about it after Jack was shot, remember?" I shook my head, puzzled. "But you got slugged, not me."

Holding his head in his hands, he said, "Maybe she just hasn't gotten around to you yet."

"Could be. But I can't imagine her doing it alone. After all, she wouldn't want to break her fingernails."

"My, we're catty."

"No, we're not: we're realistic. She's 'delicate,' even if she's hard as nails. She would have needed an accomplice—a strong accomplice with a car—unless she planned to steal our car. You still have the car keys, don't you?"

Startled, Peter checked in his pocket and nodded with relief.

I continued. "If Sue Ellen's 'turned traitor,' who could the accomplice be? Jack's dead."

"Maybe she's 'in cahoots,' as they say, with whoever killed Jack."

"You mean the men in white? Why would they want her to join them? And why would she want to? Besides, they stole her gold coin."

"That was by mistake, remember? But I don't mean them, I mean the other guy. The one who murdered Jack."

"Are you sure you're feeling all right?" I asked, examining his face closely. "The men in white killed Jack because he killed Mateo. At least I think so."

"Either way it makes perfect—or, rather, perverted—sense. Even if the men in white didn't kill Mateo, they could still be after you."

"Except that nobody knocked me out or kidnapped me. And I still have the medallion."

"Something must have screwed up their plans." Peter took another sip of chamomile tea and grimaced.

"A white-robed man came into the church after Sue Ellen left, and I had the feeling he was coming over towards me, so I left."

"So maybe it is the guys in white. But how would they, whoever they are, have followed us here?"

"Elementary, my dear Watson. Sue Ellen has been telling us which road to follow ever since Astorga."

Peter nodded slowly. "But what if we hadn't agreed with her? Or what if Sue Ellen wasn't 'in cahoots' with them?"

"Maybe they put a tracer on the car," I said.

"When?"

"In León, maybe, or in Ponferrada when they thought they stole the medallion but found out it was just a gold coin."

"Sue Ellen's gold coin."

"That's right. We know the men in white are still after the medallion. So it could have been the men in white who knocked you out and made off with Sue Ellen."

"By mistake?"

"Maybe. Or maybe they just like blondes. Spaniards have a weakness for blondes, you know."

He winced. "I wish my head didn't hurt. Then I could think straight. So why'd they knock me out? Unless they're just gratuitously nasty."

"Because you got in the way while they were mugging Sue Ellen. Or because they felt safer with you out of the picture. After all, you're strong and competent—"

"Thank you, my dear. At the moment I feel like a limp dishrag."

"That's a temporary state of affairs," I said reassuringly.

Peter took another sip of tea. "But imagine, for a moment, that it was Sue Ellen and an unnamed accomplice who knocked me out, not the guys in white knocking her out. Sue Ellen follows me to the hut, sees me enter, sneaks in behind with her strong-arm buddy, and gives a muffled scream to lure me into the corner. I go down like the proverbial ton of bricks. But why stop there? Why not wait till you came in? Or find you and steal the medallion? Something—or somebody—must have interfered with their plans. The guys in white?"

I closed my eyes for a moment and reviewed the recent events. "First things first. Peter, why did they knock you out? If Sue Ellen has betrayed us and joined up with somebody else, why wouldn't they just wait until we found the treasure? That's what Jack would have done, and he and Sue Ellen think—thought—alike."

"Maybe it was just too good an opportunity to pass up. If we were both out of the way, they'd have the key to the treasure and no interference."

With a worried frown, I replied, "There's a flaw in your logic, but I can't put my finger on it." I started to draw a diagram on the tabletop.

After a few minutes, Peter finished his tea and said he felt much better, so we went to look again for Sue Ellen. The fog had lifted and now we could see the surrounding countryside spread out far below. It looked like a small-scale version of Switzerland: steep green mountains dotted with scattered settlements. But no cows. And no Sue Ellen.

We looked inside the *pallozas* and outbuildings again, and we kept running into the tourist group and Father Raimundo, but no one had seen her, or rather, no one admitted to having seen her.

"It's as if she vanished into thin air," I said uneasily.

"Into thick fog, to be more precise."

Peter slumped against the stone wall in the courtyard. "I think we should leave."

"But how can we leave without knowing what happened to Sue Ellen?" I protested.

"Whatever happened, it can't be good. If she's 'in cahoots' with somebody else—and I wouldn't put it past her—they may still try to get the medallion from you. If she isn't 'in cahoots' with somebody, then someone has lured her away, presumably by force. In other words, kidnapping. Possibly murder." He stood up wearily. "But forget about Sue Ellen for the moment. Let's talk about you."

"Me?"

"You, my dense little companion," he said, smiling grimly. "Don't forget the medallion."

"Of course. The medallion."

"Even if the men in white had nothing to do with these most recent events, by now they know that Sue Ellen's coin is not the medallion. They'll be after you again." Hesitantly he said, "Why not give me the medallion?"

"But why, Peter?" I asked, puzzled.

"Well, they wouldn't think I had it, would they? So it would be safer."

Uneasily, I stroked the medallion and looked at him. He wouldn't meet my eyes. "I think I'll keep it, for a while anyway."

Sounding hurt, he asked, "Surely you aren't suspicious of me, Noa?"

"Of course not."

"I should hope not. After all, I've just been brutally bashed in the head as a result of my efforts to keep you safe. Really, Noa, my only concern is your welfare."

I stared at him. He sounded sincere, but so had Jack.

"Of course, I'd like to find the treasure too, but that's unimportant compared to your health and safety." He looked around nervously. "The longer we wait, the more time they—whoever they are—have to make their plans. So let's get out of here."

"I feel as if we're deserting Sue Ellen. Maybe she's bound and gagged somewhere in the back of a *palloza*, or in the trunk of somebody's car—"

"My dear, there's not a thing we can do about it," he replied firmly. "Besides, look at the bright side. This way, we don't have to deal with her peculiar brand of wit for a while. And, as an added treat, you can have me all to yourself."

"Promises, promises. But I suppose you're right."

We walked over to the red Escort, and he started to get in on the driver's side of the car. I stopped him. "I'll drive."

Gingerly holding his head, he meekly got in on the passenger's side. The early morning chill had been replaced by heat, so we rolled down the windows to cool off the car. Then we checked the map: 80 miles to Santiago. I turned on the ignition.

A tall, hooded figure in a white robe suddenly appeared out of nowhere and stepped in front of the car. He held his hand up to halt us. We waited nervously while he strode over to the driver's side.

In a deep, resonant voice, he said, "I am here to help you."

"Who are you?" I asked nervously.

"A friend." Sonorously, he repeated, "I am here to help you."

"What makes you think we need help?" I retorted.

"You have found something, have you not?"

Peter replied, "So what if we have?"

"And you are looking for something, are you not?"

"So what if we are?"

"We should join together on this quest."

I snorted. "Give me one good reason."

"There are evil forces at work. We can protect you."

Peter turned to me and whispered, "He's got a point."

I whispered back, "But isn't he one of the evil forces?" I asked the hooded man. "What do you want from us?"

"The medallion and the secret to its use."

"How do we know you won't betray us?" I asked.

"Trust me."

"Hah!"

Peter said suspiciously, "What happened to Sue Ellen?"

"Sue Ellen?"

"The blond. The one you mugged at Ponferrada."

"Oh. Her. I have no idea." He looked around, as if listening for something.

Peter whispered, "I think he's stalling—"

Then the man in white reached into a pocket in his voluminous robe and started to take something out.

Peter yelled, "Floor it!"

I thrust the car into reverse, backed quickly out of the driveway and, tires squealing, sped down the road, leaving the hooded figure standing alone in the middle of the driveway, one hand dangling at his side.

Thirteen

We fled down a roller-coaster road that swung up and down and around the mountains, past straggly settlements strung along the side of the road, past slate-roofed stone houses that seemed to grow out of the ground. Road signs gave the distance to Santiago and the next settlement, often a single house with a name emblazoned over the door.

We sped by Fonfría, Biduedo, Filloval at 40 mph, the fastest I could drive on the narrow, winding roads. An old man dressed in black sat in a chair outside an isolated house, watching the road. Villagers working in their gardens turned and stared as we drove by.

Coming out of the hills and around a bend, we reached Triacastela and, within minutes, drove through it. In the rearview mirror I saw a large pedestal with a wrought-iron pilgrim standing on top.

Tires screeching as I swung around a tight curve, I barely missed hitting a group of children riding their bicycles down the middle of the road.

Peter shouted, "Watch out!" just as I took evasive action.

Shaken, I pulled over and wiped my sweaty palms on my jeans.

"Nobody's following us," he said, "So you can slow down and negotiate the curves on all four wheels."

"But the man in white *must* be following us," I protested.

"Not necessarily. He wouldn't have to if he knew where we were going."

I took a deep breath and let it out slowly. "Of course. Sue Ellen must have told him."

"Could be."

"But he acted like he didn't know anything about her."

"My dear, your naïveté never ceases to amaze me. To think that after all you have been through—murder, mugging, and malice—"

"I thought the three M's were motherhood, martyrdom, and—"

"Don't interrupt. To think that you still retain your childlike innocence and your abiding sense of trust."

"You make me sound like an idiot," I retorted.

"I am filled with admiration for those who can maintain their illusions in a disillusioning world—"

"Peter!"

"At any rate, if someone were following us, he would have caught us by now, despite your awe-inspiring driving. So please, my dear, slow down."

"You take all the fun out of it." After checking the rearview mirror I pulled onto the road again.

"Is all Spain this primitive?" he asked, staring out the window. "I don't think I've seen even one tractor. Only oxen and carts."

"The villages look primitive, I know, but inside most of the houses you'll find large color TV sets. Many of the young people have punk haircuts and listen to the latest rock music. And they probably go to all-night discos on weekends."

"Appearances are deceiving," Peter replied offhandedly.

They sure are, I thought.

Soon we reached the monastery of Samos, nestling in the lush, rolling hills. A sign at a small gas station/café across from the monastery indicated they served *parrilla*, the Spanish equivalent to barbecue.

"I think we need gas," I said, taking my foot off the accelerator. "Besides, I want to get something to eat. I'm famished."

"'Hunger soothes the savage breast—'"

"You've got it wrong. It's 'Love soothes the savage beast.'"

"I don't think so."

"It doesn't?"

"No, you've got it wrong."

"Right or wrong, I'm still famished. Do you think it's safe to stop?"

"Why not. They're probably waiting for us in Santiago. Even if we're being driven like lambs to the slaughter, we don't have to hurry."

"And to think I was looking forward to eating lamb chops," I replied.

A young man emerged from the station and, wiping his hands on his faded jeans, proceeded to fill our tank. After paying for the gas, I parked the car next to the café. We got out and stretched, standing for a moment in the dappled light that filtered through a huge chestnut tree. Birds chirped in the branches, and two weary pilgrims with their shoes off rested beneath its shade. With a sigh, I turned and walked into the café.

Dusty bottles of liquor de Samos, a liquor produced by the local monks, were lined up for sale on a shelf behind by the cash register, and bull-fighting posters adorned the rough gray stone walls of the building. A fire blazed in a massive fireplace in the corner.

A plump, blonde-haired woman in a patterned housedress sat behind the counter, playing with a baby on her lap. When we walked in, she put the baby in a blue-and-white carriage, complete with furled, ruffled umbrella. We sat down at a Formica-topped table, and she came over and recited the menu: salad, French fries, and *parrilla* with or without Argentinean sausage.

"What's that?" Peter asked.

"It's like *chorizo*," I explained, "but without paprika."

"Sounds good."

We both ordered "with sausage" and, after relaying our order to the kitchen, the woman set the table. Her husband—the same man who had filled the car with gas—entered, carrying a plate heaped with assorted marinated lamb chops and kidneys, beefsteaks, and sausage. He placed them on the grill over the fireplace. Soon the air was filled with the luscious scent of garlic-drenched barbecued meat.

I started to laugh as he filled our plates. "We certainly are taking everything in stride. Murders, muggings, a possible kidnapping—and we sit calmly eating lunch!"

Peter smiled. "Why not? Never miss an opportunity for a good meal, that's my philosophy." After savoring a piece of steak, he commented, "This really is marvelous, and so unexpected, here in the middle of nowhere."

I nodded in agreement. "The condemned ate a hearty meal."

"All the more reason," Peter said, signaling the cook for more.

Surfeited, we complimented the cook and his wife, paid the bill, and left. A large white tour bus had pulled up beside our car, disgorging a stream of chattering pilgrims who had come to tour the monastery. We waited impatiently for the driver to move.

More green hills, more narrow winding roads, and we reached the industrial town of Sarria. Perched on a nearby hill were the ruins of an ancient castle. Ten miles further, we drove over a great bridge across the River Miño to Portomarín. From the road, we could see the fortress-like church that dominated the village. Its huge stained-glass window filled the upper third of one wall. I remembered reading that most of the town had been submerged when the reservoir was developed. Although all of the homes were lost, the important monuments were moved, stone by stone, to higher ground.

We drove on through rustling eucalyptus groves and past pastures in which dairy cows munched rich green grass. Every so often we saw pilgrims hiking on narrow trails that intersected the highway. Our paved Camino de Santiago snaked through the valleys, but the pilgrims on the traditional Camino walked up and over the hills and through the forest.

We raced past Hospital, Ventas de Narón, Portos, Vilar de Donas, and Rosario, missing the atmospheric cafés, the medieval churches, the Roman bridges, the stretches of still-existing paved Roman road described in the guidebook.

"This isn't exactly how I planned to follow the old Camino," I said, ruefully.

"Next time on foot, right?"

"I just hope there is a next time. Maybe I should make a vow to Santiago," I said, half seriously.

"Or his Knights. Where are they when we need them?"

"Why them?" I asked.

"Remember, the Knights of Santiago protected pilgrims on the Camino."

"But Peter, it's *their* treasure we're after. If they still existed, do you think they would protect us? Or kill us?"

"A mere quibble."

"Easy for you to say," I replied thoughtfully.

At Palas do Rei our progress slowed to a crawl: the town was en fiestas, celebrating its patron saint's day. Roadblocks were put up at street corners, and a uniformed policeman wearing white gloves directed traffic onto narrow side streets. Vendors had erected stalls in the middle of the street and were selling everything from bath towels to brightly colored dresses, from hand-painted pottery to ice cream, from cattle to caged birds.

The odor was pungent, a mixture of sweat, garlic, seafood, and manure. The noise was impressive: people bargained, argued, and greeted one another at the tops of their voices to the accompaniment of raucous music provided gratis by vendors of cassettes and tape recorders.

As we drove slowly by, three young girls, perhaps ten or twelve years old, dressed in shorts and T-shirts, rhythmically clapped their small hands and danced on the sidewalk to the sound of flamenco music played on a tinny-sounding tape recorder. Perhaps someday they would be dancing in the *cuevas* in Madrid. Which suddenly reminded me: I wondered what Fred had wanted to talk to me about the day Mateo was killed. Had I actually seen him in San Marcos in León? If so, what did he want?

We continued on, past Aldea de Riba, San Xulián do Camiño, Leboreiro, Disicabo, Melide.

Peter looked back every so often to see if we were being followed.

I glanced at him. "See anyone?"

"Not a soul."

"Sue Ellen must have told them we were going to Santiago."

Holding his still-aching head, he replied, "Not necessarily."

"Not necessarily what? Not necessarily Santiago?"

"Not necessarily Sue Ellen. After all, the men in white were able to follow you before Sue Ellen came along."

I gave a start. "I'd forgotten that." I gripped the wheel tightly. "But they still might need her to tell them about the medallion."

"Look at it this way. Either she's 'in cahoots' with them—"

"Or they killed her." My heart started to pound audibly—at least it was audible to me. "Peter—" I broke off.

"Mmm?"

"What about going to the police?" I suggested hesitantly.

"And tell them what?" he scoffed. "That we lied to them in León?"

"We didn't lie to them."

"We 'withheld evidence,' if you want to be precise. Just what do you suggest we tell them?" He continued relentlessly, "That one of our fellow conspirators has vanished? After all, she might have disappeared, and probably did, of her own free will."

"You've got a point," I conceded.

"Do we tell them that mysterious men in white robes keep accosting us?"

"It does sound a bit weird."

"Maybe we should 'come clean' and tell them about the gold medallion you took from the library and about the treasure hunt. Then they might hold us for questioning, or whatever it is they do, for a few years or more. And, having claimed the medallion, they might use it themselves to find the treasure."

"I get the idea," I replied testily.

Peter glanced at my tight-lipped profile. "My dear, don't be miffed. Your heart is in the right place and your instincts are admirable. But this is an imperfect world, and it's a dirty game we're playing."

"I know, I know. 'If you can't stand the heat—'"

"Actually, I was thinking more on the line of 'out of the frying pan into the fire.'"

"Do you think our goose is cooked?"

"'What's sauce for the goose—'"

"I give up," I said with a sigh. "I'm simply no match for your brilliant repartee."

With a smile, he reached over and nibbled my earlobe.

"Peter—don't! That tickles," I protested. "And I'm driving."

Soon we reached the small town of Lavacolla, a sprawling collection of low, whitewashed houses, two-story cement buildings, and vacant lots.

"The name Lavacolla comes from the Latin 'to wash one's private parts,'" I told him. "Pilgrims used to stop at the Lavacolla River and ritually cleanse themselves before they continued their pilgrimage to Santiago."

"Shall we?" Peter looked at me and grinned.

I patted his knee. "Don't leer. It distorts your mouth. We'll do it next time, when we come here on foot."

"You really are serious about that. And just when are you planning to make this excursion?"

"As soon as possible. After all, if we find the treasure and come out of this alive, it's the least we can do."

"I thought you wanted to walk the Camino because of a hidden streak of masochism. Little did I suspect you had deep religious convictions."

"Let's not use the word 'conviction,' shall we? It reminds me of the police. Actually," I continued, "I don't know if I have any religious convictions, but I do know I have a growing desire to go on the pilgrimage. Especially if we survive."

"It's a deal."

Startled, I glanced at him, then maneuvered quickly to avoid hitting an overloaded oxcart that had suddenly pulled out in front of me.

A few miles further we reached the village of San Marcos, spread out at the foot of a hill. Peter pointed to some pilgrims who were following a trail up the side of the hill instead of following the highway to Santiago.

"That's the Monte del Gozo, the Hill of Joy," I explained. "In the Middle Ages, pilgrims would race each other to the top of it for the first glimpse of the cathedral spires of Santiago, some three miles away. Whoever got to the top first would get to take the sur- name Roi or LeRoi, which stands for 'king.'"

"It's amazing how educational this trip is," Peter said with a laugh.

"Ah, Peter, you find humor in everything. That's why I love you so."

Startled, he asked, "What did you say?"

I didn't reply.

Suddenly we came around a bend in the road and in front of us was Santiago de Compostela, its cathedral spires outlined against the sky.

We followed the Calle de los Concheiros, the Road of the Pil- grims, into town. The street split, and I chose the road that headed uphill towards the cathedral; after several forks and twists, we ar- rived at a dead end and, fortunately, a vacant parking place. On our right was a four-story-tall granite wall; on our left was a two- story arcaded building filled with souvenir shops. Next to it was a staircase and a stone retaining wall. The towers of the cathedral were barely visible above.

We climbed the worn steps and emerged at the Plaza del Obradoiro. Three- and four-story-tall, lichen-covered granite build- ings surrounded the huge square. Bright, harsh sunlight reflected from the stones, and the edges of the buildings shimmered in the heat.

Next to us was the Hotel de los Reyes Católicos, the luxury *parador* where the police had made reservations for three of us. Now there were only two. Uneasily, I remembered the Agatha Christie novel about ten little Indians, and then there were nine, and then eight . . .

182

Shielding my eyes, I looked at the brightly painted wooden carts displaying tourist souvenirs in front of the hotel. While I watched, a band of red-and-black costumed men paraded down one of the narrow stone streets into the plaza, playing eerie, Celtic-sounding music on drums, flutes, tambourines, and a *gaita*, the Galician version of the bagpipe.

Directly across the plaza was the enormous cathedral. A line of pilgrims snaked up the huge double staircase leading up to the main entrance. From where we stood the cathedral looked like a gaudy wedding cake covered with stone filigree and splotches of lichen. Bells of assorted sizes dangled from numerous towers, and a plethora of statues of Santiago adorned the rooftops, windows, corners, niches, doors—

Frustrated, I turned to Peter. "How will we ever find what we're looking for?"

"Just what are we looking for?"

"That's the problem. I'm not really sure." I pulled the copy of the letter out of my bag. "I quote: 'Only the true pilgrim who follows the Milky Way will reach the treasure, and only if St. James guides him. I have made a key to the treasure—.' I figured out that the thirteen Roman numerals and symbols on the medallion corresponded to the stages on the pilgrimage road. So we looked for symbols scratched on the wall next to statues of Santiago in order to figure out where to go next. Are you following me?"

"Of course. So what's the problem?"

"The problem is that Santiago de Compostela is the last stage on the Camino de Santiago. It is numeral XIII. So where do we find the treasure?"

"That's a problem all right." Peter rubbed his left ear and stared at the line of pilgrims. "Noa, let me see the medallion."

I took it off and handed it to him. Thoughtfully, he turned it over. "What's the design on the back?"

"A labyrinth inside a scallop shell."

"Any idea what it means?"

I shook my head. "It's a labyrinth inside a scallop shell."

"You're repeating yourself."

"I thought enlightenment might strike if I repeated it."

"Did it?"

"Not that I can tell."

He slipped the medallion back around my neck.

"Whatever it means, it's all we've got to go on," he said. "Let's see if we can find that design next to a statue of St. James."

I pulled out my camera and aimed the telephoto lens at the cathedral. Then I said in disgust, "I can't see a thing. But obviously, whoever hid the treasure would not have left clues so high. After all, they had to work quickly and secretly—"

"And, obviously, whoever was looking for the clue wouldn't be able to see it if it was so high. So we can save a lot of time by only looking at the more accessible figures."

"That was something Jack never figured out," I commented.

"Oh?"

"He didn't seem to think things through very well."

"Ah. A 'shoot from the hip' sort, was he?"

"You might say that. I wonder, Peter, if that had anything to do with it."

"With what?" he asked, puzzled.

"With Mateo's murder, if it *was* murder."

"What had anything to do with it?"

"The fact that Jack didn't think things through. He tended to act on the spur of the moment. Maybe he did kill Mateo. But if he did, I think he killed Mateo without really meaning to. Maybe he was frustrated because Mateo wouldn't tell him about the letter, so he got upset and threatened him, not realizing he had a bad heart."

"I wonder if we'll ever know."

"Not that it matters," I admitted ruefully. "Mateo's dead either way. But I'd rather think that my charming companion wasn't a total sociopath—"

"What difference does it make?"

"I want to think I'd have 'picked up' on something like that. It's like those awful news reports about a serial killer, and the next-door neighbors say, 'Gee, he seemed like a regular guy to me.' That's really disturbing. You don't want murderers to seem like 'regular guys.'"

"Evil should somehow show in the face, or in the eyes. Is that what you mean?"

"I mean I'd like to think I'm a good judge of character."

Peter flashed me a sardonic smile. "Sometimes it is hard to see behind the mask. But that's what a mask is for, after all."

I replied warily, "You sound as if you know."

"Of course I know," he said, laughing. "We all wear masks. But that doesn't mean that what's behind the mask is evil. Some of us wear a mask for protection, because we are so vulnerable. And some of us wear a mask because there is nothing—nothing at all— behind it. And that's what we want to hide."

"And what about you?"

"Me?" He smiled again. "Didn't I ever tell you about my career in the theater?"

"Not that I remember."

"I should tell you sometime. It's an amusing story."

A yellow tour bus pulled up and parked in front of the hotel. Taped across the back window was a sign, "Peregrinación des de Burgos a Santiago." A noisy group of gaily dressed pilgrims from Burgos got out and headed en masse over to the cathedral. They joined the line moving slowly up the main staircase.

Looking at the increasingly long line, I observed, "Talk about bad timing. It'll take an hour just to get in the door."

"Let's walk around and see if there's another entrance."

On the east side of the cathedral we came to the Puerta Santa. Perched over the Holy Door were not one but three identical statues of Santiago as Pilgrim.

I started to giggle. "They must have had an assembly line for these statues. Maybe they were 'cheaper by the dozen.'"

"Feeling a bit punchy, are we?" Peter asked.

"Seriously, these can't be the right statue. There are too many of them and they all look alike."

"What do you suggest, Sherlock?"

"Let me think a minute." I took the guidebook from him, turned to the last pages, and skimmed the text. "When medieval pilgrims reached Santiago de Compostela they entered through the main west door and saw the Pórtico del la Gloria, the Doorway of Glory, an elaborately carved, three-arched entry. Then they placed their fingers on the column of the Tree of Jesse, which represents the genealogical tree of Jesus. Then they entered the church itself and paid homage to Santiago by embracing a larger-than-life-size statue of the saint."

"They did what?" Peter asked, surprised.

"It's considered an act of devotion," I explained.

"No accounting for religious observances, I always say."

"And then they went down into the crypt and said a prayer over Santiago's bones. Actually, Santiago's and several other peoples'. The bones were mixed together and hidden from attacking Englishmen in the 1600s and misplaced. They were only rediscovered and verified as authentic by the Church at the end of the nineteenth century."

Peter took me by the arm and started towards the main entry. "This is the 'ritual itinerary,' so to speak, that your letter-writer would have followed?"

"That's what the guidebook says."

"Sounds good to me. Let's try it."

While we waited in line to enter the cathedral, five backpack-carrying pilgrims in hiking boots came up behind us. The two women and three men dropped their travel-worn packs on the pavement and eagerly began sharing their adventures on the Camino. I overheard them commenting on how difficult it was to be in a city, surrounded by people, after weeks of walking through the wilderness. Someday, I promised myself, I'll know what that feels like. I'll walk the Camino.

A French tour bus arrived; on the back window was the sign, "Pélerinage à Compostele." I wondered whether this was the same bus Jack and I had seen in Santo Domingo de la Calzada, just a few days before. It seemed like a lifetime ago. I realized, with a shock, it *was* a lifetime ago: Mateo's lifetime. Jack's lifetime. And maybe Sue Ellen's.

French-speaking tourists/pilgrims joined the line, pushing and shoving in their eagerness to get into the cathedral. The foot-pilgrims hoisted their packs up the steps one by one behind us.

Peter looked around nervously. "We're too exposed. If the men in white—or anyone else—are after us, they'll see us standing here for sure."

"We don't have any choice," I said, trying to sound calm. "Besides, maybe we'll be less noticeable this way. There are lots of people waiting in line."

The line moved surprisingly quickly, and soon we entered the cathedral. Once inside we saw the twelfth-century Pórtico de la Gloria, carved with dozens of life-like figures of the apostles, angels, musicians, prophets, animals, and other creatures. A faint blush on the cheeks of some of the figures was all that remained of the original bright paint that had covered them.

The center support was the Tree of Jesse, an elaborately carved column of intertwining people and imaginary beasts. Seated solemnly on top of the ten-foot-tall pillar was the life-sized figure of St. James. Following tradition, we pressed our fingers into the hollows in the column, hollows worn by centuries of fingers pressing into the stone.

Then we followed the other worshipers down the aisle through the soaring central nave towards the larger-than-life-size figure of Santiago sitting on a throne behind the main altar. The air inside the cathedral was hot and stuffy; it smelled of a thousand years of accumulated candle wax, incense, and sweat.

. As we got closer, we saw that Santiago was seated under a huge, golden canopy that included angels, more statues of Santiago, golden flags, flowers, curlicues, and bundles of what looked like gold arrows tied with gold ribbons. On either side of this elaborate confection was a staircase that led inside the cupola and behind the imposing figure. People went up one side of the staircase, embraced the saint, and went back down the other side.

Mass was being said, but the words were inaudible because people in line kept chatting and fanning themselves with folded newspapers or elegant, hand-painted fans. Angrily, a black-robed priest hissed at the crowd to be quiet. There was a temporary drop in the noise level.

We kept looking around uneasily but no white-cloaked men appeared. Neither did Sue Ellen. Within ten minutes we had climbed the narrow staircase to the cupola. At the top, a perspiring young man in a white shirt, tightly knotted tie, and dark wool suit handed us a prayer card, and he gestured to us to complete the ritual. So, like millions of pilgrims before us, we put our arms around the statue and kissed the scallop shell on the back of its jewel-encrusted neck. It felt surprisingly cool. I only had a moment to look for symbols before we had to make room for others.

We waited in yet another line to go downstairs to the crypt beneath the altar. Once there, we knelt for a minute in front of the carved silver casket containing the relics of Santiago and his disciples. The line behind us kept moving and people were jostling for space. When we came back to the main floor of the cathedral, the Mass was over and people were leaving the cathedral.

"See anything down there?" Peter asked.

"There just wasn't time," I said, frustrated. "Besides, I'm not sure that's the same casket that was there in 1493. The guidebook said the bones were misplaced several centuries ago and only rediscovered at the end of last century."

"Oh. Another minor consideration." He rubbed his ear again. "What next?"

I looked around slowly. "Santiago is supposed to lead the way, right?"

"Right."

"So where's he looking?"

"I beg your pardon?" He asked, puzzled.

"Where's the big gold statue looking?"

"Towards the Pórtico de la Gloria."

I took off at a trot, bumping against people as I went. Peter followed close behind.

Soon we reached the side of the Pórtico that faced the altar. There, crouched on the floor, was the kneeling statue of Master Mateo, the twelfth-century master craftsman who was responsible for designing the cathedral. We examined the statue and the wall behind it but found nothing.

Peter asked gloomily, "Well, what next, my dear? Pick and shovel? Crystal ball? You did bring one, didn't you?"

I didn't reply. Instead, I walked around to the other side. There was the statue of St. James, seated on top of the Tree of Jesse. Peter followed.

"You know, Peter," I said thoughtfully, "this is the only other really significant statue of Santiago in the cathedral. And it's in the other statue's line of sight—if we pretend it has x-ray vision."

We stared up at the figure of St. James. One hand held a staff; the other held a scroll. I walked up to the figure and turned around, trying to see where its gaze fell. There was nothing on the wall or the floor.

Peter looked around. "So where's the treasure?"

"I don't know," I replied tensely.

"Surely it can't be buried under the floor, can it?"

"I suppose not. After all, whoever hid the treasure had to do so quickly—and secretively."

"Obviously," he observed.

I retorted, "There must be another clue. Maybe we have to look beneath the statue to find it."

We examined opposite sides of the column. Finally, hidden in the dark recess near the bottom of the column, I saw a small, carefully scratched outline of a bird on a boat.

"This must be it!"

"But what is it?" Peter asked, puzzled.

"The next clue to the treasure."

"I meant, what does a bird in a boat mean?"

"It must tell us where the treasure is."

"But where is that?"

"If I knew that—" I slipped the guidebook under my arm and reached into my bag for the letter. "'Only the true pilgrim who follows the Milky Way will reach the treasure, and only if St. James guides him—'"

"Are you sure this is the clue?"

"It must be."

"But it's so obscure. You can't even tell what kind of bird it is."

Exasperated, I declared, "It has to be the clue."

"How do you know it's not just some medieval graffiti? Maybe this whole thing's a wild goose chase."

"This is no time to give up! I'm sure this is the answer, if I could figure it out. Just give me a minute of silence."

While I reread the letter, Peter looked back towards the altar. Suddenly he exclaimed, "I think I see Juan."

"Who?"

"Sue Ellen's friend from León. Maybe he knows something. You wait here. I'm going after him!"

"But Peter—"

He took off running.

Trying not to wonder what Juan was doing here, I concentrated on deciphering the clue. Staring at the symbol, I repeated the words of the letter and stroked the medallion around my neck. I thought to myself: a bird on a boat. What kind of bird could it possibly be? What had Peter said? Something about a wild goose chase . . .

All of a sudden, I knew the answer. Without thinking, I called out, "Peter! I've got it! We've got to go to—"

At that moment I felt a cold metal object press against my ribs. A steely voice whispered in my ear, "Shut up."

Instinctively, I turned to look at the man holding me close, but he jammed the gun into my side. I gasped in pain.

Fourteen

He hustled me down the steps and across the plaza. Terrified, I tried to get free, but he kept the gun jammed into my side. I twisted around to look back at the cathedral, and I thought I saw Peter and a white-cloaked man standing at the top of the staircase. When I looked again, Peter—if it had been Peter—and the man were gone.

Lock-stepping me across the plaza, my captor headed toward a gray Renault parked in front of the hotel. Using the remote, he unlocked the car doors. Then, keeping the gun pointed at my stomach, he pressed against me in a lover's embrace. Suddenly, the lights went out.

When I woke up, I was seeing stars—and they weren't in the Milky Way. Instinctively, I tried to touch my head with my hands. They were tied together with a dirty piece of plastic cord. I looked around. We were parked on a deserted side street.

Seeing me come to, he growled, "Don't try anything heroic. Killing you would be a pleasure, after all the trouble you've caused me."

I looked into my kidnapper's ice blue eyes, then quickly looked away. For a moment I had felt the way a rabbit must feel, mesmerized by a snake. Careful not to look into his eyes again, I examined the rest of his face. Bushy white eyebrows, pencil-thin mouth, florid complexion. Maybe, I thought, he has high blood pressure and the excitement will give him a stroke. Hah. Not likely. His snow-white hair curled around his ears and down his neck; his beard was closely trimmed.

I realized with a shock that he looked vaguely familiar.

He must have guessed what I was thinking, because he smiled a tight-lipped, humorless smile. "So, you remember me."

"How could I!" I retorted. "I don't hang out with criminals."

He chuckled at a private joke. "Appearances can be deceiving."

"You look like a criminal. Kidnapping me—"

"I am not what I seem."

"You mean you're not a kidnapper? Then untie my hands," I demanded.

He ignored my request. Instead, he continued pompously, "I am many things. A chameleon. A master of disguise."

"Next you'll tell me you're a 'gentleman thief.'"

"That too, if circumstances permit. Unfortunately, they do not."

His voice sharp as a stiletto, he demanded, "Tell me where the treasure is."

My mind raced frantically but kept circling back to the same question: Did he plan to kill me? Kidnapping was one thing, but murder was something else—wasn't it?

If he planned to kill me, he wouldn't do it before we found the treasure. After all, he needed me to find the treasure. Wasn't that why he kidnapped me?

I closed my eyes, trying to formulate a survival strategy. I had to buy time. But how, and how long, could I stall? If I led him to the wrong place, Peter might never find me. Of course, if Peter didn't figure out the clue, he'd never find me anyway. Perspiration dripped down the back of my neck, but, since my hands were tied, I couldn't wipe it off.

My captor repeated ominously, "Tell me where the treasure is. Now."

I took a deep breath and let it out slowly. "Why should I help you?"

"Because I'll kill you if you don't," he said in a matter-of-fact tone.

"You'll kill me anyway," I said, my voice shaking.

"Not necessarily," he said with a smile. "At least, that's what you have to hope."

"If you kill me you won't find the treasure."

"Don't push your luck. I'll find it with or without you. Sooner or later."

Defiantly, I declared, "I don't know where the treasure is."

"You do know. Tell me. Now."

He jabbed the gun into my side and I gasped with pain.

"I don't know!"

His eyes narrowed, he demanded again, "Tell me now or else you'll learn what pain *really* feels like!" A cruel smile spread slowly across his face.

Just then I heard a muffled sound from the back seat and turned to look. Something was struggling to get out from under a blanket.

"What's that?" I asked, nervously.

Glancing in the rear view mirror, he gave a nasty chuckle. "It's about time she came to. You might call it a little insurance, just to make sure you behave."

As I turned around to watch, the blanket moved some more and, after much wriggling, the person beneath managed to push it off. Rumpled blonde hair appeared, plastered over a sweat-soaked forehead, followed by mascara-smudged eyes, a swollen face, a mouth gagged shut with a pastel-colored silk scarf.

It was Sue Ellen, trussed up like a chicken, her legs tied behind her and fastened by a cord to her hands.

I whispered, "Sue Ellen?"

She nodded and looked at me with pleading eyes.

Puzzled, I asked, "How'd she get here?"

"I ran into her, so to speak, in O Cebreiro."

"But why did you kidnap her?"

"I was going to kill her, but I changed my mind. I thought she might be useful."

"No, I meant, why did you kidnap *her?*"

"It's one more way to make sure you cooperate." His eyes flicked back and forth between the road and the rearview mirror.

"What do you mean?"

"Elementary, my dear. If you don't lead me directly to the treasure, I'll kill Sue Ellen."

I thought a moment, then asked suspiciously, "How do I know she isn't 'in cahoots' with you?" I seemed unable to keep my mouth shut. Nervous, I guess, about the gun pointed at me.

"What a devious mind you have!" he said, appreciatively. "Read my lips. If you don't cooperate, I'll kill her. Maybe that's a bluff, but maybe it isn't. You decide."

Seeing my indecision, he continued, "If you don't cooperate now, and I mean *now,* I'll kill you. Both of you. Slowly. And I'll start with Sue Ellen. It's up to you."

He actually licked his lips at the prospect. I was never much of a gambler. I don't even play card games. I never could call anybody's bluff. So I decided to play along, for the time being, trying to buy some time. Maybe if I kept talking to him, I could distract him. Maybe help would come. Maybe Santiago on his white charger would ride to my rescue. Or even Peter, in his little red rental car. That would do just fine.

He was beginning to wave the gun again. I sighed, wearily. "Okay. You win. The clue was a bird on a boat. That could mean Padrón. Or Noia. Or even Finisterre."

"Don't give me that crap," he snarled. "I heard your gleeful shout. You know where to go."

"I tell you I'm not sure. I think it's Padrón, but I could be wrong."

"Why Padrón?"

"That's where the boat carrying Santiago's body supposedly landed. Since the treasure belonged to the Knights of Santiago, I think they might have hidden it there."

"Where in Padrón?"

"Where Santiago's boat landed. There must be a mooring post with a marker."

He waved his gun at me. "Are you sure?"

"No I'm not sure," I replied, "But that's all I can think of."

He nodded curtly. "Good enough." He pulled the car out of the parking space with one hand and sped away.

I let out a silent sigh of relief. It *was* all I could think of on the spur of the moment. It was somehow reassuring to realize that having my life threatened made me think more, not less, clearly.

I hoped there was a mooring post in Padrón, and I hoped we could find it, but not too quickly. In the meantime, I would try to escape. Since my hands were tied in front of me I tried to locate the door handle with my back. If I could get the door open, I could fall out. It was risky but we weren't traveling very fast .

Seeing me rub against the door, he gave a harsh, barking laugh. "The lock's flush with the door. There's no way you can unlock it."

He drove expertly with one hand. The other hand held the gun, pointed unwaveringly at me. I sat rigid, staring straight ahead.

The air in the car was hot and thick and smelled like stale cigarettes.

"It's stifling in here," I complained. "Can't you turn on the air conditioning?"

"There isn't any. And don't ask me to roll down the windows. I'm not that stupid."

We followed the highway that led to Padrón, only 20 short kilometers away, according to the road sign. I had hoped my captor would have trouble finding the route, but he had headed unerringly in the right direction.

I tried to draw him out, hoping that maybe I could distract him enough to do something to escape. "You seem to know your way around."

"I was here during the Civil War."

"Oh? On which side?"

"That depended."

A memory began to surface. I glanced at my captor. He was wearing a wrinkled button-down shirt, a soiled beige suede jacket, beige chinos, and scuffed, brown shoes. Nondescript clothing, poorly maintained. He had said I had met him in a different context. What could it have been?

Trying to sound nonchalant, I asked, "Is this your first time back in Spain?"

"Hardly. I've been back many times. I did my doctoral dissertation on the Civil War, as a matter of fact. Little did my committee suspect where I got my information. And, of course, I've returned a number of times for further research and for business."

"You're a *professor*?"

He smiled smugly. "That's right. Can you fill in the rest?"

I closed my eyes and tried to focus the faint memory. Suddenly I blurted out, "You're Nicholson."

"That's right. I'm Rupert Nicholson."

"The history professor I told Peter to call," I said slowly.

"The very one," he smirked.

"So that's how you knew about the treasure hunt. But how did you find us?"

"Your boyfriend helped."

"Peter?" I gasped.

"That's right." He glanced at me. "Not that he meant to. I followed him."

I breathed a sigh of relief. "But how did you know the treasure was real?"

"Shut up," he snapped.

I looked at the gun pointing at my side and said nothing. Wiping the sweat from my forehead with the back of my hands, I tried to relax, but it was difficult. Since I had blurted out that I knew who he was, he would never let me live. Not that he would have anyway, I realized. Still, discretion would have been smarter.

He glared at me. "You know, little lady, you have caused me a great deal of grief."

"Me?"

"You. I don't like being double-crossed."

"I never double-crossed you—"

"No, but Jack did. Because of you."

"Jack? How did you know Jack?"

"We had a little import-export business together."

"What kind of business? Drugs?"

"You malign me. Antiquities. Stolen."

"You and Jack?"

"Me and Jack. I sent him to Spain to worm his way into your confidence. You'd never met him before."

"You mean I *didn't* meet him at a cocktail party?"

"Fooled you, didn't he," he grinned. "Jack was good at fooling women."

Only half listening, I mulled over what I had just learned. It meant I hadn't forgotten meeting Jack at a party. I found that oddly reassuring. I had always wondered how I could have forgotten even a brief encounter with that charming, but completely untrustworthy, man.

"So you and Jack were working together."

"For years. But he got stupid and decided to go into business for himself."

Suddenly I remembered the phone call I'd overheard in Burgos, when Jack was talking to "Santa Claus" about a false alarm.

I looked at him with dawning recognition. "You're 'Santa Claus,' aren't you."

He said in a hard, tight voice, "You know too damn much."

Trying to soothe him, I protested, "I had nothing to do with Jack's double-crossing you."

"So maybe he did it on his own. The details don't matter. He had about outlived his usefulness anyway. But I don't like blowing my cover. And I don't like messy complications. This treasure hunt better be worth it."

I squirmed.

"Don't try to pull anything smart, like leading me to the wrong town."

"Don't worry. I won't," I said sincerely.

"You behave and we'll get along just fine. I might even let you keep some of the treasure, if you're a good girl."

I heard Sue Ellen moving around in the back seat. Was Sue Ellen in league with him? If so, when had she met him? In León? At O Cebreiro? Maybe she had double-crossed Jack and joined up with Nicholson. Or maybe she really was Nicholson's victim. But if so, why had he kidnapped her? Certainly not for "insurance." It would have made more sense to kidnap me.

My head ached fiercely, and not just where he'd hit me. Once you started thinking deviously, I realized, it was hard to stop. I rolled my head back and forth, trying to relax enough to think straight. Not that that would make any difference, I thought in sudden despair. Whether Sue Ellen was a victim or a conspirator, Nicholson was going to kill me anyway. And then I wouldn't know or care what happened to Sue Ellen.

I watched the lush green hills and the rough stone houses rushing into and out of view. We were getting to Padrón much too quickly.

Suddenly we came up behind a ox-cart heaped with hay. Nicholson swerved to avoid it and I was thrown against the door, then the dashboard. I put out my hands to protect myself, but they were bound and I banged my wrists against the glove compartment.

Damn it! I wasn't going to let it end like this, not without a fight! I looked at Nicholson and the gun. My legs were free. I could kick him hard in the knees or swing my bound hands like a club at the steering wheel. If I succeeded, we would have an accident— probably a serious one. And if I didn't succeed, Nicholson would shoot me for trying. He wanted me alive to find the treasure, but he might shoot now and regret it later.

I decided against trying to wreck the car. Better to wait until a less risky opportunity presented itself, one based on deceit and cunning rather than on violence. Besides, I admitted to myself, hope—or self-delusion—springs eternal.

I still didn't really believe he was going to kill me.

Abruptly, we reached the outskirts of Padrón.

Nicholson demanded, "Where to?"

Pretending defeat, I replied in a flat voice, "The mooring post where Santiago's boat landed."

"Where's that?" He growled.

"By the river, I suppose. I've never been here."

We followed the road through town to the river and a small harbor filled with little fishing boats. Nicholson pulled up to a parking spot in front of an ancient stone bridge.

He turned to me. "We're going to get out and find the mooring post. You are not going to try to run away. If you do, I will kill Sue Ellen." He shoved the gun sharply into my stomach and I fought an urge to retch. He smiled grimly. "Believe me."

Reaching into the back seat, he threw the blanket over Sue Ellen again. She mumbled something from beneath the gag.

"Aren't you afraid she'll suffocate?" I asked.

With a derisive snort he replied, "She's a survivor." Turning back towards the blanket, he said, "Pretend it's a sauna."

In one swift movement he got out of the car, pulled me after him, and set the automatic door lock. Then he pressed his thick, heavy body against mine and forced me back against the car door. Shielded from view, he unfastened the cord that bound my numb hands. I rubbed them together rapidly, trying to restore feeling in them. Soon they began to tingle painfully.

He held me for a moment in a tight, smelly embrace. "Don't forget," he threatened, "I've got the gun pointed at you."

I was determined to ask for help no matter what Nicholas threatened. When we approached an old, grizzled man fishing off the side of the bridge with a long bamboo pole, I lunged toward him, yelling, "*Ayúdame! Ayúdame*—Help me, Help me!" For the life of me, I couldn't remember how to say "I'm being kidnapped" in Spanish.

The fisherman looked at me, puzzled, then grinned and pointed at his ears. He was deaf. Unperturbed, he went back to fishing.

Nicholson jerked me back by the arm, practically throwing me off balance, and forced me to walk down the narrow, tree-lined sidewalk that led alongside the river. Was he going to shoot me, I wondered, under the shade of the spreading chestnut trees?

I tried to break loose but he held on tight. Gripping me in what looked like a passionate embrace, he whispered in my ear, "I'm warning you! One more stupid move and I'll shoot. This gun has a silencer. Nobody will hear. Trust me."

I *hate* it when someone says "trust me."

Grabbing me tightly around the waist, he forced me to walk along the river. There was no mooring post.

He shook me fiercely. "Where the hell is it?"

"How the hell should I know!" I spat. "There's supposed to be a mooring post. The guidebook said so."

"You'd better come up with the right answer fast or I'll kill you and your little blonde-haired friend."

Just then I saw a white-robed monk standing by the riverside, gazing calmly at the colorful boats bobbing up and down on the green-blue water. For once I was glad to see a "man in white," even though he probably was unrelated to the ones who had been following us.

I pointed towards him. "Ask him. He ought to know."

Nicholson glowered at me. "Don't try anything stupid. I've got my gun in my pocket and it's pointed at you. First I'll kill you, then Sue Ellen."

We approached the monk. I thought Nicholson wouldn't dare shoot me in front of a witness, so here was my chance. But what about Sue Ellen? Was it a bluff? Suddenly, Nicholson bent my arm behind my back so hard I thought it would snap in two. The pain left me speechless.

Smiling benignly, he asked the monk if he knew where Santiago's mooring post was. The monk nodded in a friendly fashion and pointed towards a nearby church. Nicholson thanked him and dragged me away to the car. He shoved me in.

I glared at him and rubbed my aching arm.

"I warned you! Don't try anything else or I'll kill Sue Ellen. And then I'll kill you," he said, his voice cold as ice.

We drove over to the church of Santiago and parked in front. Then Nicholson yanked me out of the car. Holding me again in a close embrace, his gun in his jacket pocket, he half-carried, half-dragged me to the church. Just as we got there a pudgy, bald-headed priest came out and locked the heavy wooden door with a large wrought-iron key.

Nicholson asked, "Is the mooring post of Santiago inside?"

The black-frocked priest nodded and turned to leave, but Nicholson held out his free hand to stop him.

"We came all the way from the U.S.A. to see it."

"Come back tomorrow," he said, indifferently. "The church is closed for the day."

Taking a wad of crumpled pesetas out of his pants pocket, Nicholson said, "Surely you'll let us in."

The priest looked at the money and hesitated.

"My wife is not well," Nicholson continued, "and Santiago is her patron saint. It would be terribly unkind to make us wait another day." He pressed the money into the priest's hand.

The priest looked at me. I did not, in fact, look well. The pain in my arm was excruciating. With an abrupt nod, he put the money in a pocket in his robe, turned back to the door, unlocked it, and ushered us in. He pulled the heavy door closed behind us.

The large stone church was full of shifting shadows and flickering shafts of light that filtered unevenly through the dust-streaked windows. My nose twitched; the air reeked of burnt wax, stale incense, and mildew.

The priest walked quickly down the central aisle, reciting by rote, "In Roman times this town was called Iria Flavia, and it was here, to the River Sar, that Santiago's boat was miraculously transported by angels in 44 AD. The original church was built on this site in the eleventh century. It was destroyed by the Normans and then rebuilt. It was rebuilt again in the eighteenth century."

We followed the priest to the end of the aisle; worn red carpet covered the steps leading up to a wide stone dais. An elaborately carved Virgin in a gold brocade robe was perched on top of a marble-topped cabinet in the middle of the dais; her long white veil hung down over the front of the cabinet. On either side were two three-foot-tall bronze candlesticks.

"There it is," said the priest, pointing with a flourish at the altar.

We looked but saw no mooring post.

Nicholson said ominously, "Where? I don't see it."

With a smile, the priest walked up the steps, lifted the Virgin's veil, and unfastened a secret latch in the cabinet. A door swung open. There, hidden inside, was a battered stone post.

"The mooring post was moved here during the Civil War to protect it from damage," the priest explained.

Dragging me with him, Nicholson walked up to the priest. He slid the gun from his pocket, stepped behind the priest, and smashed the butt of the gun down on his head. There was a dull thud. The priest let out an odd hiss, like the sound of a deflating balloon, and crumpled to the floor, knocking over several of the candlesticks. They clattered as they fell.

Bright red blood pooled out from beneath the black robe and soaked into a corner of the carpet. Nicholson kicked the priest and the candlesticks to one side.

He turned on me viciously. "The damn post was moved here during the Civil War. So where the hell is the treasure?" He pointed the gun at me. "Time's up, sweetheart."

I tried to run, but he grabbed my arm and jerked me towards him. Thrown off balance, I fell to the floor. He loomed over me, waving the gun.

I cried out, "I swear I don't know!"

"In that case, I might as well kill you now rather than later," he said calmly.

"Wait!" I cried, hands raised in a foolish attempt to block the bullets.

"I thought that would help you come up with the answer." He waved the gun again. "Quit wasting time! Where's the treasure?"

"Give me a minute, for God's sake!" I got up slowly, holding my throbbing arm. I wondered if my elbow was dislocated or merely sprained. Not that it mattered. After all, I might soon be dead. Somehow, I would have preferred to die intact.

Gasping with pain, I said, "I thought the treasure would be where the mooring post was. Maybe it still is. Maybe it's buried where the mooring post used to be."

"It would have been discovered when they moved the mooring post. I would have heard of it," he snarled. "Try again."

Trying to calm myself, I started to stroke the medallion hanging around my neck. The treasure had to be somewhere in Padrón. I was certain that the Knight of Santiago had hidden it near the landing place of Santiago, not at Noia, where Noah's ark landed, and not at Finisterre. But where in Padrón? I had guessed about the mooring post, and that had delayed us a while, but I knew I could stall no longer. This time I had to find the right answer or Nicholson would kill me now, rather than later.

Every clue had been connected with a statue of Santiago in a church along the Camino. But the last clue had been different. The scratched carving of a bird on a boat had led us to Padrón. And then where? I had headed for the mooring post, but that was wrong. I rubbed the medallion again and closed my eyes, tracing the deep engravings with my fingers. On one side the symbols stood for the thirteen stages of Santiago. On the other was a labyrinth in a scallop shell.

As if coming out of a daze, I opened my eyes and calmly informed Nicholson, "It's here. The scallop shell on the medallion means that the treasure's hidden in this church, the church of

Santiago. The labyrinth indicates where the treasure is hidden inside the church. All we have to do is find the labyrinth."

I took my charm necklace off—after all, it hadn't done me much good—and held it out to him. He grabbed it and looked at the medallion in the faint light. "So this is the famous medallion."

"I'm surprised you didn't take it from me earlier," I said acerbically, still unable to keep my mouth shut.

"Why bother? I knew it would be mine eventually, and in the meantime you would use it to find the treasure." He slipped the necklace into his jacket pocket. "You'd better be right this time. You're running out of time."

He kept the gun pointed at me as we inspected the columns and the walls of the church, looking for the labyrinth.

After a short time he grew impatient.

"You're stalling." He pointed the gun at my head. "What—or who—are you waiting for?"

"Nobody! Despite my heartfelt prayers," I said, sarcastically, "Santiago and his Knights aren't likely to come to my rescue."

"What about your friend in the red Escort?"

"What about him. He doesn't know where to go."

Nicholson laughed. "I owe him a favor. Renting that car was the stupidest thing he could have done. It made following you a piece of cake. Of course, the tracking device I slipped under the fender didn't hurt either."

Startled, I asked, "When did you do that?"

"At Ponferrada."

"Ponferrada? You mean *you* were the one who stole Sue Ellen's gold coin?"

"Not me. I wouldn't have made such a stupid mistake. It was easy. I followed you out of León, saw which way you went at Astorga, and took the highway to Ponferrada. It was a lot faster than your backcountry road. Then I just waited at the outskirts of town. When I saw you coming, I followed at a distance and saw where you parked the car. When no one was watching, I attached the tracking device."

"Why?"

"Just in case." He waved the gun impatiently. "Don't just stand there. Find the maze!"

"You mean, the labyrinth," I replied, taking inordinate pleasure in being able to correct him.

"Maze, labyrinth, what's the difference. Find it!"

Ignoring his irritation, I replied, "A labyrinth is a kind of maze, but a maze is not a labyrinth. A labyrinth is a spiritual tool, a maze is a puzzle. There is a difference." Not that this difference mattered in terms of my life or death. Not that there was any point in baiting the bear. But, in some odd way, it made me feel better to correct him: a trivial moment of power in the midst of near-powerlessness.

I looked anxiously around the church. Where could the labyrinth be? I tried to remember everything I knew about church architecture. It wasn't much. I promised myself—and Santiago—that if—no, not if, when—I got out of this, I would pay more attention to the subject.

Vaguely, I recalled something. "Didn't some medieval churches have labyrinths laid into the pavement?"

"Damned if I know."

I walked slowly back up the central aisle, looking at the stone pavement. Then I climbed the steps to the dais and pulled aside the worn red carpet in front of the altar. There it was: a large paving stone carved with the same design as the medallion. "Bingo."

Nicholson stepped up beside me and began caressing the shiny barrel of his gun.

In desperation, I pleaded, "Look, I'm pretty sure the treasure is hidden under there, but for all you know, I'm bluffing. Or wrong. You wouldn't want to kill me before you made sure, would you?"

Nicholson kept rubbing the burnished barrel of the gun.

"You might need help getting the paving stone loose or digging up the treasure," I babbled. "It would be a mistake to kill me now."

"I told you I don't make mistakes." Keeping the gun pointed at me, he bent down to examine the paving stone. It was mortared solidly in place. He stood up and wiped off his dusty hands on his pants. "There're some tools in the trunk of the car."

Grabbing my arm so tightly that I cried out, he jerked me along beside him to the front door, opened it, and peered out. No one was in sight. He dragged me to the car and opened the trunk. Sue Ellen had managed to toss off the blanket again. She looked up at me, tears streaming down her grimy face. I was sure she wasn't working with Nicholson. She looked much too miserable, and much too scared. I tried to smile encouragingly, but I don't think I succeeded.

Nicholson handed me a chisel, hammer, pickax, and shovel. Keeping the gun pointed at me, he herded me back into the church.

Soon I was kneeling beside the paving stone, using the hammer and chisel to loosen the mortar that held it in place. My arm throbbed fiercely. Every time I hit the chisel, a wave of nausea swept through me. Of course, that wasn't the only thing that made me feel queasy. Once I found the treasure, I would be dead. I had no illusions that Nicholson would turn into a real Santa Claus and give me part of the treasure for being such a good girl.

He leaned on the corner of the altar, just out of my reach. The priest, sprawled nearby, groaned and started to move. Nicholson bashed him on the head again. He stopped moving.

Out of the corner of my eye I saw movement in a shadowy corner of the church. I immediately looked down at my work. There was no sound except my labored breathing and the tap-tap-tap of the chisel. Or was there? Did I hear a faint shuffling sound? Maybe it was just rats. Or bats. I let the chisel slip and dropped the hammer; they clattered noisily to the floor.

"Damn!" I exclaimed.

"Get back to work," Nicholson demanded.

I paused for a moment and looked around, wiping the sweat from my eyes. Someone was slowly working his way up behind the thick stone columns. If only I could keep Nicholson from noticing.

"Professor Nicholson," I said, brightly, hoping to distract him, "I just don't understand how you got into crime. After all, you're a professor of history at a respected university."

"You know what that's like." He gave a harsh laugh. "Damn committee meetings, idiotic students. Little money. Little respect. No freedom. Who wants to live like that?"

"I suppose you got started before that, though, when you were a traitor in the Civil War."

"Don't make me angry," he said, in a voice that grated like chalk on a chalkboard. "You can make this easier or harder on yourself. The choice is yours."

Apologetically, I replied, "I didn't mean to offend you. I'm just trying to understand what makes you—or Jack—the way you are."

He relaxed a bit and leaned back against the altar. "Anyone can be a professor. All it requires is a little bit of talent and a lot of perseverance and drudgery. But it takes real intelligence and imagination to lead a life of crime and not get caught. There are, however, advantages to being a professor. That's why I put up with the stupidities of academia."

"Oh? What are the advantages?" I kept chipping away at the mortar, making as much noise as I could to disguise the activities of the person sneaking behind the columns.

"A legitimate excuse to travel, for one. Access to museums all over the world. Entrée into the social circles of well-educated cultured snobs who have lots of money and few brains. Nobody suspects a college professor of anything criminal—except plagiarism."

Deferentially, I murmured, "I never thought of it that way."

"Of course you didn't. Nobody does. That's why it's been such a sweet cover all these years. And such a good life." His voice turned vicious. "Until you came along and wrecked it."

I glanced up at him. His face was contorted with rage. Suddenly he started to smile and pointed the gun at my head.

In a cheerful voice, he called out, "Come out come out whoever you are or I'll shoot the little lady."

After a moment's pause, Peter stepped out from behind a nearby pillar.

Nicholson turned his head and looked. "Ah, the red Escort driver—"

I took advantage of the momentary distraction and threw the hammer at Nicholson. It gave him a glancing blow on the shoulder. Letting out a grunt of pain, he turned and shot in my direction. I felt a sharp burning in my thigh.

Peter ran up to the dais and jumped Nicholson from behind. Nicholson twisted suddenly, throwing him down on the cold stone platform. Peter dragged him down with him. They rolled around, locked in a deadly embrace. Peter tried desperately to get the gun, but he just couldn't do it.

As far as I could tell the bullet had just grazed me, cutting a slit in my jeans, but bringing almost no blood. I picked up one of the bronze candlesticks and waited for an opportunity to clobber Nicholson but they kept rolling around and I couldn't get a clear aim.

Suddenly Nicholson kneed Peter in the groin. While he writhed in anguish, Nicholson stood up. He pointed the gun at me.

In a chilling voice, he said, "Drop the candlestick or I'll shoot your interfering friend."

Nicholson dusted off his clothes while he kept the gun pointed at Peter. He motioned for him to get up. Slowly, Peter stood up and limped over to me.

"How disappointing for you," Nicholson sneered. "You thought you'd save your lady friend. Instead, you botched it." He grinned at me. "See what I mean about academic types?" He gestured with his gun toward the implements on the floor. "The job'll go twice as fast with both of you digging. Get to work."

Peter and I exchanged a look filled with fear and affection. He reached towards me, but Nicholson started waving the gun again. "Not a chance!" he jeered.

With a sob, still sitting on the floor, I grasped the chisel, then looked around for the hammer. Nicholson kicked it in my direction. Peter picked up the pickax and started to work.

Nicholson leaned back against the altar and watched.

Peter whispered to me, "Don't—"

Nicholson pointed the gun at him. "Shut up."

The only sounds in the church were the chip-chip-chip of metal on mortar, and, occasionally, a tuneless humming emitted by Nicholson.

After half an hour of hard work we managed to wiggle the heavy stone slab loose. Wedging the chisel beneath one side, I lifted the slab up by the edge. Peter grabbed the other side of the slab and pushed. It made a sound like chalk grating on a blackboard as it slid and then settled onto the dais.

A thick cloud of ancient dust rose up from the hole. Nicholson walked over and looked in. Beneath the platform was a mass of rubble.

"Rubble!" Nicholson exploded. "You're still holding out on me, you bitch!" He pointed the gun at me and cocked it.

"No, No!" I protested desperately. "The whole platform is filled with rubble. That's how it was supported over the floor. The treasure has to be here. You've got to believe me!"

His voice ragged with fatigue and pain, Peter said, "She's right. The treasure must be buried in the rubble."

Nicholson wiped the sweat from his forehead. "Get back to work," he snarled, gesturing with his gun at the shovel.

Peter picked it up and starting shoveling out the rubble. Using my lacerated hands to move piles of sharp stone fragments, I bit my lips till they bled, determined not to let Nicholson know I was in pain. Every so often I sneezed from the dust and wiped my nose on the back of my hand. Soon my face was streaked with dirt.

Suddenly there was the clanging sound of metal striking metal. Peter dropped the shovel, and we brushed the remaining rubble off the top of a tarnished box. It was two feet long by one foot wide. Stretching out on his stomach, Peter worked the coffer loose with his hands and shoved one end up towards me. I grabbed it and, muscles straining, lifted the heavy box onto the stone dais. It scraped as metal slid against stone.

Nicholson smiled grimly. "Put it on top of the altar."

Peter stood up and lugged the box to the marble altar top, placing it in front of the statue of the Virgin.

Nicholson pointed the gun at us and cocked it. The sound reverberated in the silent church. "If I weren't such a nice guy, I'd kill you now. But I'm really not so bad. I wouldn't want you to meet death unrequited. I won't deprive you of seeing the treasure."

"What if we just leave quietly and let you have all the pleasure for yourself?" I suggested hopefully. "We'll just forget this ever happened."

Laughing harshly, Nicholson replied, "Always the joker. I'm no fool. Why should I trust you to keep your mouth shut? You know too much." He pointed at the coffer. "Open it."

"What's the matter?" Peter sneered. "Afraid of a curse?"

"Open it."

Silent and weary, we stood in front of the treasure chest. Nicholson stood at the corner of the altar, close enough to see what we did, far enough away to be out of reach.

In the faint light that filtered through the dusty air, we examined the coffer. I brushed off the dust that had accumulated for centuries. The box was made of silver, with scallop shells carved in high relief on all four sides and the lid. The lid was gold, inlaid with precious stones in the shape of the cross of Santiago. A rusty lock kept the top securely fastened.

"It's getting dark in here. Light the candles." Nicholson demanded, tossing a gold cigarette lighter at Peter.

Peter picked up two of the fallen bronze candlesticks, replaced the thick candles, and lit them. A gentle, golden light suffused the altar.

"Open it." Nicholson ordered, his voice shaking slightly.

Peter hit the brittle lock with the hammer, and it shattered and fell to the floor. As we lifted up the lid, the hinges squeaked, and a hint of lavender wafted into the air. When I saw what was inside, I gasped in amazement. Nicholson leaned closer to get a better view.

Inside was a short gold and ebony staff with the sword-like cross insignia of Santiago. Next to it was an elaborately bound manuscript. On the embossed leather cover was a gilded image of Santiago riding a horse. One upraised arm held a flag, the other held a dagger with a ruby in the crosspiece. These gorgeous works of art rested on top of a jumbled pile of gold coins, glittering stones, and jewelry.

I took the staff and the book out of the chest and placed them gently on the marble-topped altar. Then I picked up an enormous cabochon-cut ruby and polished it on my T-shirt. It glowed in the fading light.

Nicholson said smugly, "Well, well, well. The treasure of the Knights of Santiago. I knew it had to be something special." He turned to us with a grisly smile. "Thank you for your help, even if it lacked in graciousness. And now the time has come to tidy up loose ends. I'll start with you, then finish with Sue Ellen." He paused a moment and leered. "She might be fun for a while before I kill her. She'll be willing to do anything to save her life, including betray her friends. I know. She already told me."

He brought the gun up, kissed the barrel, cocked it, and aimed it at me. Peter grabbed a handful of jewels from the treasure chest and threw them at him. Startled, Nicholson raised his hand to protect himself and took a step backward.

Just then we heard a strange whistling sound. In slow motion, Nicholson collapsed onto the floor. He jerked once, then lay still. A jewel-encrusted dagger stuck out of his back.

Fifteen

Peter and I clung to each other while a tall, white-robed man strode towards us from the dark recesses of the church, his sandaled feet making no sound on the stone pavement.

He gestured at the treasure and in a deep, commanding voice, announced, "That belongs to me."

My voice trembling, I whispered, "Who are you?"

"The Master of the Brotherhood of the Knights of Santiago, the true heirs to the lost treasure."

In unison, Peter and I said, "Haven't I seen you before?"

Solemnly, the hooded man replied, "Several times."

"Was it you at O Cebreiro?" I asked.

He nodded as he looked at the open treasure chest. Reverently, he picked up the staff and book.

Peter asked, "And at Santiago?"

He nodded again.

"But aren't there more than one of you?" I asked. "It seems to me I've seen you in an assortment of sizes."

"We are thirteen, the descendants of the original 'Trece' that governed the Order of the Knights of Santiago until it was so despicably destroyed by Ferdinand and Isabella. They turned the Order into a sham by electing their own leader and taking the power and wealth of the Order for themselves. But we hid from them our greatest treasure."

"You mean, these gold and jewels?" Peter asked.

"Not those," he said dismissively. "Those are mere worldly baubles. The greatest treasure of all is that which made us the Knights of Santiago: the Staff of Office and the holy Rules of the Order." He pointed a long, skeletal finger at the book. "This volume is the original *Reglas*, written when the Order was first founded in 1175 and signed by Pope Alexander III himself. And this is the true Staff of Office."

Cradling the ebony staff, he said, "In 1493 the last true Master, Alonso de Cárdenas, commanded one of my ancestors to hide the greatest treasure of the Order from those who would use it to destroy the Brotherhood. At great risk, this courageous Knight succeeded in hiding the treasure. Unfortunately, he was treacherously slain before he could tell the Master how to find it. And the Master died soon afterwards."

Puzzled, I asked, "But where do you come in?"

"For nearly five centuries it has been the sacred charge of the Brotherhood of the Knights of Santiago to find the hidden treasure. My ancestors established themselves at stations along the Camino de Santiago and dedicated their lives to discovering the treasure. I and twelve others have solemnly vowed to carry out their sacred trust."

Astounded by such single-minded devotion, I exclaimed, "All those centuries dedicated to one cause?"

His obsidian eyes glittered. "It has given a holy, sacred purpose for our lives."

I shivered, disturbed by such fanaticism, and changed the subject. "Was it your Brotherhood that searched our rooms in Burgos?"

He nodded.

"And mugged me in León?"

"Yes." His voice mournful, he continued, "One of our brothers was seriously wounded in the attempt. We pray daily for his recovery."

Peter interrupted, "You could have killed Noa!"

"We do not kill, except *in extremis*. We avoid violence as a rule, although we are a military brotherhood." He smiled a bit shyly. "You may have noticed we were not terribly effective in our attempts at violence."

I nodded.

"We are out of practice. Several of the Brothers are old and frail."

"Brother Mateo—was he one of you?" I asked.

"He was my father."

"Your father? I heard him speak of you—"

"My father spoke of you also."

Defensively, I said, "I was very fond of him. When we found him dead, we did what we could. I thought he'd died of a heart attack. Later, I began to wonder. But I still don't know for sure if he was murdered. And if he *was* murdered, whether it was by the white-robed man or Jack." I paused, thinking it through. "But the man in white was one of your Brotherhood, wasn't he?"

The Master nodded.

Afraid to hear the answer, I asked, *"Was* Mateo murdered?"

He nodded again.

My voice breaking, I said, "So Jack killed Mateo. But why did the man in white run away?"

"Because his first and most sacred charge was to find the treasure, and he suspected that Jack knew where it was," he explained patiently. "If our Brother had told the police, it would have meant we might never have found the treasure. As it is, my father's murder has been avenged. Jack was killed by the man who lies dead at your feet."

I took a step back from Nicholson's motionless form and tripped over the priest. He moaned softly, then passed out again.

"Why did you approach us at O Cebreiro?" Peter asked.

"Because I knew that you and Noa were not bad people. Adventurous and greedy, perhaps, but not evil. You had gotten involved in something much more dangerous than you realized. We knew that Jack was part of an international smuggling ring. When he was killed, we knew that someone else—someone unknown to us—was loose on the treasure hunt."

I added slowly, "You knew Nicholson killed Jack and you saw him kidnap Sue Ellen."

"I knew it after the fact."

"So when you tried to stop me in the cathedral," Peter said, "You were really trying to help."

The Master smiled. "That is true. But you managed to get away, and I wasted precious time finding your trail. Fortunately, we spotted your red car parked down the road from this church, and Nicholson had asked one of our Brothers for directions to the mooring post."

I looked at the white-haired figure lying motionless on the stone floor. "You said your Brotherhood doesn't believe in killing, but you killed Nicholson."

"That is true. But it is our sworn duty to defend pilgrims on the Camino de Santiago and to slay infidels. You will soon be the former—"

How did he know I planned to walk the Camino?

"And he was the latter. After all, the Brotherhood is a military order, even if the Brothers are used to being in the 'reserves' rather than on active duty."

I was still bothered by something. "Your father left a tattered note, something that seemed to say, 'the Brotherhood . . . beware.' How do I know you guys really are the 'good guys'?"

Peter looked at me in shock, and I realized I had been indiscreet, to put it mildly. After all, this man had just killed Nicholson. Why risk antagonizing him? But I refused to be satisfied with partial answers. I had been through too much to be intimidated any longer. I had faced death and survived. Besides, I suddenly realized, one could be honest out of bravery, not out of stupidity. Heart thumping, I waited for his reply.

After a minute, the Master spoke. "It took courage to tell me about the note my father left, and I am grateful that you did. I think that as my father lay dying he was trying to warn the Brotherhood. Unfortunately, the words he wrote were easily misunderstood. What he must have been trying to say was, 'Tell the Brotherhood to beware of Jack.'"

I nodded slowly.

The Master put the staff and book back inside the coffer and closed the lid.

"What happens next?" Peter asked warily.

"The Brotherhood has friends in high places. All will be taken care of quickly and discreetly."

Impatiently, Peter responded, "I meant, what happens to us?"

"You?" He seemed puzzled. "You must leave immediately."

"You're letting us go?" I said in amazement.

"Of course. I have nothing against you. In fact, because of your fortuitous discovery, our sacred treasure has been returned to us after 500 years." Sternly, he continued, "But before you leave, you must swear a vow of secrecy."

We looked at the imposing hooded figure, heir to 500 years of fanatical duty, and nodded. The Master bent down beside Nicholson. Bracing himself with his sandaled foot, he pulled the bloodstained dagger out of his back. The body moved, and we heard a tinkling sound as my charm necklace and a set of car keys rolled across the floor.

The Master picked them up and handed Peter the keys. "There is someone waiting for you in the car. Leave the keys in the ignition when you are done."

Ignoring my lucky charms, he looked at the medallion, turned it over, then held it for a moment pressed between his hands. With a sigh, he said, almost to himself, "So this is the medallion for which at least two of our Brothers have died." He gazed at me, then solemnly placed the necklace, with the medallion, around my neck. "Never forget where greed can lead you."

Then he held out the bloody dagger and told us to place our hands on top of it. I stared at the jewel-covered crosspiece, embellished with a simple scallop shell. Peter and I placed our hands over the wet metal blade.

"Repeat after me. In the name of Santiago, we vow never to reveal what has occurred."

In slightly shaky voices, we repeated, "In the name of Santiago, we vow never to reveal what has occurred."

The Master handed me the dagger. "Keep this as another memento—and as a reminder of what awaits those who betray the Brotherhood." He gestured imperiously towards the door. "Now leave."

Peter supported me as we limped down the aisle and out the door. Arm and arm, we hobbled over to a nearby bench and sat down.

The sun had just set. As we watched, the sky deepened from turquoise to teal to blue-black. The Milky Way spread across the heavens, dropping its stars on the hills behind the River Sar. I breathed deeply, filling my lungs with the fresh night air. Insects chirped in the grass, and birds—or maybe bats—rustled in the trees. I could hear Peter breathing deeply beside me.

After a moment, he reached for my hand. "Well, my dear, this has been quite an adventure. I regret I ever suggested you should lead a more exciting life."

"Do you really, Peter?"

He leaned over and ruffled my hair, which had come loose from its coil. "Of course not. It's been marvelous." He paused a moment. "I can hardly wait until we walk the Camino together. What an adventure that will be."

"You'll really walk the Camino with me? I thought you just said that to soothe me."

"I meant it as much as I meant that vow we just made."

"It only seems right, somehow," I said softly. "After all, we owe Santiago a great deal."

I looked at the cross-shaped dagger, glittering in the moon-light. For the first time, I realized it was made in the shape of the Cross of Santiago. "Talk about a double-edged sword." Then I said thoughtfully, "I wonder what will become of the Brotherhood."

"What do you mean?"

"Seeking the lost treasure has been their raison d'être for 500 years. What happens now that their quest is over? What will they do? They can hardly become a public Brotherhood of the Knights of Santiago, can they?"

"I wonder. As the Master pointed out, there are still pilgrims—and infidels—on the Camino."

"Maybe you're right."

He kissed the palm of my hand. "Noa, I want to make a propos—"

Just then we heard a loud thumping noise coming from the Renault. Sue Ellen had managed to prop herself up against the side window and was pounding on it with her head, trying to get someone's attention.

"Shall we leave her there?" Peter asked, with a grin.

I laughed. "It's tempting, but I suppose not."

We unlocked the car and let her out.

Epilogue

"Quit tickling me!"

"Don't you want me to wash your back?"

"That's not my back."

"I'm reassured that you can tell the difference."

"I'm not that far gone."

"That's a relief."

"I love the way the soap smells, like warm, bittersweet chocolate."

"I prefer the way it feels, like whipped cream on your satin skin."

"Hungry, are we?"

"That depends."

"Peter—"

"Mmm?"

"It's a good thing the police made the room reservation for us."

"Why?"

"Because the hotel didn't dare cancel it, even though we arrived so late."

"And looked so disreputable."

"You concocted such an outrageous story. I couldn't believe it, but they fell for it."

"Not only fell for it, but gave us a luxury suite—"

"With a bathtub big enough for two. What a wonderful way to end our search for the treasure of the Brotherhood."

"And what a delightful way to start our quest for another treasure."

"Just what did you have in mind?"

"Get out of the bath and I'll show you."

"Now?"

"Now."

"I thought you'd never ask."